The Flood of '64

Also by David Long

Home Fires
Early Returns (POEMS)

The Flood Of '64

Stories by
David Long

The Ecco Press
New York

Copyright © 1987 by David Long
First published by The Ecco Press in 1987
18 West 30th Street, New York, NY 10001
Published simultaneously in Canada by
Penguin Books Canada Ltd., Ontario
Printed in the United States of America
Designed by Reg Perry

Library of Congress Cataloging in Publication Data
Long, David, 1948–
The flood of '64.
Contents: The last photograph of Lyle Pettibone,
Compensation, Cooper Loftus, (etc.)
I. Title
PS3562.04924F5   1987   813'.54   86–19687
ISBN 0–88001–127–0
ISBN 0–88001–108–4 (ppb.)

Publication of this book was made possible in part by a grant
from the National Endowment for the Arts.

First Edition

ACKNOWLEDGMENTS
"V-E Day" was published in the Sewanee Review (Vol. XCI,
No. 2, Spring 1983). Copyright 1983 by David Long.
"Cooper Loftus" was published in the Sewanee Review (Vol. XCIII,
No. 3, Summer 1985). Copyright 1985 by David Long.
"Great Blue" first appeared in Tendril Magazine.
"Alex's Fire" first appeared in Cut Bank.
"The Flood of '64" and "The Last Photograph of Lyle Pettibone"
first appeared in Antaeus.
"Soltice" first appeared in Northern Light.

The author wishes to thank Sandra Alcosser, Ed Harkness,
Sara Vogan, Bob Wrigley, and the many others who helped,
as well as the staff of the Glacier National Park library.

For Susy and her boys, and for my mother

Contents

Until we die our lives are on the mend.
—Richard Hugo

🙚 *The Last Photograph*
of Lyle Pettibone

I took this early on a Sunday morning, the 26th of August, that blistering summer of 1917. I was using a Brownie Autographic, bought for $18 at the Stillwater Mercantile—you can see where I scratched the date and hour along the bottom of the negative. The people who'd been up all night were gone. Others would soon be rising and dressing for church, and stories would crackle through the streets, but I was alone then, or nearly so, crouched on the rails at the west edge of Stillwater, shivering. I could still smell the fire on my clothes, and the first light, when it finally arrived, came thickened with smoke. I made the picture, folded in the bellows of the camera, and walked back along the tracks toward home.

You asked me how I got started . . . it was then.

I was twenty-one that summer, caught between working as my father's factotum at the Dupree Hotel and being conscripted for the war. Some boys I knew had already left their jobs and shipped out; some others had fashioned hasty marriages . . . I'd see them walking through Depot Park with their pregnant wives after supper, heads bent to the grass. I wasn't so gung ho on the war myself. When the *Clarion* ran the first cull of Sperry County names, three hundred to the man, I was mortally relieved to skim to the end of it without seeing mine. But the relief wore thin before long. Flanders was falling, Russia was going to hell, American recruits were funneling into Pershing's army by the thousands. As for matrimony, the only girl in Stillwater I'd cared for had gone east that May to study piano in earnest. Her name was Marcelle, and she wore a French braid that hung down her back like a bullwhip. Her picture shone at me mornings from the bevel of my shaving mirror. In her last letter, she told of going to the Opera House in Chicago to hear Irma Kincaid perform Chopin. *I know you'll think I'm just being dramatic, Willy, but Irma Kincaid has changed my life.*

I spent my free time staring at the town through the Brownie's viewfinder, developing what I saw in a room off the cold storage under the Dupree. I had a picture of the mayor with his foot planted ceremoniously on the running board of his new Saxon roadster . . . schoolchildren poling their raft down McAfferty's Slough . . . drifters sleeping under a wagon behind the Pastime. "What do you want to take pictures of old bums for?" my sister Ellen would scold me mildly. "There's enough unpleasantness in life without going out and *scrounging* for it." "That's not what I'm doing," I'd tell her, "I'm just keeping my eyes open."

One afternoon I sweet-talked Ellen into sitting for me with her clothes off. We went up to an empty room on the top floor and I made dozens of pictures of her lolling on her quilt pretending she was one of the women on Calhoun Street. She was never a beauty, but her skin was white as bar soap, freckled pleasantly across the bosom, and she was capable of a wicked droopy-eyed smile. "How's this, Willy?" she'd ask, draping herself in a new travesty of wantonness. "You're one to reckon with, all right," I said, and we had a high time, the two of us, there under our father's roof. But when I mentioned the developing and printing, Ellen suddenly glazed with worry and told me she wouldn't allow it. "You have to promise me you won't print them," she said.

"You looked awfully good," I said. "Trust me."

"I'll trust you to never *ever* print those pictures," she said, and threw her robe around herself. "I'm not fooling."

And so I left her glaring out over the roofs of Stillwater, on the edge of tears. Later, I made the negatives and looked at them by myself against the lightbulb, then put them away in a drawer and never printed them up, more's the pity.

Of course, I took my father as well: a florid, girth-heavy widower of Scots–French-Canadian stock, a man burdened by an ungenerous nature and nagging social aspirations, burdened, too, by a daughter who drank and a son he called a runt and a dreamer. . . .

But here's the first picture of Lyle Pettibone. He's down in front of the Montana Cafe, around the corner from where the IWW headquarters had been till that June, when the troopers had come after hours and shut it down. He's just endured another set-to with Wilbur Embree, who was on the town council, and E. C. Doyle, the banker, one of that high-minded crew that came to the hotel at noon every day to pack away one of Ellen's heavy lunches and smoke Cuban cigars with my father. By the time I got across the street, the shoving was done and Pettibone's copies of *Solidarity* were strewn down the boardwalk. Winded, hat aslant, he collected the papers in silence, waiting for the other men to get on with their rightful business. Men like Doyle and Embree thought harassment of unionists *was* their rightful business.

Pettibone was a tall man for those days, sober-looking as the Lutheran pastor, but it wasn't God on Pettibone's mind that summer, or not as yet. You can see his sawtooth of a nose, those chiseled-out cheeks. His voice was the same, sharp as a sickle, rife with a union spiel that either sickened and terrified you, or sliced through all the built-up half-dead parts of you to a place that was still tender and ripe for such radical encouragement—depending on how you fell in the scheme of things. I'd heard where Helena had whistled through an ordinance to ban Wobbly organizers from public declamation, but Pettibone had spoken on our streets for weeks, and up in Depot Park as well. I'd watched him with his long arms thrown open to the sky, and I'd watched the people watching him, people of all kinds, in all kinds of costume, but mostly men I didn't recognize, shading their eyes, listening hard, and a few at the back I did know, taking notes.

They blamed the fire on him. Of course they did.

They'd been expecting something like it and then it happened and there was no question who was behind it and what it meant. All summer the *Clarion* had wailed and prophesied against the Wobbly Menace. Back in July, when trouble broke out down in Arizona, when they loaded Wobbly miners onto cattle cars and rode them out to the Mexican border and dumped them without so much as a tin cup full of water, Will McKinnon wrote that it wouldn't surprise him if citizens all through the West declared an open season on IWWs. He said we'd have a reign of terror. He wasn't personally in any position to advocate such a perversion of justice, but the deaf could've heard him pardon it. He worked that vein so hard, none of the *Clarion*'s right-thinking readers could've harbored any doubt that the IWWs were enemies of the flag, a plague on the country's war effort worse than slackers or pacificists or the few outright cowards dodging conscription. Of course, the Anaconda Company owned McKinnon, owned him outright, as they did damn near every other editor in Montana, then and for a long time after, but that was a distinction lost on me at twenty-one. The town was afraid, you could feel that for certain. Myself, I was restless, and some afraid too, though not of Pettibone or what he said, not yet.

Well, I made that picture of Pettibone on the boardwalk and it wasn't until I started to thank him that he came to his senses and glowered at me.

"What're you doing?" he wanted to know.

It was so obvious I didn't know what to say. Nobody'd ever cared one way or the other if I took their picture, except that time with Ellen.

"Who's this for?" he said.

"It's not for anyone," I said. "I mean, it's for me."

He gave the street a sidelong check, but commerce had resumed around us.

"I liked hearing you talk the other day," I added suddenly . . . unaware until right then that I'd even listened. An illicit pleasure came crushing over me, so palpable Pettibone couldn't fail to witness it. He laid a hand on my shoulder and bent to squint me in the eye.

"You did," he said, solemn and testing, both. "What did you like about it?"

"I don't know," I said. "Sounded fair, what you were saying."

"We should live so long, you and I," Pettibone said.

Then he asked who I was. And I told him, leaving my father and his well-regarded name out of it.

"Willy the photographer . . ." Pettibone said. "You know there's going to be a strike . . . at the mill, here in Stillwater."

All I'd heard so far was the wary grumbling talk of the lunch crowd at the hotel, and McKinnon's.

"I want you to come out to the mill and take some pictures," he said. "I think it would be very good if you would help us this way. You think you're up to that?"

I told him I was.

I told him he could count on me.

But a week later, when the strike came, I was back at the hotel re-shaking the back roof with my father. He could've paid to have it done—there were plenty who wanted a day or two's wage—but he was deviled to do for himself. He hauled his prosperity up the ladder, puffing and swearing at me. You'd think these would've been prime days for an innkeeper, Stillwater swelled out with newcomers as it was. A generation earlier there was woods here, and people still called it Stumptown sometimes, but no one worried anymore that Stillwater would prove another flash in the pan. Even so, these were not peaceable days for my father. Too many of the passers-through couldn't afford the Dupree. Some were family men who'd lost homesteads east of the mountains . . . *honyockers* they were called, immigrants lured West by the Great Northern to farm 320-acre parcels of dust. Many were single, though, with no change of clothes, and—to his mind—unhealthy ambitions, or no ambitions at all. Anyone with a whisper of an accent, or a complexion darker than his own, he suspected of being an agitator. He rented rooms to strangers who could pay, but kept his eye on them, using spies like my sister and the hired girls who served them dinner. What he did with such intelligence as he came by, I didn't know.

We worked side by side on the roof all morning, and I itched to be out at the mill where I didn't belong, but I kept my tongue. I watched the traffic on Main and around the corner on First Street, and it passed for an ordinary day of high summer, though it was hard to pin down what was ordinary anymore. Just before lunch, my father pounded his thumb and cursed the Lord and flung the hammer across the alley, end over end . . . shattering the back window of the Mercantile. He stood on the ladder glaring down into the jagged hole, slack-jawed, as if now he'd surprised even himself.

We'd had strikes before, but nothing since 1909, and the tension was sharper now. What Pettibone was talking about was a general strike Big Bill Haywood and the Wobbly brass had called for the whole Northwest: pickers and harvest hands, miners, mill workers, and bindle stiffs who worked out of logging camps. They wanted five dollars for an eight-hour day and respectable living conditions in the camps. They wanted to run their union without being harassed and shot at and picked up for every kind of petty charge from vagrancy to suspicion of sedition. And they wanted the ones already in jail let go.

They were perfect fodder for the Wobblies. Nobody else was going to stand up for them, that was for damn sure. Timber beasts, people around here called them, illiterate footloose rabble. The mills and camps went through men like cans of beans. The Wobbly talk about One Big Union struck home. *An injury to one is an injury to all,* Pettibone and men like Pettibone said. *Live to be an old man or woman and hear the whistle blow for the bosses to go to work.* It sounded glorious, this talk, but the rest of it, the politics, the trashing of capitalism itself, that was only a far-fetched dream. They'd slept forty or fifty or sixty to a bunkhouse, doubled on straw-covered slabs, their clothes still rank and wet in the morning and no match for the ferocious cold. To a man they'd had lice and dysentery, and plenty had bronchitis they couldn't shake even when the summers finally came. And there weren't any over thirty with two hands full of fingers.

The Wobblies said you can forget about the sweet by-and-by, strike now, and they did.

For a few days, the *Clarion* ignored the strike, except for McKinnon's mighty editorializing, calling for federal troops to root out the IWWs. Then on the 20th of August he announced that the strike had proved a grand failure. But it hadn't . . . or it hadn't yet. For a time, it tied up three-quarters of the mills in the Northwest. But the strikers were isolated —nobody but the Lumbermen's Association and men like McKinnon knew for a fact how far it had gotten.

Now something let loose in McKinnon, and when it let loose in him it let loose all over the county. Other IWWs before Pettibone had stood up and said this wasn't their war, but this was Pettibone's favorite string to harp on. "Stay home," he preached to his people. "Fight your real enemy, fight the bosses." It was too much for McKinnon. *My friends,* he wrote, *treason is treason.* Nothing short of rounding up every last one of them would do, but authority was dragging its heels.

It was a dry summer, as I said. The streams ran low and the sloughs caked over and the grain heads shriveled before harvest. Out east of the mountains it was worse, of course, because the land was infinitely drier there to begin with, but even here in the valley the long afternoons of sun and the promise of a poor crop added to the strain. Early in August, a timber fire started up in Idaho, near the Canadian line, and burned eastward for eight days. It was far away, but you could smell it every morning and see the haze backed up against the mountains to the east. Someone called it sabotage, and a few probably believed it, though surely lightning had touched it off. The forest was government-owned up there, and the Wobs had no kick against that.

Anyway, sabotage was on people's minds. I never heard Pettibone favor it, for his thoughts were on the strike by then, and on the problem of keeping Wobblies out of the conscription. But others had. They called it soldiering on the job. Grain sacks would come unsewn. Shovel handles would break soon as they were passed around. Spikes would appear in logs bound for the headsaw. Whole shipments of cut timber would turn up four inches short. And nobody to blame. Hit the boss in the pocketbook and play dumb, that was the idea. But by that August sabotage had come to explain *anything* going haywire, from polluted wells to derailings of Great Northern. There were some who'd swear the drought itself was a Wobbly trick.

That Saturday, a week into the strike, the town was stuffed with people. Common sense said it was too hot to sit in the movie house, but some were braving it to watch Myrtle Stedman in a five-reeler called *Prison Without Walls*. There was a benefit for the Red Cross out at the Pavillion. At the hotel, we had a wedding party in progress—the Upshaws, important friends of my father, had married their oldest girl to a fellow from Spokane. The groom's mother was a disciple of Temperance so the cut-glass bowls on the buffet held a strawberry punch, but the men excused themselves now and again to work on flasks or bottles of ale my father'd stowed in crushed ice under a tarp on the back porch landing.

Earlier he'd called for pictures, and I'd lined the celebrants up and frozen them for posterity, still fresh. But now it was stifling inside. Even the cut flowers were droopy on their stems. The dining room was cleared of tables and Mort Pickerell's string band played and the guests danced. My sister Ellen looped freely about the room in the grasp of the groom's brother, her shoes off and her eyes half-shut. My father and Matthew Upshaw and the groom's father presided over it all, smiling heavily and dabbing at their foreheads with handkerchiefs.

I'd had enough of noise and pleasantry, and I thought I'd expire without some air. I headed out toward the kitchen and slipped up the back hall to my quarters on the third floor where I could sit in the window with my feet out on the peak of the porch roof. It was nine-thirty by my watch, just growing dark. The sky west of town was still aglow and overhead was a smear of deepening blues. Some of the mill workers had taken their last roll of wages over to Calhoun Street, I imagined, but most were down below, drinking. Men were spilling out the doorways of the Pastime, the Grandee, the Silver Dollar, and already there was yelling.

From up here, the town didn't look like so much, a few streets of commerce, a grid of frame houses stretching north to the Great Northern yard, south to the elevators, a little cluster of lights on the valley floor you could imagine snuffed out by the Lord's little finger. In a while, the evening wind came across the roofs. I stretched and breathed it in, expecting the smell of hay . . . not creosote and burning pitch. I jerked my head up and caught sight of the train yard. All up one siding, boxcars and flatbeds loaded with lumber were shooting out flames, full-blown at the western end, just getting going down by the station. For an instant, it seemed I was the only witness . . . then a few figures broke into running, and the headlamps of a few cars veered into Depot Square . . . then, all at once, the people on Main Street began to know.

I hustled back inside and bolted into the hallway and down through the back wing . . . but a door opened in front of me and a man backed out, latching the door gingerly, as if he'd left someone sleeping. He straightened and saw me and stopped short.

It was Pettibone. What was he doing there? *My God!*

"William," he said. He looked enormously tired. His shoulders drooped and his hands hung from his sleeves like skinned rabbits.

"The train's on fire," I said.

The words didn't reach him at first.

"The train," I said. "The whole . . . all the lumber's burning."

There's no picture of Pettibone in the hallway, gazing down at me in bewilderment . . . except as I've called it to mind so many times. They say action was Pettibone's long suit, action and oratory. Still, with such a picture in hand, you'd see how the real man was given more to brooding and intellection. You'd see the incomprehension letting down into understanding and disappointment and weariness.

Then, standing opposite, we heard the fire bell. Pettibone returned a wayward suspender to his shoulder and peered over me at the empty hallway.

"I thought we were going to have pictures of the strike," he said.

"Well, I didn't make it," I started in, but Pettibone wouldn't have any use for cowardice, so I shut up. *I'll make it up to you,* I was thinking.

Pettibone shook his head. He turned and went back into the room and threw the bolt.

By the time I got to the fire, things were already out of hand. Not only were the cars burning, but a storage shed had caught, and the fire had leapt from it to a snarl of weeds and torn across them like a dam burst to a garage on Railroad Street. From the platform I could hear the popping glass and the whoosh of air, and from all sides commands and argument flaring and jumping from man to man. They'd managed to get some of the cars unhitched, but by the time they could get an engine jockeyed to the right track it was pointless to try and pull them all apart.

Some councilmen had arrived, and volunteer firemen, and men who worked the yard for the Great Northern, but for all this authority, nobody was in charge. A couple of hundred others pressed around, many come straight from the dance, the women in summer linen with flowers or hair ribbons worked loose, the men holding their jackets and staring. Through this crowd soon pushed some stalwarts of the Lumbermen's Association, including two of the mill owners, brothers named Kavanaugh, who'd made it in from a lodge on the lake with remarkable haste.

One boxcar was wheat, and two flatbeds were ties soaked in tar and creosote, but the other twenty-four were stacked full of contract lumber. The two Kavanaughs halted on the platform, observably angrier—and more stupefied—than the rest of us. They searched the line of fires, then turned and searched the line of flickering faces. In a moment they set off down the spur for a closer inspection, but the heat and the down-swooping coils of black smoke stopped them short, and they stood silhouetted in the cinders finally, gawking with the rest of us.

The firemen had now turned to that tongue of blaze threatening Railroad Street. The pumper and the chemical truck were pulled up at the edge of the heat. The south wall of Kramer's car barn was eaten away and smoke came chuffing through the roof shakes. If they knew that railroad bums sometimes slept off bad weather or liquor in Kramer's loft, it didn't figure in their attentions. They sprayed down the sides of the next building up the line, some of the water turning instantly to steam. For a handful of minutes, the rest of that scraggly block—and who could tell what else—hung on the whim of the wind.

Then the crowd's first amazement burned off. The men in front got tired of standing around. Helplessness offended them. Shoving broke out by the depot doors. By the time I could worm myself near, one man had been wrestled to the pavement and another was being restrained by a beefy Sperry County deputy. They held the man down with a knee at his neck, like a calf for branding. In no time they'd been through his pockets and found his red card and showed it around to everyone, and the same with his friend's.

"No law against being in the union," the friend said, but he was a small man and surrounded.

"Don't give me law, mister," the deputy said.

Someone reached in and kicked at the down man's ribs, and the struggling started up again. A third man, who'd been standing by, was shoved forward.

"Here's another one," somebody yelled.

The depot door opened and the county sheriff stood illuminated by the fire, a man tall as Pettibone but solid as a steer. He eyed the boxcars, then popped open his watch and had a look at that, closed it with a patient click, then came striding down through the people to where the trouble was, one hand on his holster. Out the door behind him came the two preened heads of the Kavanaughs, but they slipped away into the commotion, and that was all I saw of them that night.

Maybe it was the sheriff who said it, or maybe the word was spat from some other mouth, but I heard it clear enough. *Pettibone.*

I won't say I fit this all together right then, for I was a slow blossomer in most all things, matters of deceit included. But I worked my way out from the people and the rising clamor at the station and headed down through the alleys toward the Dupree.

I ran up through the shadows onto the back porch and my boot sent an empty bottle ringing across the landing, but no one was left to hear. The party had gone astray. Some of the guests had dashed off to the station, not being able to stand not going any longer, and some had come back and were loitering in the big room wondering what kind of mood to take up now. The bride and groom had departed. There was no sign of my father. Even the band had left their instruments on top of the piano and were gone.

I ran up the two flights of back stairs and down to the door where I'd had my sudden audience with Pettibone. No one answered my knocking. I put my ear to the door, but was breathing too hard to hear. Next thing, without a thought, I had my third-floor key out.

The curtains flapped into the room indifferently, those strips of cheap poplin my father assigned to his dollar-fifty rooms. The bed was stirred-up, cigarettes were snuffed out in a water glass on the window sill . . . that was it. I tried to fix Pettibone there in the room, that dark lankiness and agitation. And who it was *with* him, and what would possess him to trespass under my father's roof, so near the authorized gaiety downstairs. It occurred to me with a cold rush that I didn't know the first blessed thing about men like Pettibone, where they could find their respite in a town like ours, where they could turn when they had to.

When you thought of Stillwater, you thought of the railroad. You saw the depot in your mind's eye, looming at the end of Main, huge, white-painted, monument to the wheeling and dealing that secured us the GN's northern route, when everyone expected it to dip south to Sperry. It'd been my duty, since the age of fourteen, to loiter there, outside on a baggage cart by summer, inside on the curved walnut benches by winter, waiting for the train to disgorge guests for the Dupree.

But tonight, by the time I'd returned, the depot was ringed by men with guns.

Some were police and some were National Guard, and some were just men from town. They'd started rounding up Wobblies. The jail was too puny for such a job, so they were herded into the depot's generous waiting room. I climbed up on the back railing and stole a look through the stationmaster's window. Fifty or more of them were in there, packed together under the lights. They looked like they were waiting for a train, but where they were going they didn't need bags.

I tried to wiggle the window up enough to stick the Brownie through . . . but someone suckered me back of the knees and I fell from the railing and my head careened back against the concrete. The noise and the lights went dead for a moment, then came pounding back with the bang of my heart. I got up on all fours, but crumpled again with an awful pain and dizziness, and was a moment later hauled up by the back of the shirt and marched around into the light on spidery legs, then searched. The man was in uniform, no one I knew or who knew me. He stood me against the depot wall while he composed himself. I could feel the fires on my face. Burning like that, it seemed like they could burn forever. Nothing in focus, I strayed a few feet toward the tracks, but he had me again and prodded me past the windows and thrust me in.

The smoke was worse inside, trapped under shafts of heavy electric light. One guardsman had the door and there was one in each corner and one more perched in the ticket window with a shotgun cocked over his forearm, five in all, against a roomful of herded-up men.

"What you waiting for, bohunk?" the one at the door said.

I stumbled out into the middle. The nearest men looked

me up and down and saw they didn't know me and turned
back to themselves. I found space and collapsed to the bench
and held my head. Slowly, the pounding lightened and my
thoughts began to clear. I looked at the faces around me
. . . and remembered the camera, felt it dropping from my
hand again, falling away into the trampled shadows.

The door snapped open in a while and another man was
driven inside. A languid wave rolled through the hanging
smoke and broke against the far wall, then the air settled
again. He was middle-aged, this one, with a dazed, swollen
face and the tails of his shirt blood-soaked. He was as lost in
here as I was. I realized then that I knew him, or recognized
him, from the photo I'd taken behind the Pastime, when he
was sleeping under Von Ebersole's wagon. He was no Wobbly, this one.

For a time it was quiet. The heat grew and pressed in on
us and the room took on a mean smell. Some of the men
wouldn't sit down anymore.

"You," one was saying, up and staring the nearest
guardsman in the face. "How old you supposed to be?"

The guardsman was hardly older than me, a moon-faced
boy in a clean uniform that didn't fit. He jockeyed the gun
around in his arms and squinted off above our heads at the
other guards, but the haze isolated him.

"Look at what they get to point guns at good union
men," the man said, louder, narrowing in on the boy and his
gun. Another two steps and he could wrap his hand around
the muzzle. I couldn't tell how people would act anymore,
what they'd give the most weight to at any particular moment.
I could see how the first shot would be touched off in panic
and self-regard maybe, or would just expel itself like matter
in a boil, then the others would have their reason and they'd
lace us in a crossfire, and we'd be in no shape to say boo about
it afterwards, though the guards would say plenty enough and
McKinnon would write it up in a high style and people would
believe it gladly and completely.

"Sit down, Blue," somebody called out.

This Blue rocked back on his heels and turned to us. He

was drunk, or he'd been started that way when they'd caught up with him. His mouth was chapped with tobacco, his eyes flat and watery as he tried to light on the one who'd yelled at him.

"Shut him the hell up," someone farther back shouted.

Blue shook his head, stranded between us and the guard. "You pukes," he said. "You ain't worth boot grease."

There was nothing of Pettibone in him, nothing of entitlement or pride, I understood then, and got a sick feeling for us all.

Pettibone could've said what they were doing: penning us up until morning when they could march us out in the daylight past the stench and ruin of the lumber train and load us onto cattle cars just readied for the purpose, the idea not even fresh, stolen from the Bisbee, Arizona, copper mines, or over at Everett, Washington . . . and haul us out of the valley and the county and the state on the suspicion of sabotage.

Pettibone could've stood up and told them—*us*—it wasn't his fire, and engendered a silence around him, in which every one of us at the station—Wobbly or no—would get clearheaded and remember that we weren't individually or in concert stupid enough to bolt up the line of train cars with gallon bottles of kerosene and punks, with the sun barely down and the town crawling with people and no realizable good to come from it, only trouble, which had materialized in force. It's true, Pettibone, by himself, or with the rest of us solidified around him, wouldn't have been able to *stop* the deportation, any more than he, or any of the others, right up to Big Bill Haywood himself, could stop the War Department from shipping IWWs off to Army camps, but with him there the men could've known the extent of what was going on and not gone at each other, empty-handed and down in their hearts. But, of course, Pettibone could not have risked being there himself.

The filigreed hands of the station clock said one-forty. The door to the tracks cracked open then and the sheriff pushed his way in, a gang of deputies in tow.

The room got quiet again, man by man.

The sheriff looked around for something to stand on, then just raised his voice. "Listen like this mattered," he said. "You're going to line up against that wall for me, that one with the bulletin board on it," he said. "Fast and orderly would be a good way."

After a decent interval, the nearest bunch rose as if their bones hurt and moved grudgingly toward the wall. A few more straggled over and I joined them and then most of the rest came, leaving Blue alone, slouched on the last bench, talked out. The boy guard moved in on him, happily, and pointed the gun at his face.

The sheriff drifted over to the two of them.

"Where's Pettibone?" he asked Blue.

Blue didn't say anything. He looked from the sheriff's face to the snout of the gun and down to his shoes.

The sheriff nodded. He picked his watch out again, opened it and turned to compare it with the clock on the wall.

"All right," he said. He motioned to the boy to get Blue up and standing like the rest of us. Blue swung his arm out to bat the gun barrel away from his face, but the boy swiveled the butt around and cracked him in the temple and he went down across the bench and lay there, derelict.

The sheriff walked back over to us. "Where's Pettibone?" he said to the first man.

The man said he didn't know.

The sheriff watched him impassively. "If you knew, you'd tell me, wouldn't you," he said.

The man didn't say anything.

"I know what kind you are," the sheriff said, still eyeing him. "I know what you'd do."

He moved down the line, one deputy following along with a note pad, taking names. When he got to me he stopped and scowled.

It wasn't Pettibone, I thought, the sheriff hulking over me. *It could not have been Pettibone—even carried out by someone else's hand, could not have been.*

"Well, Mr. Dupree," the sheriff said. "Looks to me like it's time for you to get on home."

And like that, like sleight of hand, or worse, I was outside again, where it was cooler and the air was less concentrated and the crowd had been broken into factions and dispersed. The fires were still going but I didn't want to look at them anymore. I started back to the Dupree, despite myself. Where else was I going to go?

It occurred to me that I might walk up to that third-floor room and find the door open and the bed clean-made, and no vestige of Pettibone except in my imagination . . . my father's tremulous baritone reiterating in my mind's ear how untrustworthy I was, how weak to give myself over time and again to the made-up instead of the certifiably real and necessary. But if all that milled lumber was burning and the depot was full of men to be locked inside cattle cars, then anything else could've happened, I was thinking. Salmon could come raining down out of the sky. I was halfway down Dakota Street near the Chinese laundry before I remembered the camera.

I knew I'd find it ruined, the lens shattered and the bellows ripped like a rag, but I had a sudden fierce desire to secure it and carry it home. I snuck back through the elms to the dark side of the depot and pawed through the heavy shadows beneath the railing, and down in the gap between some packing crates and the wall, then out on the grass, though that was too far for it to have flown. I was kneeling there, stupefied, my hands wet with dew, when a flurry of raised voices from up on the platform drove me back behind the boxes. In a moment, three men came past, one in uniform, the others decently dressed, men I knew I'd seen before but didn't know. They couldn't decide whether to run or walk fast. They crossed to a car waiting along the park and two got in. The other leaned down and kept talking, his free hand flitting like a huge bug against the streetlight.

Finally the headlamps came on and the two men drove off and the third stood looking after them, then did an about-face and peered back at the trainyard and up at the putrid

orange halo above it. Then he was gone too. I pulled myself
up by the lid of the packing box and it came free in my hands,
and there, swaddled in shavings, was the Brownie.

Try these other pictures: Pettibone and the woman—for it
was now, in my mind, surely a woman, hard-faced comrade
and lover under the guise of a traveling widow, whose room
he had visited in the hotel—hurtling in a car away from Sperry
County toward shelter and counsel at the Wobbly cabal in
Spokane. Or Pettibone alone—just as likely—striding west on
the GN tracks toward that skinny part of Idaho that should
still have been Montana, satchels in either hand swinging like
ballast, long legs hitting every second tie in perfect cadence.
I could see him halting every little while to listen—for what,
for dogs? They didn't have dogs, these officers or citizens who
were after him, or have need of them apparently. Pettibone,
his head cocked east, just the dimmest smudge of sky-reflected
firelight glancing off his face, would hear only the yap and
howl of a coyote, most of the timber wolves having retreated
to British Columbia by our time, and the clamor of the town
not carrying much beyond its boundaries, and the worst of
that just spoken and confirmed between men in voices not
meant to carry. . . .

Or picture any of the others I dreamed up, still hidden
in the lee of the depot, the camera folded against my shirt, not
twenty feet from where the sweating-out of Pettibone's actual
whereabouts continued, the sheriff's shadow obliterating each
man's night-beaten face in turn. What they'd have in common, these pictures, would be Pettibone in flight, for I
couldn't shake the image of him in the upstairs hallway, face
abruptly unleavened by the news I'd delivered and all the
implication he wrung from it in a few consecutive instants.
Battles are won by the remnants of armies, that was a Pettibone
refrain, lifted maybe from an Old Testament litany of suffering and endurance. *Outnumber, outsmart, outlast them. . . .* I
could only imagine him using his head start like a weapon.

And as for the Wobblies inside, it wouldn't matter if they
knew or didn't know, if they broke ranks or not . . . whatever

any of them said, it could be taken as more sabotage, more red-inspired trickery. These thoughts in mind, I tried out a new idea: that I might be forgiven for not telling what I knew, the truth about Pettibone and the fire . . . that my silence might even be strategic, the better part of valor. All of which was consoling . . . but missed the point entirely. For I'd managed all night not to ask myself the question that counted.
    If it wasn't Pettibone's fire, whose was it?

McKinnon was right: it was the end of the Wobblies in Sperry County, beginning of the end even in Butte, union town above all others. "The expected has happened," he wrote in Monday's paper, the rest of the state and the Northwest looking on, meaning not the fire itself, which he decried separately, but the work of the twenty or so free-lance men who located Pettibone and took him into their collective custody, at roughly the same late hour of the night that the sheriff finally concluded that not one of those miserable Wobblies in the depot actually knew where Pettibone was.
    Deportation by boxcar, that must've been the heart of the plan, as conceived, for the cars were too readily at hand, paid for by the sacrifice of a *portion* of the lumber train—but not the whole of it, certainly, and not those car barns down Railroad Street, and not the railroad bum charred to futility inside one of them. Nor the combustion of anger—most of all that—in no time surpassing their design. McKinnon played it straight. He passed the buck to Congress for not protecting industry, then turned his vitriol on Pettibone for a last time. "Hysterical," McKinnon said of Lyle Pettibone, "mentally unbalanced, preying on uneducated, unsophisticated laborers. . . ."
    I left Stillwater.
    The rest I know you're familiar enough with: the staff work I did those years for the *Post-Dispatch,* then my great fortune at meeting Roy Stryker who added me to the group he had at the Farm Security Administration, Dorothea Lange and Russ Lee and Walker Evans and those others making pictures of the tenants and croppers blown out of the Dust-

bowl . . . all of it, I can see now, fitting together, aiming me toward that day in 1941, outside General Tire in Akron, when some union men swarmed and beat down a strikebreaker, which was the shot they gave the Pulitzer for.

It's luck who gets the prize, that's an article of faith. But I took it as an honor, regardless . . . because even then, forty-four years old, older even than Pettibone had been, I would still sometimes hear my father's grinding deprecations of me and be tempted, despite the evidence, to believe in them . . . and because luck's not enough to explain what I was doing at General Tire that day, that change of shift. The tire workers, ganging in union regalia, with balled fists and nightsticks, and smiles burning into frantic bloom on their faces . . . and the scabs, this one here cut from the pack, bent double under one thickness of overcoat, nothing showing but a bony hand aimed at the sky like half a prayer. They knew what they were doing, all of them. And I knew my business by then as well, for it's a man's duty to find what he's good for, if he finds nothing else worth the cost of learning it. In all his days, in all his dogged sucking up to men of property and office my father never found this out.

That Sunday morning in Stillwater, after I'd talked myself home along the tracks, holding the folded Brownie inside my shirt, I slipped down into the cellar of the Dupree where it was cool and no one ever came—except my sister, in search of potatoes for the kitchen, or communion with her private store of red wine hidden among the Ball jars of Sperry County cherries. In a few minutes I had the film stripped, developed, and hanging by a clothespin to dry. I sat down in the dark and touched the clotted lump at the back of my head. I heard the morning commencing above me, the wince of guests reaching the bottom tread of the front staircase, one after another, pausing on the foyer carpet, struck lavender by sunlight spewing through the transom, then crossing onto the bare floor of the dining room where the tables had been restored. I heard the hired girl's feet clipping back and forth to the kitchen, Ellen's dragging by the stove. I heard the waste water come coursing down the pipes and in a while I heard the church bells start in. Gradually, the dining room grew quiet. I got up and turned on the light and passed the negative before it. There they all were . . . the bride and her earnest groom, the mothers, Matthew Upshaw and my father and their friends, everyone shoulder to shoulder, dignified before the camera . . . and there at the end of the roll, Lyle Pettibone, uninvited, hanging from a trestle just west of town.

⚝⚝⚝ *Cooper Loftus*

Cooper was welcome in the main house for breakfast but never came. He kept to the wellhouse, where he slept on a foam mat Bram and his sister Kelly let him have. From its single window he could see their lights come on downstairs, the smoke beginning to pour from the kitchen chimney. It didn't laze off into the air now that the mornings had turned, but held its shape, gray against gray. Jerking the cold and the sleep from his shoulders, he watched for Kelly's face to show in the light above the sink, and when it did, he stopped looking, and started waiting for Bram to stride across the pea gravel to the barn and fire up his old International and sound the horn. Then he trotted down past the sheep yard, the hood of his sweatshirt up, his elbows hugged to his vest, and Bram leaned over and cracked the door for him and he climbed in where it was starting to get warm.

He was a head taller, Bram, thin as a fence board, except for his arms, which masonry work had thickened like burls. He was long all over, long hands, long quiet clean-shaved face, with cropped-off hair the color of an old nickel, though Cooper figured he couldn't be more than forty. Where mornings were a fight for Cooper, Bram settled into the day first thing. Nothing seemed to surprise him . . . whatever happened, he looked like he'd already given it some thought. Cooper read more there too, sadness maybe, but he had no business messing with that.

They didn't talk much in the truck. Sometimes Bram snaked out an arm to soften the radio and told Cooper if he was planning on staying in the valley he ought to know things the locals knew—that, for one, the crowned field above town where the new hospital and the doctors' offices had sprung up once had a buffalo herd grazing across it, a hundred-something head bought and hauled there by the Cripps family, whose name was on half the things in Sperry, from the biggest bank to the cemetery. Or for another that this slice of lowland they crossed on the other side of town, full of junk trees and pastured horses and thrown-together houses, was all flood plain, all under threat of washing away come another freakish spring like the one they had in 1964.

Bram would take a final squint over at him and add, "Sometime you'll thank me for all this useful stuff," then put the volume back up.

Cooper watched the road and let most of it drop into his slow-waking head unhindered. He didn't mind Bram's talking at him like that. It wasn't a hard voice to listen to—it was high and decent-sounding and unrushed. Surely it wasn't *Bram's* fault for thinking Cooper was a regular person who made plans.

Up on the scaffold the blocks glittered with frost. Cooper's fingers were crimped and stiff inside the gloves, but by coffee he couldn't see his breath anymore, and by lunch he was as limber as he was going to get. The air had a sweet hazy smell. Down along the sloughs, the aspen were already fluttering gold, the maple and the cottonwood looked green as worn-out dollar bills. He could see mallards flocking, and those yellow-headed blackbirds they had in this country. It was exactly the kind of day that couldn't last. Even Bram stuck his head up now and then, letting his eyes sweep down the valley, not saying anything.

They capped off the chimney about four and loaded the staging in the back of Bram's truck and Bram told the rest of his crew to take off. Down to T-shirt now, Cooper watched McElroy's 4 × 4 jounce through the cattle guard and down off the hill, disappearing behind its own storm of dust.

Bram came over noncommittal for a minute, his eyes still

searching around in the sky, then got down to what he had to say. Cooper'd seen it coming since way last week, looming up like a change in his private weather.

"Now Coop, I got to tell you about Toby," Bram started in. There wasn't work for five, that was what it came down to, and Toby, Bram's friend and oldest hand, was coming back Monday, the torn rotator cuff healed to where he could lay bathroom tile. The truth was, Bram said, once this job on the hill was finished he'd have a tough time keeping four of them occupied.

"You don't have to say nothing," Cooper said.

"Well, I know I don't," Bram said.

Nobody knew better than Cooper the break Bram had given him, nearly eight weeks' work so far, cash under the table and no questions asked.

Cooper'd hit the valley in early summer, with five twenties and change left from day work in Washington state, knowing full well the woman wouldn't be there anymore. Shelby, her name was. Four winters ago, when Cooper was twenty and had a future, she'd been a dinner hostess on the mountain, as finely turned-out a woman as he'd ever touched. But *four years,* he must be a total idiot. Not finding the least flicker of her, that was what made sense. He gave up looking the second day, then got to worrying that he might actually find her if he knocked around Stillwater long enough . . . find her married, find her not wanting a thing to do with him. So he caught a ride down to Sperry, which he thought would be easier to disappear into, and it was.

The Washington state money petered out in no time, and though the nights were easy now, in the forties with the winds not so fretful and the scent of fruit blossoms dropping down on him wherever he'd curled up, a new tiredness overtook him. He woke lame and coffee didn't cheer him. Getting through a winter on the loose had taken all he had. Not chancing more than a couple or three nights in the same place . . . talking back the fear that got going in him like a sick headache as every afternoon the light started to leak out of the clouds once more . . . being rocked from sleep by any kind of noise ten times a night, then giving up when it still wasn't daylight and going outside and walking and staying away from people, sometimes passing a lighted pay phone at that hour and asking himself if there was someone left he could call. Yes, he figured he ought to be grateful down in his bones that winter was through. But it didn't work that way. Now he felt like he was throwing his weight against a wall that was no longer there.

It was right then that Bram had run onto him, needing another hand to help buck a few-odd acres of hay and alfalfa. Theirs was a patchwork place, Bram's and Kelly's, close in to town, flanked by crab apple and windbreak poplar, with a steep side hill and deep woods in back. Three dozen sheep, a couple horses, chickens—it just bordered on being too much to manage with their outside jobs. Next Cooper found himself installed in the wellhouse. Pretty soon after that he was learning mud work from Bram.

Bram took a bottle out of the jockey box and offered it. He wasn't much of a drinker, neither was Kelly, but he offered anyway, like something he ought to do. Cooper didn't much go for the stuff straight himself, but he took a little and handed it back.

"I can ask around," Bram said.

You been good to me, that's what needed saying, but Cooper came up short of uttering it.

"Sure," he said.

He knew better than to get his hopes up. Another winter was coming, and it would thin out crews all over the valley before long. At least those others, Cooper let himself remember once again, they'd be getting some unemployment, some benefits.

"This doesn't change anything else," Bram said. He attempted a smile but it didn't take. It looked to Cooper like he had some more to say, but maybe it was just the borderline kind of day it was . . . it made everything sound half-said.

Dinner was another story. Cooper had a deadly hunger by that hour, the sugar food and the coffee burned out of him, and his thoughts spitting like hot grease. Most nights Kelly cooked, food Cooper hadn't eaten in years: summer squash steamed crisp and sprinkled with Parmesan, stuffed tomatoes, carrots ten minutes out of the ground glazed with brown sugar. But some nights Bram went upstairs and showered and came back in good jeans and a shirt fresh from the cleaners, and made a fire and put on lamb steaks from one of their Suffolks.

Cooper would borrow the downstairs john and wipe his face and arms clean and join them on the deck. He took a beer if they offered, nursed it along, waiting for the coals. Kelly was the one to talk at that hour—nothing earth-shattering as far as Cooper could tell, what needed attention around the place for the most part, another dose of thuricide for the garden, some goop for the sheep, one kind of telephone message or another. Bram sat slumped in the canvas chair, knees off at angles, the can of Rainier resting at his belt buckle. Sometimes he'd say as much as *Oh, that can keep.* Sometimes he only nodded, rubbing his eyes with the heel of his free hand.

Cooper sat back, listening, trying to keep out of the way. He didn't know what to make of these two. Kelly leaned back with her arms out against the railing, the low sun hitting her back. She was a hand taller than Cooper, almost Bram's height, with the same rangy legs, the same crop of hair gone to silver too early. And her face . . . his mother would've called it *homely as a mud fence,* a little goggle-eyed, with roughed-up skin and none of that cheerful-because-God-loves-me look his mother talked up—but Cooper guessed she looked all right. She didn't get him feeling edgy right off, which was something, but then what difference did it make, for she had at least ten years on him. It wasn't like he had to be *interested* in her.

After the silences she'd start up again, maybe letting loose of some business from when she and Bram were kids there, like the night she got herself locked in the root cellar.

"It was around dusk," she said. "Pretty much had to be summer sometime because it was stone empty in there, in the cellar."

"It was the same week as Dad's birthday," Bram said.

"August then. Well, I guess I had some complaint. I guess I just had to get off by myself for a few minutes. I kept pulling on the door, inching it in, you know, until *click,* there goes the latch . . . one of those sounds where you know exactly what you've done to yourself."

Cooper had to wonder how much of this was for him. He looked off toward the garden, at the strange elastic shadows of the sheep looping across the grass. He tried to picture this tall grown-up woman little, stuck in the dark.

"We thought the wild animals had got her," Bram said, smiling now.

"You were worried sick," Kelly said.

"Not me."

"I know you," Kelly said.

"Dad was," Bram said.

His eyes came up to Cooper. "It was after midnight when he finally thought to look up there . . . and here she's curled up on one of the shelves. Dreaming her dreams."

Kelly looked at her brother for a second and didn't say anything, then stared off.

"I swear you sound like him sometimes," she said.

Cooper couldn't tell if this was teasing or something else.

"Like Dad?" Bram said, a little of the smile remaining. "I could be guilty of that."

Kelly craned her head toward Cooper. "You should've seen the old man," she said. "It was something, how he mothered this place. . . ."

Her voice tailed off. Later on in the summer, on a night when weather sent them inside, Cooper first saw the yoked pictures of their father presiding over the kitchen, the one on the left from when he was years younger than Bram . . . up on the back of an Appaloosa, mountains showing over his shoulder, kind of a goofy-looking boy, Cooper thought at first, except for the eyes, which even at that distance seemed to glint with confidence, and they weren't so changed in the other picture, a studio sitting from when he was old, the confidence having gone to kindliness and strength. Then from time to time Cooper heard mention of the stroke, which spared him having to ask about the wheelchair ramp still angling off the back door. He could feel how they missed him, how they kept bumping into him in their thoughts. His own father hadn't much figured in Cooper's life, unless you counted that bloodless authority his mother summoned up when Cooper pushed her too hard. "If your father was here," she'd get going, her eyes the size of buttonholes, "how disappointed he'd be, how really bad he'd feel about you. . . ." To the point where Cooper couldn't conjure him up, even for the sake of pleasure, without considering his own host of shortcomings first.

Before long the dragonflies came swooping down from the elms, weeding the mosquitoes out of the air. Kelly brought the plates out and they served up.

Then came another little silence. Bram dipped his head and said a blessing. It wasn't fancy, just a thank-you-kindly delivered in Bram's workaday voice, what you'd say to somebody who helped you push your car out of a snow bank. But that first time it caught Cooper off guard. About to panic, he stared at Bram, sure this was it, this was the kicker, that they were planning on getting him wrapped up in some religion. But then they were eating, just going on with things, not paying him any special attention. He let out his breath and looked down at the food and, finally, took a bite.

Most nights after dinner he put on a pair of Bram's gloves and walked out into the alfalfa and moved pipe for the next day's irrigating. After that he went back up to the wellhouse and sat in the doorway flipping through old Eddie Bauer catalogs Kelly saved, or just staring at the mountains past Sperry until it got dark enough to sleep. Some nights he heard the radio playing in the big house, but didn't know which of them was listening to it. He didn't know what they did in there at night. The music leaked out through the screened windows . . . it killed him how he couldn't quite hear what the songs were. He'd go in and lie down, but it carried through the boards, making him think of the cars pulled up along the river outside of La Grande, the radios all tuned to the same station, the music beating out across the water to where he sat on the rocks, watching from a hopeless distance.

One night when Bram was gone in town, Kelly appeared at the corner of the wellhouse, fresh from the garden, one arm wrapped around a colander full of raspberries. She came and squeezed down beside him on the sill and tumbled a few berries into his hand.

"You want to help me celebrate?" she asked him.

Now what, Cooper thought, but before he could do anything, she was telling him about being married.

She'd been nineteen, he was a builder from up in Stillwater, someone Bram had brought home.

"A big Swede with a red beard," Kelly said.

"You like beards?" Cooper asked.

"I liked *his,*" she said, laughing at herself, Cooper thought. "All, you know, fiery, out of control . . . and he had great eyes, Cooper, and . . . well, he had things to recommend him, all right."

She pointed downhill toward the crab apples. "Look there," she said. "There under the shade's where we had it. . . . Dad was in his chair. It was a pretty day, not a cloud. Well, you should've seen Bram all dressed up. . . ."

Cooper felt immediately stupid as she went on telling him this. He hadn't given as much as a second's thought to her having any life except the one tied to the place, to Bram. But then he thought, why shouldn't she? God, he hated it the way he never got past how things looked first off.

"No kids, I guess?" Cooper said.

Kelly looked at him, shook her head lightly. "I'll tell you what, Cooper," she said. "It just didn't get that far."

Cooper groped for something to say, ended up sticking the raspberries in his mouth.

"It's all right," she went on, but it sounded like she didn't mean it.

What happened? he wanted to ask her. *What messed it up?* This is the part he had to know, had to really get a handle on . . . because already he saw her as someone who knew what she was doing, like Bram, already he'd let part of himself begin to trust her.

So in a little while he forced himself to say it out loud, to ask her.

She didn't answer. He could feel her shoulder against his. When neither said anything for a little while, Cooper got to thinking about that girl he'd known, that Shelby, got to remembering how the skin on her shoulders had been suntanned even in the middle of winter, smooth as a wood carving, and how he'd been allowed to run his hands over it all he wanted to, just that one night, but that was all of it he could remember. What kind of things she said to him in bed, what kind of smell she gave off . . . it was all gone.

Then he felt her hand, Kelly's hand, as it closed on his leg, just hard enough, and he looked down across that enormous space and saw her fingers against the denim like streaks of light, and felt the same pop and whoosh of fear as when Bram had said his grace at table, the same wrenching from being yanked two ways at once. But then the hand was back folded with its mate, and she was saying, her voice low-pitched and peaceable, "Well, it gets a little wrong sometimes, huh Cooper?"

That Friday at quitting time, after Bram had delivered his bad news about the job, and the two of them had drunk on it, they climbed into the truck and started off home like nothing had occurred. Bram hunched over as usual for a clear shot at the windshield, one hand cupped on the shift knob. Cooper tried to shuck down and close his eyes, but the road coming off the hill was more pointy shale than dirt, and after the third time his head slapped the door frame, he sat up and held on, beginning to think about how Bram had told him things would stay the same out at the ranch. He came to understand, shortly, that Bram could *not* have meant it like it sounded, that it was only his way of being civilized and not spelling out what Cooper ought to know on his own. In Cooper's experience, the only things that stayed the same were who you were and what you'd already done.

When they came to a rolling stop at the county road, Cooper suddenly cracked his door and jumped out, skidding down onto one knee in the loose gravel.

Bram slipped the truck out of gear and stared at him through the open window, blinking slow, half-curious as a bay mare.

"We're going to see you back at the house?" he said.

Cooper turned away.

He didn't know what possessed him sometimes. It felt funny standing there, wanting to get back in the truck. He started walking. Nothing happened for a few steps, then he heard the International rumble onto the pavement and felt its wind swirl around him, then fade as he picked his way along the scruff of the borrow pit. He watched it lumber up the rise, the tangle of scaffolding in back shooting off spears of light.

He'd lied to them from the first day.

A summer ago, sinking into the dark plush of a guy's van, out on the Interstate east of The Dalles, the name *Cooper* had stumbled off his tongue, and he'd gone ahead and used it when he'd had to ever since . . . even here with Bram and Kelly, though he'd have been the first to say it wasn't right. Now, evenings, when he'd hear Kelly call from the deck, the *Coo-per* bounding off the side hill to where he was setting pipe, tired as he was, he'd think he could walk back to the main house and tell her he was Stuart Norgren out of La Grande, Oregon, and see if anything tumbled along after it . . . but by the time he'd get back to the yard, he'd have shied off that idea.

The real Cooper Loftus was legend back in La Grande. One twilight—long ago when Stuart was still working his mind on fractions and state capitals—Cooper Loftus had ambushed his own father with a haying fork, half-blinding him and tearing the flesh of his cheek and puncturing his voice box in one blow, an act Stuart could scarcely bring himself to believe, even when Simon Loftus appeared downtown every Saturday morning for years after, helped out of his morbid mud-splattered Coupe de Ville by another son, with the waxy scars and the eye patch bearing witness.

Cooper Loftus was the name his mother used to chastise him, to shrivel him, the fine point in her telling of the story being the retribution visited upon Cooper, not a month after the act itself, occurring at a bridge abutment outside of Yreka. "This is precisely and exactly what happens," his mother said. *God,* could he hear it in his sleep, her voice like surgical steel. "The Lord says you may count on it, Stuart. Don't you believe you're a special case, my man, don't you believe it."

What he wanted was to go back to when there'd only been the warnings, the time before any of it had materialized. *Trouble rides in threes,* that was another thing his mother said, to go with her talk about the wages of sin. He didn't think he'd paid much attention to these pronouncements of hers ... but after the third trouble (the one involving the Thunderbird and the crippling of Farris Mackey, a county deputy who'd screamed along behind him until his cruiser caught a front tire and flipped like a soda can), when Stuart learned that he'd used up whatever charity he was due in the world, beginning with his mother's, then he started to understand how much of her thinking had sunk in.

What he wanted was to go back and find out what he'd been thinking that last time, because the evening had started reasonably enough, some games of eight-ball downtown with Skip Kostas (Skip had driven, of course, because Stuart's license had been pulled) ... then, funny thing, Skip was drinking with this girl named Debbie Arnoux that Stuart'd been out with one time that summer, so Stuart drifted next door to the Long Branch, which had a grill, and when he was through eating they were gone.

Even then he wasn't mad, just a little high, a little disappointed and bored—he was trying to be honest about remembering these facts, but it was hard because he'd had to repeat them so many times for the record. Anyway, there'd been a song caught in his ears, J. Geils, *oh ... oh ... love stinks,* that chorus, over and over, in time with his feet on the pavement (he always left this part out of all the re-telling because it didn't seem like a fact, though now it kind of did). He kept walking down across from the switching yard, but it was too cold for what he had on—his windbreaker was back in Skip's pickup. So he stopped in at the Eagles bar, which had a scattering of older men he didn't know, drank another can of Lucky, took a leak, and walked out the back door, more or less in the direction of home.

That's when he saw the T-bird . . . turquoise, vintage, simonized religiously. The seats were white vinyl, glowing under some arc lamps. The keys were in it, *of course they were,* and on the passenger seat lay a present for somebody, wrapped in silver paper. He backed off and walked down the alley and around to Main and stood waiting to cross but the traffic was loud and steady, this being a Friday night and there having been a home game earlier, which the Tigers had taken.

So he *didn't* cross and then he was scuffing back to the car and getting in—this is the exact part he wanted to retrieve, the moment when he slid across the vinyl and the engine fired under his touch so smooth he ground the key a second time, because it could tell him . . . but no, God, wasn't that bullshit, that idea there was something special about that moment? If he was bad then he was bad all night—he'd harbored the badness, nourished it, like Cooper Loftus had one twilight on his father's ranch. Anyway, out in traffic, he had a vision of himself heading out 80 North toward Cannon Beach. He had to laugh—three hundred miles inland and he'd never laid eyes on the ocean except in pictures. He saw the car stopped on a bluff, a wilder blue than even the seawater.

Early morning was how he saw it, not a soul around, the radio delivering something spacy and uplifting. He'd listen until his head was right, then get out and run down to the beach and . . . something, that was as far as he saw it. But he drove past the cutoff to the Interstate and out into the valley to a spot by some dumpsters where he'd gone parking with Debby Arnoux that time. She had thin lips, that's what he remembered now. They were dry and didn't give under his. He'd gotten some beyond the kissing with her, but nothing caught fire. He picked up the package on the seat of the T-bird and shook it—it was heavy but it didn't rattle. He started to open the card, but suddenly couldn't bear to know what it said. He folded the flap in and tucked it under the silver ribbon, hoping his thumbs hadn't smudged it too badly, then he circled back toward La Grande, about twenty minutes too late.

Now he walked down through the middle of Sperry, stopped in at the cafe where Bram sometimes bought them maple bars in the morning, but didn't recognize anyone and slid out again without eating. The pickups were stuffed with high-school kids now, their tunes thumping past him through rolled-up windows, and couples were heading toward the Chinese place on the corner, already spiffed-up for the evening. It was no time to be downtown looking worked-out and gritty-eyed, with blisters coming on both heels and bad thoughts sliding around loose upstairs. He zigzagged off through the west side until the neighborhoods finally thinned out. People's lights were on by now. Their fires were going and the woodsmoke made a low thin roof just above the tops of the trees.

He thought he could make it to the wellhouse without them seeing . . . and it wouldn't take him any time to get his things together. But Kelly must have caught him edging across the field, the last of the sunset lacquered on him, because she was standing with the storm door propped open when he hit the yard.

"You want to come inside, Cooper?" she said. It wasn't a question.

He followed her up into the kitchen.

"You missed dinner," she said.

"I don't need anything," Cooper said.

"Lucky for you, I saved you a plate," she said. "In the oven."

It was about twice what he could eat—chops and stuffing and gravy. Kelly had the Missoula paper spread on the table, but once Cooper sat down with the food she stopped reading and watched him.

"Good?"

Cooper nodded, but it was hard to keep eating with her eyes on him.

"Listen, Cooper," she said in a minute, "Bram feels kind of tough about this afternoon."

"He doesn't have to feel bad about me," Cooper said.

"Well, you know Bram's kind of a serious guy."

She got up and poured coffee in a pair of mugs, dosed hers with two-percent and set the other by Cooper, giving him a squeeze on the shoulder before she went back to her reading.

When he was done he took the plate to the sink and ran water on it. It was all the way dark now and his face shone back at him from the kitchen window. He remembered mugging in the upstairs mirror back in La Grande, staring into his own eyes, the scruffy brows bunched-up, serious as the world. Now it looked like nothing, a white balloon on a string he could just let go of. The water ran warm on his hands, then suddenly hot. He dropped the plate and grabbed his hands back, balled them and crammed them under his arms.

"Cooper?" Kelly said.

"Can I use your phone?" he said.

He wished she'd turn those eyes off of him.

"You don't have to ask," she said.

"No, I was thinking could I use the other one."

She nodded at the stairs. "Just don't be calling Hong Kong."

Salem was a grunt, every ounce as ugly as they'd cautioned him. After lasting a few months inside he'd been transferred to a work crew, and it was a lot nicer to be out in the sun working his muscles. Sometimes he could even picture it being just a job, something like the Army, but he didn't say this to anyone. Most of the time he just did the work and kept his mouth shut. On the day he and the two others walked off the crew he had maybe a year to go and had given exactly no thought to flight.

The three of them—St. James and Carboneri were the other two—stayed in a pack that afternoon, going southeast by hedgerows and cuts in the land, but then they came into the open at a fork in the county road. Someone had carpooled from that point and left an old blue Datsun marooned there. They'd talked about getting up into the National Forest land and taking their chances, but now Carboneri was smashing the side window. Stuart balked . . . his heart wouldn't go back to normal and for the last hour he'd kept trying to be sick and be done with it. Even so, he knew one thing—that he'd had enough of hot-wired cars, of things that didn't belong to him.

The two men didn't waste any cajoling on him. The Datsun spun off onto the pavement and was gone.

The fluke in all of it, even weirder than what'd gone wrong to let them loose in the first place—he was upstairs on Bram's bed now, the telephone in his hand, the room dark, some bluegrass music filtering through the floor register, up there remembering how it was to be stranded at that cross-roads in his prison issue, feeling absolutely overmatched by being a fugitive, sure in his heart he'd be back at Salem in worse trouble than ever before the sun set—the fluke was that Carboneri and St. James had been caught not an hour later, and he hadn't been. Not then, and not for the three days he waited in a moldery dug-out space among a farmer's leftover hay bales, and not using a made-up Social Security number all over eastern Washington, and not crossing over Idaho and into Montana, and not to this day.

He was going to keep his mouth shut until the last minute, until they were actually here for him. He'd explain that Kelly and her brother were good people, that they didn't know about him . . . but as soon as he'd gotten to the bottom of the stairs and seen them in their kitchen—Bram leaning against the sink working on an apple, Kelly not doing any-thing, just standing around agreeably—right away he hated himself.

"Oh, Jesus, I did something," he said. The words just lurched out of him.

Kelly moved in on him, so fast he flinched and would've had his hands up to shield himself, except he couldn't get them out of his pockets quick enough.

"Don't lose it now, Cooper," she said, her fingers smoothing down his arms where they shook. "It doesn't mat-ter what you did."

Cooper's face was burning. "You're crazy," he said. "It matters, *God.*"

And then he told them, working backward from what he'd just done on the phone, as much as he could get out in one burst.

"You called the sheriff?"

Off to one side he could see Bram finishing the apple, turning it to get the last bit by the stem, nodding like he had in the truck, then dropping the core into the compost jar and squinting over at the wall clock.

"Just this minute you did?" Bram said.

Then Cooper saw Kelly fit the story together and felt her hands all at once turn stiff where they'd been soothing him.

"I can't believe this," she said. "Why'd you do a thing like that?"

Cooper sat.

He'd have as much luck telling her about the Thunderbird, as much luck illuminating the heart of Cooper Loftus.

She stood over him, the huge eyes fixing him.

"God, I'm tired," he said finally, "I'm just . . . real tired."

It didn't change how shaken, how badly let down she looked.

"I can't do this anymore," he went on, hands clamped between his knees. "I can't."

Waiting chews the heart out of everything, he'd have to tell her. He'd have to tell her it'd gotten past waiting for the sheriff, gotten past mattering who it would turn out to be, had gotten more like holding his breath all the time, bracing for the next trouble. And they didn't come in threes either, that was just something people like his mother said. They came one after another, not riding down out of the sky, but appearing endlessly out of who you were.

And he'd have to tell her, once he understood it himself, how their kindness had finally gotten to him and broken him, and why . . . but by now Bram had crossed in front of his sister and had laid a hand on Cooper's shoulder.

"Listen, Cooper," he said, "we'll handle the fine points later, OK?"

The next thing he knew, they were on their way up

through the wet grass to the wellhouse. Cooper felt himself carried along between the two of them like deadfall on the river. They crowded inside and scooped everything of Cooper's up and rolled it inside his bedroll and snugged it with a length of baler twine. Then they slanted down by the lower sheep pasture toward the root cellar.

Bram worked the latch and kicked at the door where it stuck on the concrete.

"Lord," he said, sniffing, ushering them in, "I forget how it stinks in here."

He handed Cooper the light, a heavy Ray-o-Vac with a huge steady beam. He took a step back and stood in the door mouth, looking downhill toward the road from town.

"This won't take too long," he said.

"You're wasting your time . . ." Cooper started to say, but Bram cut him off, almost fierce. It was a whole other sound he'd never heard from Bram.

"No more of that talk," Bram said. "That's all finished. That's a thing you're leaving behind. As of now, tonight."

The voice scoured through him. His arms flagged and the light slid down the door jamb to the concrete.

"No," Bram said, *"you look at me,* Cooper . . . Stuart." Like a reflex, Cooper jerked the light back up so it bored a hole in Bram's chest.

"You're all right," Bram said.

Cooper couldn't move. He couldn't say anything for a minute. There wasn't the least sound in the root cellar, not even down inside him where it was never quiet. When he drew a breath his body bristled with shivers, and when they melted, he was no longer cold, no longer sure he was doomed.

"Now get comfortable," Bram said.

Cooper backed slowly in against the far wall and let himself slide to an empty place on the floor by the seed potatoes.

Finally, his voice restored, he said to Bram, "Don't get yourself in trouble. . . ."

"Don't worry," Bram said. He gave Cooper a quick

smile, then set his face and loped down toward the house, leaving Kelly the job of shutting him in.

But instead of stepping outside and shouldering the door, Kelly got her fingers on it from the inside and wiggled it in until it latched.

She came back to where he was.

"I know you can use some company," she said. "It's not so good in here alone, huh?"

Cooper swung the light so it bounced off the ceiling and lit her face. The disappointment had burned off, leaving it still and handsome. He saw nothing there to trouble him, no grudges or hungers he couldn't understand. He shoved over and made room for her to sit by him and in a moment she did.

He looked down at their legs poking out along the floor past boxes of onions and winter squash—hers sticking out a little farther, so gangly, with the boot tips pigeoned in. In a moment he flipped off the light and let out a long breath and heard it break into a sudden laugh.

 *Clearance*

I'd gotten myself nerved up in the night.

Fay would've said, if she'd known, I had no business going up in the mountains alone, a man with young kids, a man not equipped with above-average bravery. But I let the crackle of the fire and the tin of Dinty Moore's and the stack of dry wood by the tent distract me. Sometime late I zipped myself into the bag and watched the coals glow blue through a thickness of ripstop nylon, not thinking of anything special, baseball at first, the status of the VISA bill, then how jittery Matty, my older boy, looked before launching into his back dives. Outside the stars pummeled down. I was comfortable and reasonably tired, but before long my thoughts got away from me, bounding past the recent trouble with Fay and gravitating toward worst things, zeroing in, ultimately, on the noise a sow grizzly would make plundering down out of last season's huckleberries toward the tent. I'd lost some ground these last couple of years since my father died. Already this spring Mr. Allred, the man who brought us eggs, had been pinned under his tractor, and the aide in Fay's classroom had been told she had a melanoma on her ankle. *Why not me,* I'd learned to think. But all I heard all night was wind coming southeast over the saddle, scouring through the scrub pine.

When I woke it was afternoon. The fire was cold. That last hour before sunup the light overhead had appeared promising, but now the sky was thick with coils of heavy, dark-bottomed clouds. I knelt, rubbed water on my face. The ridge was pocked with alpine lakes. Clayborn, Lynx, Aspen, the two Pearls. Some were too marginal for names, shallow glacier-made gouges that froze solid. Most, though, ran deep enough for a crop of cutthroat or grayling.

A remnant of ice floated near the deep end, mottled and flecked with reddish algae. Yesterday, when I'd stopped above the last grade, the lake had shone up gaudy as a god's eye. Under this afternoon's clouds that fluky ultramarine had gone to black. The wind tore across it, not slapping up white-caps but flashing off into trails of fine erratic shivers. A patch of meadow lay beyond the outlet; it was too early for color, though. The slope to the left was all scree, emptying into the lake. Above the scree, couloirs of broken shale shot another few hundred feet to the summit.

In the eight years since Fay and I'd moved back to Sperry, I'd made this trip late every June, in the company of my two oldest friends, Pat McSherry and John Rittenour. One year there'd been a drive on at the aluminum plant and McSherry hadn't been able to take time off until into July and by then the lake was completely clear of ice. Even so, the three of us were the only ones there, and the fish struck like they were starved. It was just over seven miles from where the Forest Service road quit, slow going early in the season. The shadowed stretches were still bermed with corn snow, turning to a heavy slush by afternoon. Even last year, when Rittenour finally married again, and drove out with Holly and her daughter to visit family in St. Paul, he got back in time and we came as always.

The second morning we scrambled up the mountain. Rittenour led, climbing with light, quick hand holds. McSherry came next, stubborn as a pitbull. I followed, not in a hurry, watching their heads bob against the sky. The snow was off the south face by now and the rock was mostly dry—there were a few bad spots, up along the cliffs, but we'd worked out a route and stuck with it. The peak was small, sheared flat as a poker table except for a cairn climbers had built over the years. We'd collapse around it, draw up our knees, try to catch our wind.

McSherry's face would be flushed and sweaty. He'd complain about his knees. He'd say he was an old man and wasn't going to climb anymore. We all joked about being old men, but we didn't feel that old yet—I didn't anyway. I was just forty. There was nothing wrong with my knees. I had a good head of hair left, my weight was OK. Fortune, or whatever, had been kind to me, Fay had to remind me sometimes, though in the everyday course of things, Fay wasn't a big believer in Fortune. *It's not in the lap of the gods, Averill,* she'd more likely say. Whichever, it was true I'd missed the war, never broken a bone, never been stitched.

Beyond this summit lay a slice of backcountry valley, then other peaks, silt-colored, chopping north into British Columbia, each band thicker in haze. Even the mildest days had a cool wind, smelling of lichen or, I thought, the rock itself.

"I'm spending the rest of my life right here," I announced once, so close to happy I didn't know anything sensible to say. Rittenour nodded, fluffing out his beard. "We'll tell Fay what you decided on," he said softly.

McSherry snorted, took a long pull off the water bottle.

In a way, I meant that about staying on top, but pretty soon—I don't know—I'd get to kicking the loose stones around, skimming them out into the air.

"Let's head down," I'd say.

"Christ Almighty, we just got here," McSherry would say. "You don't know what you want."

That was other years.

In that first friendly light today I'd traced the whole route in my mind, consoling myself over the lousy night. But now, with the clouds boiling low overhead, it seemed remote and dark, no place to be alone. A fine mist had begun to coat my glasses. I pulled a space blanket from the pack and covered the woodpile, and after that I told myself I'd better fish.

Fay'd already taken the boys down to her mother's outside of Hamilton, standard procedure once school got out. I had to admit I didn't mind having the house to myself—it was only for a few weeks, after all. Some weekends I'd drive down after work on Friday, in time to help Fay get the boys to bed, then the three of us would play cards, or just sit outside and talk until it was too dark. Fay's mother had been widowed years ago, the fall Fay started junior high. Her husband had gone off for weekend duty in the National Guard and—one of those accidents that seem excruciatingly senseless—been crushed between the back of a troop truck and the armory wall. She was a plain, strong-looking woman, in the same style that Fay was, red-cheeked and long-legged, still trim from working with the horses. She must've seen other men now and then, but none were in evidence and there was never talk of another marriage. We got along, Fay's mother and I (better since the boys had been born), though I'd feel her eyes on me sometimes—gray as river stones—and believe she was on the verge of telling me things about myself.

After those weekends I'd get up around five, leave Fay sleeping, and drive straight through to the office. It was a happy-enough arrangement. But this time, this year, Fay'd told me she thought they'd stay all summer. She said it as if she was testing me.

"Well, OK," I said.

"I'll call you from the ranch," she said. But she didn't and I didn't call her.

How do these things get started?

For a while I'd been willing to believe it was winter grinding on Fay and me—it's not so fierce here as people imagine, but it's diabolical, it acts like it won't ever end. I found myself taking offense all the time. I didn't like the grudging, snappish thing she did with her voice. I dogged after her, wanting to know how on earth she could talk like that to someone she loved. She sloughed it off—*You're bored, Averill,* that's all she'd say, as if it was a fault in me. Or she'd say, *Please don't buy trouble.* Weeks went by. The boys drifted around the house like a couple of lost satellites.

Fay and I still got together in bed now and then, but we seldom said a word. It was always very late, the bedroom in total darkness. At one point, over the winter, she had her hair cut in a blowzier, more modern style, and switched from her old glasses to a pair of soft contacts. It occurred to me to wonder if she was seeing someone else, and for a while—it sounds funny—I was excited watching her come and go, wondering if she'd take that sort of chance. But it was a poor idea, this suspicion, and when I finally said what I'd been thinking, one night in March, Fay said, *Averill, believe me, it's you or no one.* Her voice wasn't even angry, only, I thought, tired, as if what disappointed her most was that I'd think something so predictable.

Whatever was wrong, I'd begun to believe it was inescapable, a thing in our blood it took sixteen years to grow.

I knew I ought to use this time she was gone to see how I felt, to settle on the next move—I knew she'd be doing that down in Hamilton. But lately things had turned chaotic at the office. Every night I came home dull-headed after a day of trying to sort between the backbiting and the fact. I wasn't up to doing anything constructive. Most of the storm windows were still on, and already the grass had grown wild along the alley. Then it was Thursday night. The ball game on the cable station was over and I was out on the porch steps listening to the neighborhood settle down, watching the last twenty minutes of sunlight bleed through cracks in the back fence. The phone rang. I didn't move at first. I didn't know how we were going to act about this. I was afraid I'd say something meaner than I felt. Still, I couldn't bear to hear it keep bleating in the empty house.

It wasn't her, but Rittenour, canceling.

"I feel funny about this, Averill," he said. "I mean, we can still reschedule, don't you think?" Holly's daughter Rose Ann was having tubes put in her ears, he explained. "I thought it was going to be all cleared up by now, but the medicine just didn't do that much, so, I don't know, Holly says she wants me to go on with you and Pat . . ." I could picture him looking off, blinking, hoping not to offend. "I kind of want to be here, you know, in case . . ."

I felt this punch of anger.

But I said, "Whatever you think," then added that I was

sorry, and that I'd wait up and give McSherry a call when he got off swing shift. I went back outside with a beer. I could hear the neighbor's sprinkler slapping against his clapboards and dripping into the hedge. Farther off in the dark I heard the *ack-ack* of a plastic machine gun and the shrill taunting noises of some young boys. When that beer was gone I had another. I went inside to call McSherry and give him the news, but as soon as I heard his voice I knew I was going to lie to him.

From where I stood on the rocks, I couldn't see two inches down into the lake. I thought I had a hit once, but then it felt more like something on the bottom. All I carried was an Eagle Claw Fay's brother had lent me years ago, with a tired Shakespeare that clattered as I reeled. The others used flies, damsel nymphs at ice out. I made do with whatever was left from last year, Daredevil, Colorado spinner, I didn't care. McSherry could barely stand to be around me. Sometimes I just used niblets from a can, eating the spares myself. I lobbed a few more casts, reeled in too fast, and put the pole down on the rocks.

Without the others, I had to admit, it was only killing time. I'd never loved it anyway, the actual fishing, not like they did. I tossed most of what I caught back anymore, unless they'd managed to swallow the hook. It was a joke how squeamish I'd gotten. I set off hiking down toward the jam of bleached logs at the outlet, but it was muddy along the shore, and I found that walking felt as pointless as the next thing. What time had it gotten to be? With the sky so socked-in I could make my best guess and be off by three hours. I considered how fast I could tear down the camp, and where I'd be on the trail when I couldn't see my feet in front of me.

Still, I didn't feel like pulling out, either.

I wondered what Pat or John would do with themselves, alone up here. Fish, drink a little, nap in the tent where it was warm. Fish again later until the light failed. In my rush I hadn't even brought a bottle. I tried picturing Rittenour's airy looping casts, that lovely concentration of McSherry's, his huge hands resting in his lap like driftwood. But when I imagined my friends, I saw them under a bright sun, the leaves on the bushes uncurled and jiggling in the breeze. It was a dumb exercise. They wouldn't have come alone, either of them. It wouldn't have crossed their minds.

And I knew if I'd told them, I wouldn't have come either. McSherry would've gone silent for a second, then asked what I thought I'd prove with a stunt like this. He would've said I was a moron not to carry a gun—he never went near the mountains without a .357 Smith & Wesson on his belt. Of course, I hadn't told Fay either. For a moment, I contemplated which was worse. Back at the house I'd gotten fired up, loaded the car that night under the floodlight, making myself believe this was something necessary, even crucial (one of Fay's words), but all that was neutralized by now. It was nothing short of perverse not telling people where you were.

It took most of a matchbook to get the fire going. I boiled a kettle of lake water, sliced off a few rounds of Thuringer, emptied out an envelope of onion soup mix. I crouched on the log, warming my hands around the cup, watching the mountain, the little I could see of it. There was still a wind on top, but it was trapped above the clouds. The bushes near the tent didn't so much as twitch.

There's no way I'm going to sleep, I thought. *I'm going to lie in that tent all night again and tomorrow's going to be just like today.* God, it was bad enough at home without Fay there civilizing the bed. I could fall asleep on the couch with the TV on, but if I stripped down and got under the covers, I'd get so wired I'd feel like I should throw my clothes back on and go to the office. Sometimes I had a glass of brandy, sometimes I broke down and took a pill. Next thing, I'd be awake again, the heartbeat pattering in my ears. I'd swing my legs over the side of the bed and look at the clock. Quarter to three invariably —as if I'd been called for a purpose, then left on my own to guess what it was.

It got dark sooner than I'd figured. Already I couldn't see features in the terrain across the lake, dark shapes was all. The pine had burned into steady coals. I snugged my arms in against my vest and watched my breath.

I couldn't help it, I thought about Fay getting ready for bed, her head cocking to one side as she pulled an earring out. I thought of the nightshirt dropping down, obscuring her limbs. Forty thousand hours I'd spent in bed with her—*unfathomable.* I remembered how her stomach felt under my hand. It had more give after Ned, but still had that flat calm feel from when she was seventeen and we were first lying together by the Bitterroot. I thought about her alone in her old room at her mother's, slantways across the bed, oblivious, and in another few seconds I was picturing my own mother locked up tight and paranoid in her little place down in Arizona.

I wrenched myself up as if standing would scatter my thoughts. The only place to go was down by the lake. So that's where I was, off away from the fire, crunching stones under my boot, when I first heard the plane.

McSherry couldn't bear them. *I swear a man can't lose himself far enough anymore,* he'd say, or just get a foul look and turn his head. He didn't go into it, of course, but I knew it was one of the ways the war still got to him. I didn't have that reflex in me, though. They were only little planes, Pipers or Cherokees, and they weren't so many. From the top of the mountain, if the sun was right, I'd scan the air until I caught sight of the wings glinting across the thermals. If anything, it made me feel farther from home. But in the dark, with the wind gone and the lake flat and the birds at roost, the engine's drone sounded immense.

I waited for the lights to show, the red and green flashing from the wingtips, the strobe on the tail illuminating a portion of cloud. Nothing came but sound, a gruff, untroubled baritone, the pitch creeping up a note or two as it neared the divide. Right away it cheered and diverted me, this sound. I stood looking up like Matty or Ned, mouth open. Then, almost instantly, I felt a crushing envy—here were people who had their lives in hand. I saw them relaxed and flush, buzzing home from the city, deals cut. I stood listening, scolding myself, and then in no time I was back to Fay again, thinking I couldn't have wandered farther off course if I'd tried.

And that's what I was still doing, moments later, when the plane struck the mountain.

I kept listening, jerking my head as if there'd be more. I heard the spitting of my fire, nothing else. Even so, I couldn't disbelieve what I'd heard—already the sound, the sequence of it, was scored into my ear. Stub of sheet metal on rock, another longer shearing, wincing noise, an empty beat, then the rattle of dislodged talus kicking downslope. If I lived to be ninety —I knew this instantly—it wasn't going to change the least bit. It would come back like eight or ten other things I heard when my mind blew empty. Fay shaking me, her fingers embedded in my arm, *It's time, Averill! it's time,* in the apartment on Griswold, before Matty came . . . or my mother forlorn as a curlew, also summer, the middle of the night, *Honey, your father's . . .*

But the next part spilled together: throwing on the half-empty pack, running off down the lake, turning back three separate times before I got going right—the first for gloves, the second for my hatchet, and a third time to go back where I'd been standing when it happened, to stare up again as if I could memorize that spot in the darkness by the angle of my neck.

The flashlight threw out a thick rope of light. I kept it straight on the trail all the way down the side of the lake, dodging deadfall and standing water, trying not to run, but loping anyway, cutting finally up into the scree.

I tacked a few times, stopped for my heart to slow, then kept on, looping my free hand to the side for ballast. Higher up, the rocks had a sheen, and as I swung low, the chill rose around my face. Above the scree, I hit the foot of the wall, roughly where I'd imagined it would be. I followed it south, hoping it would meet the ridgeline. All at once I was in the clouds and my fire no longer showed below.

In another few feet I hit new snow.

Climbing, it was easy not to picture what I was looking for. My mind strayed to a story involving my father, how the family'd sent him into a blizzard to look for his uncle on the road to Cut Bank. This was back in the worst of the '30s—

my great-uncle Sumner had torn off to town to vent himself
on a government agent. The truck had left the county road
and was nosed into the borrow pit, drifted in as high as the
tailgate. Uncle Sumner was lying across the seat, his knees up
to his chest, his ear frozen to the leather. He always survived
in this story (he died many years later at the Lutheran Home,
a shock of silvery hair still hiding the disfigured ear). My
mother was the one who dredged it up now and then, a
preachment on doing what was needed, but my father, though
he didn't mind telling it, never acted like it had a point—or
if it did, it was that events were sometimes larger than you
were. I'd heard it addressed at me a half-dozen times (and at
my little brother a few more) without ever deciding which
way to see it. What remained was his voice, creeping along,
shaded with amazement. I could hear that voice now, mixed
up with my own, and all the time I climbed it never occurred
to me that I wouldn't find the plane, that I wouldn't jab the
light forward through the mist and come straight on it.

Still, I wasn't ready.

Suddenly the shaft of light fell on a section of engine.
The rock around it was bare where the snow'd melted. The
surface of the metal was still giving off twists of steam. I
reached my hand out, then yanked it back and crammed it
under my arm and started shooting the light around, but there
was nothing else that didn't belong there. I poked uphill a few
steps, then a few more, and all at once the light careened off
into an expanse of drifting cloud.

The ridgeline was sheer, hardly enough to balance on as I
stared down. The plane lay on the other side, where it had to
be, just downslope from a brief disturbance in the rock and
snow. It was right-side to, a single-engine. Except for the
crumpled wings jutting from the roof, it didn't look much
bigger than the white Corvette McSherry used to drive. The
nose was torn, balled in like scrap, but the tail section was still
sleek as a bullet. I could read its numbers without any trouble.

I yelled down, but my voice sounded puny. I called out
a second time, sharper, and hung back, waiting.

In a way, I believed I could still scramble down to the

passenger's door and swing it free, and find them only stunned—suspended there, waiting for my hand to snake in and release the lap belts. I could see them tumbling out, waking up. It was a potent feeling: their weight bearing down on me, my boots clattering in the loose shale, taking them one at a time (however many there were) down to a sheltered place on the rocks where they could rest while I got blankets . . . but it dispersed almost at once. All it took was another breath and I was crashing down toward the door. It was jammed tight, and I had to beat the safety glass with a rock until it shattered.

There were two of them in the plane, a man maybe ten years my senior, and a woman younger, Fay's age or thereabouts. The clothes were Western, new and expensive. They both wore snap-front jackets too light for the altitude and the weather. The man had been piloting. His arm was strung around the control, his face canted toward the far window, an imposing, important-looking face still slick from shaving. He could've been a rancher, a lawyer . . . I felt an instant, almost fearful deference toward him, toward them both. The woman's head was thrown back, baring an expanse of white neck crowded with strands of Navajo silver. She was blonde and the hair was pulled off her face and hung down over the seat back.

    In a moment, I wormed the flashlight into a twist of sheared metal so it shone on a mirror and diffused across the cabin. I busted out the window glass and crawled through the frame, pulled off my glove and put a finger to each of their necks. The skin felt like vinyl, not cold yet and not warm. I let my weight fall back against the leather duffles and department-store packages strewn in back. A bottle had broken in one of them, aftershave or cologne, something sharp and sweet that stung my eyes.

    I'd kept my mind clear of the moment of the crash, except to remember how glowery and unstable the clouds had looked from down at the lake as they shunted and broke against the cliffs. But inside the plane, staring uphill through the remains of the windshield, at the rock skiffed with snow, I had to wonder why it didn't explode and burn.

Or why the whole cabin hadn't been pounded into oblivion.

I kicked at the door until it released, then hauled myself out, urgently, as if the plane might still explode. I backed off, and it was only then, apart from it, that I understood how close they'd come to clearing the ridge. Ten feet maybe. And then I could see the story. He'd had just time enough to jerk back on the control, punching the nose up into the draft, but not enough for the lift to take hold and carry them over the saddle.

So they were just barely dead, I thought.

And this thought was so strange and unanswerable, for a few seconds it held back the others, but then they tumbled ahead anyway. *What would I've done if I'd found a pulse? What if one had been living and the other not? What if they'd been crazy with pain?*

I crumpled the back pages of the Lethbridge paper scavenged from the floor of the cabin and covered them with moss and laid on the deadest, driest wood I could find and drag up the hill. The fire sent up a black smoke; even the paper seemed unwilling to burn hard until I got my face down and blew at the sparks and fed in the twig tips with my fingers. Slowly it came around. In a few minutes, it burned without me. I crashed down through the loose rock toward the treeline where I could hack off some real wood.

Later, using the blade of the hatchet, I jimmied the pilot's door. I unthreaded his left arm and, bracing myself against the wing strut, tugged on his shoulders until they slumped and began to tip out.

A few minutes later I did the same for the woman.

Back in the cabin again, I couldn't find a goddamn thing to cover them with. No blankets or sleeping bags, not even a tarp. Their bags were soft-sided, sparsely packed, just enough for an overnight. I started opening the larger of the two, but as soon as I had the top splayed open I stopped and couldn't bear to keep going. I zipped it back and fitted the straps together and got out.

I'd put the man and woman next to each other, their feet toward the fire, and wedged a seat cushion under each of their heads. After that I walked around for a while, but now that I was through with the work, the chill seeped inside my clothes and I had to sit down by the fire myself.

The damage should've been massive, I knew that—so wretched that a man like me couldn't stand to look. Instead, it scarcely showed. The man's arm had broken, I was fairly certain, also his nose. It was puffy and off-center and a filament of blood ran slantwise across his cheek and down into his collar. The woman had a knot at her temple, crossed by a little furl of cut skin—I'd done worse to my own head being careless in the cellar.

Their eyes were shut. Whatever kind of clenched expression they'd had those last four or five seconds, the impact had scattered it. The faces looked incredibly vacant. It was hard to sit so close and not wonder what their names were, whether they were married or not—probably, I thought, she was a second wife, being that much younger. I could see the firelight batting off her fingers—they were spiny fingers, with glossy, evenly rounded nails, and they were empty of rings. But that didn't say much. Even Fay left her ring on the dresser some mornings. I could piece together all kinds of things back in the plane, but I was tired now and starting to shake a little. I wished I had some coffee, I wished I could hold it and feel the steam on my cheeks.

Not long after that, I heard the search planes, first one, coming east from the city airport in Sperry and passing far up the ridge, then others. The clouds were still locked overhead. For an hour or so the droning kept up, growing and twisting away while they tracked a grid above the mountains. The fire was too little to show through the clouds, I thought, realizing I was glad of it. All this felt private, of no concern to others.

After the planes had gone home, my fatigue seemed to pass into a quiet, patient sort of sadness. I wished them better weather: a night with a moon they could follow down out of

Canada, flashing on the creeks and the expanse of reservoir, on the pockets of meltwater lying along the ridge. I sent them a safe distance above the lake where my tent was, and over me, down at the edge of the water the way I'd been before, deviling myself. I let them break into the sky above the valley lights, banishing the racket of the engine with bright talk. I felt like I was in the cockpit with them, my arms looped around their shoulders, my head leaning forward between theirs.

But then, while I was lost in this wishful thinking, a chunk of talus worked loose from the ridge, skipped down and smacked the body of the plane. I shot to my feet and glared back into the dark.

It was quiet again.

Suddenly I couldn't catch my breath. My chest began to heave. Acid spashed up into my throat, gagging me. I yelled out loud, crazy things, to keep from throwing up. But I threw up anyway, the heels of my hands wedged down between the points of the rocks.

I rinsed my lips with snow. I straightened, and slowly my head grew clear. I moved back and forth through the blowing smoke and came to rest finally, staring down at the bodies. At the man's primarily. I looked at the massive chest, the face. My sympathy burned off in an instant. *I don't need to know any more about you than I already know,* I thought. I hated him. I hated him for the killing he'd done, but I hated him with a worse kind of passion, it came to me, for that string of other ridges he'd barely cleared in his life. I didn't need to hear any of what he'd have to say for himself. I knew his laugh by heart, I knew the things he said to the woman as they started out.

There was more of the night left, but I broke up the rest of the larch and threw it on and let it roar.

I pictured daylight starting over the mountains, the pressure rising and the sky coming apart. Then the helicopters dropping into the meadow by the lake's outlet, and the rescuers clattering down from the ridgeline and finding the empty Cessna, then, the couple stretched out here by the fire in their summery clothes, with cushions under their heads. Nobody'd want to speak for a moment, I guessed. One of the men would kick at the ashes for something to do, and find a strip of live coals underneath, and maybe kneel and blow on them and think *What in God's name went on here?*

I put my head down, but didn't sleep.

Sometime after eleven the next morning, I stopped at a cafe up the canyon and ordered eggs and potatoes with gravy, and sat eating and reading *The Missoulian,* running through the box scores, batter by batter. Then, for a long time, I watched the river. It was high in its banks, still fast and discolored with run-off. Despite what you hear, I thought, a man doesn't change overnight, no matter how abrupt his chastening. Still, it could begin that way. I walked out and started the truck. By the time I crossed over the upper valley bridge it was a clear, achingly bright summer's day.

I backed to the shed and unloaded, slipped the tent from its stuff sack and spread it across the picnic table to dry. After that I rolled the mower out and got it running and cut the grass along the alley fence where it came up wild. I stopped to strip off my chamois shirt, then a row later, my T-shirt. I raked the clippings and carried them to the compost, then upended the mower, took the blade off with a crescent wrench, and sat on the back steps in the sun, sharpening it, filing away the gouges. A heavy truck banged across the potholes at the end of our block, downshifted onto Ponderosa, and moved off, leaving the neighborhood suddenly still. There was hardly a shiver of wind in the new leaves. Somewhere, out of sight, a song sparrow called out across the yard and was answered.

I got up and unlocked the house. I left my boots by the door, entered the shade of the kitchen and made my way to the phone.

I let it ring a terrible, implausible number of times, feeling the sweat cool on my shoulders.

It was Fay's mother who finally answered.

"It's you," she said. She sounded a little surprised and breathless and, I thought, relieved. "Dear boy," she said, "you nearly missed us."

❧❧ Alex's Fire

A late steamy afternoon on the cramped beach behind Mendelssohn's Bathhouse. The squealing children have disappeared into hot station wagons or pedaled over the hill on fat-tired bikes, and we're left with the buzz of a last water-skier from the far side of this stale lake. *Miss Whalom,* the dwarf steamer, loiters at her moorings. Alex watches the lovers sitting on a gummy picnic table at the edge of the canopy. The boy's older than we are, nineteen maybe. The girl's our age, but nothing like the chilly tennis-playing types we've taken out this summer. Her hair's swept up into a lacquered swirl, only now beginning to release a few dark strands for her to brush away. Her suit's a green-striped two-piece that balloons in front as she leans forward, smoking, rubbing the boy's leg with a small white hand. It's nothing they do outright, only the intimacy of the touch, the way they act secluded by the wing of moist shade the bathhouse casts. We're desperate for experience, Alex and I, but the desire and patience we see in them shrinks us. Here we are, stranded between the two chunks of time that make up our lives.

In a month I'll go south for my last year of boarding school, and Alex, who's been away and come home, will begin laboring through his senior year at our town's high school. In the afternoons he'll hose the day's grit off the clunkers at the Lincoln-Mercury dealership where his father

Clifton manages to stay employed. Alex has had three jobs this summer and they've all had to do with cars. I look for him in backstreet garages—Lloyd's Radiator Shop, for one. It doesn't surprise me anymore when men like Lloyd glance up darkly from their work and say Alex went out earlier and never came back.

Alex has no special talent for fixing things, even less for knowing what's wrong with them. He has yet to figure out that the bond between young men and cars isn't absolute. His skin is pallid, oil-stained in the pores of the hands. He drives a maroon Cougar with dealer plates, which is free, but it eats at him that he can't do a thing to it. His talk's laced with words like *glasspacks, hemi's, 427's.* As for me, I just like how driving lets me feel. Pointless solitary rides through backcountry New England, the stone walls and the great maples whizzing by, the radio beating out harsh new tunes by Eric Burden or the Stones, against which I sing almost fluently. But I have no keen interest in the artistry of engines, or in pacing off the thick, still-warm tails of rubber on the road behind Alex's house.

We're not so different to look at, though: two nondescript seventeen-year-olds with limp brownish hair brushing the tops of our ears, shagging longer in front. We're neither of us unblemished or physical enough to pass for a lifeguard, or enough eccentric to draw a curious stare. We blend in. I'm the one with the black glasses, one bow wrapped in white athletic tape, Alex the one with the long horsey face, the one who's slow to smile these days, who walks with his shoulders bunched and his hands balled in loose fists.

When it's time to leave the beach for Mendelssohn's yeasty changing room, Alex shuns the lovers. Across the road from the bathhouse sits Whalom Park, an oasis of aging rides and come-ons. Standing here, we see the sun blasting through the roller coaster's webbing of whitewashed struts and crossbeams. It's a landmark, beautiful in a way, I guess. Every night there's a line, people straggling out into the midway with snocones and cotton candy, joking and bragging, and a few staring up quietly as the gears tick and the cars climb to the highest tier, followed by a cascade of screams, regular as breakers at the shore. Last year we heard that someone was thrown and killed, but he'd obviously broken the rules . . . and he was nobody we knew.

Then, that day on the beach, Alex stops abruptly, grabs my arm, and waves his free hand in an arc that takes in the whole roller coaster.

"See that?" he tells me. "I'm gonna burn that thing down."

There were crowds every night after dark—up on the midway, and down on the street where the back of the park met the lake. In the distance, a few lights burned at camps on the far shore. Alex and I worked our way down the sidewalk through clusters of girls perched on the railings or slouched against parked cars or hunched on the curb. Down from a fried-clam place at one end, past a bar and an open-faced Skeeball palace, past Mama Castiglio's, past the dance hall called Roseland, past the last fluorescent-lit soft-ice-cream stand to the dark area under the roller coaster, protected by hurricane fence. Then back.

The sidewalks were patrolled by local toughs, some alone, in immaculate black leather, picking through the foot traffic, alert for something to take issue with, others with the red lettering of the RYDERS club on sleeveless denim jackets, assembling among the bikes outside the White Horse bar. Alex knew a few, by name at least. One night we lingered with one named Angelo, and Alex said, *Here, feel,* and pressed my hand to the back of Angelo's jacket where I felt a huge knife tucked into his belt. Angelo looked off above us and said there'd be trouble later. If it came, I was gone by then. Sometimes Alex wore his own leather jacket, actually a kind of vinyl, but nobody mistook him for that breed of roving anger.

So there I was with Alex, scuffing through the snatches of music, the yells from passing cars, the noxious canned laughter spilling from the dummy outside the Fun House. And Alex was holding forth, as usual, but now I couldn't stop thinking about the roller coaster. Why the roller coaster? I didn't ask, and I didn't ask *why*, nor do I remember thinking *This is rotten, this makes no sense.* I only imagined, though far more dimly than Alex, the flames darting like excitement through the old wood, rising tier to tier, until the night sky was blasted with a light he'd never forget, a light of his own making.

We paused across from Roseland and drank Cokes in huge paper cups full of crushed ice. Alex stopped a girl he thought he knew from the beach, or maybe from the counter at Friendly's. She had long straight hair made white and lusterless by peroxide. She wore a man's blue button-down shirt, tails out, and cut-off jeans dappled by Clorox.

"You want to go for a ride?" Alex said.

"Where to?" the girl said . . . or maybe she said she had a friend waiting, or maybe she was savvy enough to snap, "Whatcha got?"

Nothing would happen beyond this. A light hand on the shoulder, endless fractions of talk. My attention wandered to the dance hall across the street.

When my folks went out to dance, it was to the country club. I see them standing in the foyer at home, my father showered, suffused with witch hazel, his tux newly pressed, and my mother in her long quiet dress trying aloud to persuade herself she'll survive the evening's clamor. When they get back it's still early. I've just gotten in myself and I'm sitting on the edge of my bed in the dark. My father's voice floats under the door, buoyant from Scotch and a few sociable hours among his peers. *Never again,* my mother says, fatigued, resentful, as I lie back, trapped a while longer in protective custody.

But now Roseland stood before me. A long frame building sheeted in painted tin decorated with a great furled rose and lettering in a script that said Roseland had survived from the park's more genteel beginnings—into this present-day noise and gaudiness so attractive to me. Downstairs was the bar, upstairs the dance floor. From the sidewalk, I could see the dancers sweep past rows of windows, speckled with darts of colored light from the mirror spinning above the bandstand. Sometimes they stepped onto the balcony and looked over the lake or down at us, from whose ranks they'd once come, but they soon disappeared inside. They were beautiful in their bright tight clothes, in the sweaty flow of fast dancing and drinking and being so unashamedly in the prime of their lives.

I must say this about Alex: he lied. Not once, dramatically, but habitually, as if his life had come to depend on little doses of it. I hated to admit this, because he'd been my friend and sometimes-confidant since grade school, and because it was so needless and transparent. Alex wasn't one of those drifty kids who lie because they can't keep things straight in their minds, nor was he any more devious by nature than the rest of us. It was just that we couldn't trust what he said he did outside our circle of friends.

On summer evenings we played music in a built-over shed down behind Alex's house. We were joined by our friend Owen, who played a Hofner bass, left-handed, McCartney style, and by Fritz, who hunched behind his partial set of drums, always just ahead of the beat, so even the slow songs scampered toward the end. And some nights Jody, Owen's lovely vulgar sixteen-year-old sister, would come too, having seized on a legitimate excuse to get out of the house. Sadly, Jody'd always been more like a sister to me, or I'd have made myself miserable over her . . . and Alex had it worse than I did.

Alex was our leader, our arranger and lead singer. He got us the occasional job at someone's barn party in Ashby or Townsend. His voice was fair enough when he relaxed, but his falsetto leaked air like a split reed, and he sneered the words. He favored three-chord songs like "Hang on Sloopy," or ones he'd written himself, which were thin on melody and rhymed only in the sense that most of the lines ended with . . . *girl.* But quality of voice didn't count for so much, because he played his guitar too loud. Owen and I would have to turn ours up to be heard, then Alex would nudge his up again, and before long the songs were all instrumentals.

One night after we'd stopped—our ears exhausted by the sheer weight of the noise we'd made, our fingers unable to come up with anything new—Alex dug around in a drawer by the turntable and produced an unlabeled 45 record and displayed it to us proudly.

"Just came in the mail," he said. "It's that group I was in up at school."

He hovered over it as it played, head cocked, as if filling his mind with glamorous memories of the recording studio. It was an old song, one of those reverberating space-age numbers done by groups like the Ventures. In fact, it *was* the Ventures.

"That's you, huh?" Jody said.

"Sure," Alex said. "Me and some others."

Jody made a face. I didn't know what was spinning through Owen's mind, but we kept our mouths shut. Maybe we thought Alex was entitled to his illusions. From time to time there were stories about prodigious tenderhearted girls from the teacher's college, stories of high-speed chases late at night, Alex saved at the last by his hot car, his cunning, his instinct for backwoods geography. As truth, his tales were hard to swallow, given what we knew of Alex firsthand— unless, somehow, there was another Alex inside him, who only appeared in the world away from us. But as fantasies, they were too tame, too predictable to capture our awe. When we were in a group I tended to let them blow by like a bad smell. When it was just the two of us, as it often was, he was more restrained. Maybe I seemed less gullible, but more likely it was that he felt some respect for the allegiance we'd made, and maybe a little fear that it would be—would *have* to be—broken.

So what did I believe? Did I think he meant to torch the roller coaster—not a boast or figure of speech or outright falsehood, but a case of actual premeditated arson, something criminal and asinine? The more I considered that day at Mendelssohn's, remembering Alex's reddened eyes uplifted to the lowering sun, which made the roller coaster look like it was already on fire, the more the answer was *yes*, passionately, despite the lying, despite everything. As we drove home one night, I told him, "You know, you don't have to prove anything to me."

But he didn't answer.

I worked on a framing crew that summer. *Good experience,* according to my father, meaning (he elaborated often) I'd know how a house was put together and not be cheated in later life, and meaning further (he didn't say) I'd get to know what it was like to work with my hands, since he had every intention of sending me to college so I wouldn't have to. I held the job that summer—and two more—neither loving the work nor hating its drudgery. If I ever thought of quitting, it was only after a day when the wood and the sun and my own hands had fought me, a passing thought, one I'd scarcely recall in the subdued air of the next morning. And if I *had* yearned to quit, if I had ever thought for a moment it was my right, I wouldn't have given in to the urge . . . partly out of fear of not living up to my father's vision of me, partly out of knowing the work was safe passage into a world I wasn't ready to meet alone.

But Alex had quit or been fired three times in three months. I have no idea what *his* father had to say about it. Clifton was a big slope-shouldered Texan whose discomfort at being stranded in New England for twenty years had been dulled by bourbon and by his dulling job at Lincoln-Mercury. He probably said next to nothing. The fact was, Alex's mother kept the family afloat. She ran a travel agency in Fitchburg and had a good grip on the business-travel market. She also, occasionally, lapsed into guided tours, skimming off the cream for herself. She wasn't exactly a tiny woman, but the clarity of her features and the insistent Old Boston snap to her voice made the contrast with Clifton all the more glaring.

For a few days the previous spring, Alex and I'd been home on spring break at the same time. There were still islands of corn snow in the side yards and the sky hung low over our heads with a terrific dreariness. His mother'd taken a group to Martinique, leaving Clifton nominally in command of the household. I was there late that Sunday, engrossed in serious talk with Alex. Clifton appeared now and then, treading the worn carpet between the room he called his office and the bar at the end of the kitchen counter, looking up from his slouch as he passed, ready to share some drinking-man's wisdom with us, but settling for a soft nod of the head, acknowledgment of how far our downbeat presence was from any true sons of his, red-blooded Texas boys he could throw his arms around and bullshit with all night long.

Alex had just dropped out of school and he'd called me over to help explain it. The truth was simple: he just couldn't cope with it anymore, but I had to admit, the truth wouldn't sound like much. Maybe he could've just walked into the office that night and told Clifton straight out, and maybe Clifton would've recognized something kindred in his son, but there was no tradition of straight talk in that family—and besides, Clifton's honest sympathy wouldn't get Alex half as far as a well-told story.

We were huddled on the couch by the open fireplace in the kitchen when the night took a new turn. The door slammed open and Alex's mother appeared, American Tourister in hand, her gray-flecked ringlets drooping and wet, a pained yet eager look on her face. Without a word to us, she marched into the office, where Clifton had whiled away a major chunk of his married life, engrossed in the *Shotgun News*.

"You slug," she said, elaborating in detail, her voice prodding him like a sharp stick.

He'd failed to leave the car at the airport, as specified. It had just slipped his mind. Alex watched the sputtering fire, head on knees, as his father offered no defense.

"Listen, about this school thing," I told him lamely, "you'll come up with something."

Alex kept his mouth shut. I left wondering what he'd say when he couldn't put it off any longer. I envied him neither his mother's anger, nor his father's sloppy charade of surprise and disappointment, nor the understanding surely taking shape in his mind that he was, in one rattled embodiment, *both* of them. In the end, Alex actually returned to school that spring, finished the year, and waited for the counselor to do the dirty work.

You might imagine Alex inviting me into his plans—the corner of his mouth squeezing into a look that's less than a smile, the look of a card player who can no longer hide his estimation of the night's luck. Or picture the two of us in his Cougar circling the park, going over such matters as timing, gaining access to the understructure, whether gasoline or kerosene would do the better job. Or hear Alex share his misgivings with me.

This would be wrong: Alex said nothing.

In fact, for several weeks I hardly saw him. Then one night Owen and Jody and I drove out to Alex's. Jody lay sprawled in the back seat, filling the car with mentholated smoke, giving us the benefit of her obscene commentary on whatever she saw out the window.

Alex was down in the shed with his guitar cranked so loud he didn't hear us come. Jody stopped at the door, which had a sort of a porthole window, then waved wildly for us.

"Look, look!" she said.

Alex was alone, the guitar slung below his belt where he beat at it savagely. He'd taken off his shirt and we could see some sores on his back as he humped and shook in front of the wavy mirror on the wall. His left hand was gripping the neck like it was a wild hose.

Jody started laughing her coarse husky laugh, the braids flopping across her chest like two weathered rope ends. She made her face long and serious and shook her hips like Alex. Owen and I couldn't help laughing too, though in a moment I turned away and walked to the car, ashamed.

It was several summers later (at a party before her wedding) that I learned what had given Jody's mockery its edge. Of all of us, Jody—at fifteen, then sixteen—was the only one who took her sexuality with anything like an open mind, the only one who seemed to *enjoy* it. Unlike her brother, ever aware of his role as the family's oldest male, she dealt with her appetites with a bright willfulness, which earlier that summer had led her into an encounter with Alex, a walk on the ridge overlooking town, which in turn had progressed from two near-siblings shooting the breeze on a warm summer night to Jody's sudden desire to have Alex down in the long grass with her. And Alex had failed her, fidgeting atop her, half-dressed and humorless, then red-faced and groaning—so that Jody's vicious imitation of him wasn't so much the way he was in the shed, but how he'd been with her on the hill, before he'd run off and left her to walk slowly home.

Then it was Labor Day weekend, end of the summer, though it came that year in the midst of a fierce hot spell. For days there'd been no trace of moderating Atlantic wind. Saturday was my last day of work. I said my simple farewells, came home, showered, letting the water run cold on my sunburn, changed into fresh jeans, and sat on the back porch with my father, listening to the Red Sox game on his transistor radio. He'd taken to offering me a Ballantine Ale now and then, so I drank with him, the long branches of the willow hanging still, a fragile dusty feeling in the light around us. It was the second game of a twinighter and the Sox were already falling behind.

"They'll pull it out," I said.

My father sighed, "Those heartbreakers."

All summer I'd worked and cleaned up and gone out, but for once, at the end of it, I felt no restlessness. It was a happy moment, the kind you wish you could seed your life with, but which is, instead, an extract, distilled and rare.

Into that soft hour came Alex, around the corner of the garage, hands in his pockets.

"Well, Alex," my father said. "How's the world treating you?" his irony subdued by the time of day to a point below Alex's threshold. Actually, my father had never cared for Alex and sometimes referred to him as *that jerk*.

"OK, I guess," Alex said, standing awkwardly between us.

My father nodded. A burst of cheering rose from the radio, then died away, but he didn't seem to notice.

"You boys have hot dates tonight?" my father asked.

"There's a dance down at the park," Alex said.

I looked at my father. "I better go," I said, though I could have stayed easily enough—in a way I wish I had.

My father nodded again as I stood. He touched my arm and said, "Have a good time," then added, "Use your smarts."

Alex did have a hot date. Once we were on the road his excitement showed. He drove slower than he had to, the Cougar cruising along in restrained bursts as he talked at the windshield. We climbed the hill that separated our town from Whalom, and from its sloping ridge we saw the last color of sunset smeared across the horizon, and below it, the park's flashy neon, reflections of each trapped together on the surface of the lake.

Her name was Fran and she was a secretary at the dealership. Twice in the last week, Alex had aced out all the salesmen for her attention. He'd taken her to the drive-in.

"She know how old you are?" I asked him.

"Sure, hell," Alex said. Then in a minute he said, "What difference does that make?"

He downshifted past the driving range and rounded the corner that brought us to the park, slowed at the traffic circle by the roller coaster, holding his hands together at the top of the wheel, peering up at the string of cars rattling by above us.

What did he say then? It was something like "This could be the night," the kind of thing he often said, vague enough its promise to mean everything or nothing. What I remember clearly is the peculiar expectant way he seemed, cool on the outside, jazzed-up inside.

We passed the park and found the house where Alex's date lived with another girl. Cars were pulled up on the grass and music poured through the screen door. We waded into the middle of a party, a few couples dancing in the pastel beaverboard living room, others straggling into the kitchen drinking beer from plastic mugs. I trailed Alex through the house as he searched for a familiar face, then out the back door where he found Fran's roommate talking to a guy straddling a big low-slung motorcycle he had cranked up to a high whine.

"Where's Fran?" Alex said.

The girl looked at him distantly, trying to hear.

"Fran?" Alex said.

"She isn't here?" the girl said. "She was here before."

The bike's owner eased off the handle. He seemed to be listening for something and paid us no attention.

"She was going to the dance with me," Alex said.

"Yeah," the girl said. "She went to the dance."

"She was going with *me*," he said. "I was going to pick her up."

"Oh," Fran's roommate said, "I don't know then. Maybe she was going to meet you."

"Sure, yeah," Alex said.

The girl smiled. "There's a keg in the sink."

Alex walked off, not back through the house but around the outside, scraping through some dark bushes to where the Cougar was parked. He got in and sat behind the wheel and smoked one of his Luckies and said nothing for a minute, then flicked his burning cigarette out into the darkness and revved up his engine. As we pulled out to go looking for Fran, the roommate shot past on the back of the motorcycle, her bare arms clutched around the man, her hair streaming out behind in our headlights like a vapor trail.

They'd blocked off the street, above the clam bar at one end, at the traffic circle by the roller coaster at the other. The band played from a flatbed parked outside Roseland, a group from Boston who'd made it big enough to have a hit record everyone remembers, but not so big they could escape playing fairs and street dances. They were bored and buried their boredom with volume, but nobody seemed to mind. People stood by the stage three or four deep. Dancers spilled out into the road and behind them others milled along the sidewalk at the edge of the lights.

Roseland was dark upstairs. A bouncer stood in the doorway of the bar below, and you could see past him to a few of the regular Saturday-night patrons holding their beer cans at their bellies as they checked the action outside for a minute, then drifted back from view.

Alex went about looking for his date.

"So what's she look like?" I asked.

Alex became very serious. "Real good-looking," he said. "Sort of dark red hair. Looks kind of like Ann-Margaret only with glasses."

We split off through the crowd. I worked my way to the back, hoping not to see her. The last thing I wanted was to tell Alex his hot date was draped around a RYDER. But the crowd was mostly strangers, dotted by a few faces I knew that summer. No Fran.

Once in a while I'd see Alex skirting the ring of dancers, stopping and squinting, then moving off against the grain. More than ever, the night seemed like a maze—I marvel we could go into it so often with our hope unblunted, believing we'd suddenly see its design and sprint free.

Just before the band broke, I ran into Jody, who'd shed a blind date. We danced. I had a pang of wishing we weren't so much like family, but it was good holding her in the midst of the noise and the drifting salty smells. A peace came over me, a return to the feeling I'd sensed earlier, sitting with my father, in the *gloaming,* as he called it, amid the clipped grass and the straining of the lawn chairs and the quick lacework of the swallows above us. Even if the night hadn't turned out as it did—under the spell of another mood entirely—I might have remembered it anyway.

When the music stopped I could no longer see Alex. Jody took my arm and we walked up to the midway, and sat on a bench opposite the shooting gallery. The families were gone now, the crowd thinned to clinging couples and packs of boys in jeans and T-shirts, and a few older men, alone.

Jody told me what a *cretin* her date had been. I sympathized. Then she stood puckishly and said, "Aren't you going to take me on the roller coaster?"

I didn't want to. The mention of it made me think of Alex, and with that came a shot of dread. And for another thing, I didn't want to admit I'd never, in all my seventeen years, been on it.

"Don't be an old fart," Jody said.

As we stood in line, I heard the band start in again. I hoped Alex had given up and gravitated to the front of the flatbed to watch the guitar players. It was a reassuring thought. But as we moved onto the raised platform, I caught sight of him darting across the midway, going from ride to ride, lurking at the exit gates, shading his eyes as he scanned the seats for Fran, his date, who wasn't in any of them.

Jody pulled my arm and we locked ourselves behind the bar and began to climb. Those next moments remain an emblem of that night: the slow tick of the gears, the fading of heat and noise as we rose, and the sight of Alex over my shoulder. He'd come to rest on the blacktop below, arms dangling at his sides, the people from the last ride drifting clear of him so he stood alone, numb-looking as we pulled steadily away. And then the corner, the tilt, the momentum that made everything run together.

I didn't see him later.

Jody and I danced again, our feet scuffing lazily across the sandy tar until it was late. The park began to close. I offered Jody a ride home, then remembered I'd come with Alex. We walked back along the lakefront, past the barricades, to the parking lot outside Mendelssohn's where Alex had left the Cougar. I half-expected to find it gone, but there it was in the shadows, and no sign of Alex . . . except the trunk was standing open.

We waited a few minutes, talking, leaning against the car, only a few feet from where Alex had watched the lovers that day. The air hung perfectly dead. Jody reached her hands around my neck and rubbed. The music was finished now, supplanted by the tinny echo of loudspeakers within the park, and finally they quit and there were only a few distant car horns, the clap of doors, and the ringing of gates shutting for the night. Jody kissed me, smiled, kissed me again, a slow time-killing kiss that meant almost nothing.

Then came the shouts, and we broke and looked back along the curved shore and saw a plume of smoke rising into the lights.

"Something's burning!" Jody said, pulling away.

She ran ahead, but I hung back a moment, confused,

staring across the road at the roller coaster. It loomed like a huge bulwark, its white struts glowing with a dull luminance.

The fire was elsewhere, two hundred yards farther down.

I caught up with Jody and we ran to where the dance had been, and discovered that it was Roseland burning. Already flames had eaten a hole in the roof and were leaping out in jagged bursts. Park employees ran down the blacktop and gathered in the street, joining the stunned beer drinkers who'd hurried out of the bar, and a few others like us who hadn't quite left yet. The upstairs windows filled with color as a section of ceiling caved in, then the glass suddenly blackened and imploded. In the distance now we heard the whine of sirens.

Then the rest of the roof was burning. We backed away from the heat and waited against the railing by the water. Jody's mouth was open but soundless for once. All around us, people were shaking their heads. *What a firetrap,* they said. *No wonder.* Deprived of its dancers and twirling mirrors, it did seem rickety, more a decrepit warehouse than a place for celebration.

I left Jody and looked for Alex among the assembled faces, but had no luck there. I backed away and made for the car again. It was only then I saw him, collapsed against the hurricane fence in the dark, head down as if he'd been in a fight.

"Alex?" I said.

I expected to see blood streaming from his nose and lips, but when he looked up I saw he was sobbing, and as I knelt I was overpowered by the stink of gasoline on him. What should I think? It seemed for a moment that he might actually be responsible for Roseland. I drew back, shaken. His face was ugly as he cried, hardly recognizable.

"What did you do?" I said. *"Tell me."*

His shoulders shook, then were still. The streaks on his face shone in the quavering light.

"I didn't do it," Alex said. "I didn't do anything."

The fire trucks came to a gritty squalling stop in front of Roseland.

"Alex," I said, touching him. "Tell me the truth."

He looked into my eyes, miserably, then past me at the halo of flames.

"Go away," he said.

And I did.

A year later we barely knew each other. I have no good sense of the grown man Alex became, about whom only a few rumors come to me, and none good. I remember him as he was that night, at seventeen: freshly brutalized by a glimpse at what his plans would come to. He *had* told me the truth. He'd done nothing at all. Roseland burned to the ground, but not by his hand, instead a victim of tattered wiring and neglect.

So I see how the fire mocked him that night. I see him crouched in the hot litter-strewn crawl space under the roller coaster, waiting for his moment to come. The two tartan Thermos jugs, hidden earlier in the Cougar's trunk, lie empty beside him, the gasoline splashed on the undersides of the old supports, and some spilled on his jeans. I see him taking the specially bought butane lighter from his breast pocket, where it says *Alex* in red script, and flipping it from hand to hand. He hears the timbers straining overhead, the last cars roaring through the intricacy of track and wood, the screams bursting into the night . . . then the silence, in which he feels his heart beating right up in his throat, as it finally dawns on him that either way, either way he doesn't win.

✺✺✺ Great Blue

Paul's grandfather cut the engine and the boat coasted into a dark cove on the far side of the lake. It was a sweet late time of the evening. Paul sat in the bow, his chin rubbing on the top of the life preserver. He was happy his grandfather had picked him to fish with tonight, and not let any of the other cousins come. They were older, they'd gone out with their grandfather plenty—they already knew how the bats careening above the boat kept from striking your head, they knew about the ice age that gouged these lakes, they knew the story of Father Marquette's trek through these woods along Lake Superior, three-hundred-some years ago . . . not that his grandfather acted obliged to improve every spare moment with grandfatherly wisdom. No, he could be a stony quiet, the cousins all knew, not to be budged by their best antics.

The other cousins lived downstate, no more than a day's drive from camp, but Paul had flown back from Montana, alone. He'd come just once before, a rushed pilgrimage he and his mother had made at the tail end of last summer, a few clear days cool enough for a jacket around suppertime. It was hardly long enough! Everyone seemed lost in the work of closing things up for the year, and his mother was still coaching him on names by the time they left. Still, camp haunted him all winter: the lake, darker than Montana lakes, long and

cinched in at the middle by two points overgrown with blue-
berries; the five cabins spaced along the edge of the pine
woods; all the people kin to him in one fashion or another.
And the grandfather he'd been named for. So this year his
mother had set it up so he could stay at camp as long as he
wanted, living with Aunt Hallie, her next-youngest sister, and
Uncle Ray and their two girls. "Miss us, will you?" his mother
had teased him in the car. Out on the water now, he did miss
them a little, but it was a feeling he could bear.

"You put me in mind of your mother," his grandfather
said after a while. "I'll tell you, Paulie, I see her best up here,
your age or thereabouts."

His grandfather's voice wasn't loud like his uncles', but
it seemed to roll and echo out from the middle of him.

"One summer," he said, "she wore long pants and a long
flannel shirt with the cuffs snapped, a blue—I think it was a
baseball cap, with her hair crammed up underneath it. All day
every day, hot or no. Not a one of us could talk her out of
it. She was so serious, your mother . . . how we tried to get
her into a swimsuit. No dice. I said, *Shirley, you afraid of poison
ivy? Or yellowjackets? Something of that nature?* But no, it wasn't
that."

Paul smiled and waited for his grandfather to finish, but
he didn't.

"She swims a lot now," Paul offered finally.

"That summer feels like a hundred years ago," his grandfather said. "I think she just wanted to be *prepared,* set for
things. You're a little that way, too, are you?"

Paul stared down at the fishing gear. He guessed maybe
he was. He didn't much like surprises, he liked to know what
he had to do—traveling by himself, for one thing. At the
airport in Sperry they'd boarded him first, along with a
woman strapped into a wheelchair; they'd let him take a window seat in the first row, and when the others walked on,
there in Sperry, and in Great Falls and Billings, he tried to act
like it was nothing to fly. He watched the mountains for a
while, but out over the plains the clouds thickened and didn't
break, so he brought out his book, *The Voyage of the "Dawn*

Treader." He'd read it straight through half a dozen times at least, but he'd given it to his mother to hide from him so he'd have it again now. He skipped ahead, reading certain pages at a crawl. He pictured the "Dawn Treader" in full sail crossing a sunny expanse of ocean—then out of nowhere they strike a patch of darkness . . . the crew pulls a raggedy man from the water, he screams for them to turn and fly back where they came from. *This is the island where dreams come true,* he tells them. *Not daydreams: dreams!* Paul closed his eyes, then stared out at the tops of the clouds, at the bright endless sky, considering what it would be like for his dreams to be real, and fighting off the squeeze of panic by turning from the window to another place in the book and making himself read.

He lifted the anchor over the side of the boat and ran the rope through his fingers until the weight settled on the silty bottom. There were no cabins on this side of the lake. The firs reached the water's edge and the forest was heavily shadowed. The reeds at the shore rocked with the boat's last ripple.

Paul held his pole ready but waited for his grandfather to make the first cast.

"Your uncle had some luck over here last night," his grandfather said. "Not that it's ever the same two days running."

He sat in the stern, straight-backed, his eyes almost as drained of strong color as the sky. He wore a canvas cap with a long stained bill. Under it, Paul knew, he was bald as a hen's egg. His arm drew back, his lure skipped once and sank near the reeds. In a moment Paul made his own cast and began reeling in, trying to copy the even whirl of his grandfather's wrist. He hoped they'd get something, hoped actually that it would be his grandfather who did, so he could see what to do exactly—all he'd ever caught were little panfish that jiggled in the air at the end of his pole. He wouldn't mind too much if they didn't, though. So far, the mosquitoes hadn't found them. He heard the hum of another boat far-off, but it was peaceful in the cove as the light began to pass from the lake.

Suddenly, just to one side of where he'd been staring, came an explosion of water and reeds and wingbeats, so startling him that his pole rang against the aluminum gunwale. A great bird rose and skirted the water, its wings dipping in long fluid strokes. He was transfixed.

"The great blue," his grandfather said. "Our heron. You've never seen it before?"

"I . . . no," Paul said. "I've heard them talk about it, I guess."

His grandfather spread out three spiny fingers and held them up to Paul. "Some morning before the others are up," he said, "you go down and look in the shallow water in front of the cabins, in the sand. You'll see where it's been."

The bird leveled off just above the treetops, tracing the outline of the lake, as if to mark off its territory before dark. The sharp beak jutted ahead, the legs trailed behind thin as pencil lines. Paul felt the goosebumps shoot down his legs and tried to wipe them away through his jeans. Minutes passed before he thought about fishing again. When he looked over at his grandfather, he saw that he'd been crying.

There were always secrets at camp. Some were even his: one afternoon last summer, walking along the bluff above the big lake, he'd spotted Aunt Leah's oldest girl—Lara, with the shiny black hair—down on the sand with a boy who was visiting another of the cousins. Paul had watched her suddenly jump up in front of him and strip off her T-shirt so he could look at her—even last year Paul knew she'd never do anything like that back at camp, but he kept it to himself, remembering all winter exactly how she'd stood with the waves curling behind her and how the boy didn't move at all except to run his hand through his hair over and over. Other secrets he glimpsed because the adults still felt free to talk in his presence—over a drink on the screened porch of his grandfather's cabin, called The Folly, or at the stove of Aunt Hallie's or Aunt Leah's: who'd broken her word, who Grampa Paul was going to have to lend money to, whose grown-up child was having mental problems. Sometimes he could tell they'd gauged him wrong, and that he shouldn't listen anymore, but those were the times he most wanted to hear it, the times he wished they'd say the parts they never said out loud. Even so, it amazed him that he fit in as well as he did, that all it took was having the mother he had. Only rarely did the cousins ever draw back from him, making him feel there remained a few things he hadn't a right to yet.

He slept on a pallet in the cabin's loft. Aunt Hallie and Uncle Ray had the bedroom; the girls, Billie and Gwen, shared the hide-a-bed below him in the front room. Curled in his bag, he'd hear the soft-spoken tallying of the cribbage hands at the kitchen table, then the sounds of the game ending, and the last relations slipping off to their cabins. Someone would reach up and shut off the gas lanterns and they'd gutter for a moment, then go quiet. In the dark, he'd hear the two girls whispering, sometimes breaking into talk or laughter loud enough to draw a muffled yell from Uncle Ray. Or he'd hear their bare feet slapping as one, then the other, got up to use the pot. Tonight their voices were different, though . . . hushed, pointed. He lay still, afraid to move his head against the railing.

". . . only because he's dying," the boy heard.

"It's pretty weird," Billie said.

"Uncle Duff said they'd have to build the cabin over. It's all rotten underneath, it's so *old.*" She rolled over and the rest was swallowed by her pillow.

After a long silence, the older girl said, "I think it's *creepy.*"

Outside, pine boughs grated on the gable screen. He had no trouble sleeping at home. He read as long as he wanted; next thing, light would be speckling down through the horse chestnut leaves and his book would be over on the bedstand, the page marked. But the dark at camp brought raccoons with red-glowing eyes and claws that scuttled across the porch boards, and it sent wind flying down off Mt. Charles, whipping the lake up, leaving the shore strewn with foam. Men didn't use the pot, so if he couldn't stand it anymore, he'd talk himself down the stairs and back toward the outhouse. He'd never make it the whole way. He'd stop beyond the woodpile and go there, then find himself looking up through the blowing limbs of the pines at the stars, so needle-bright and endless that he imagined himself falling out into them . . . until he'd look away and hurry back to the porch steps, hating himself for not being brave.

But now these worries vanished. He waited in the loft and thought, *Who's dying?* For a minute or two, his mind beat with wondering, then, just as suddenly, he was gone.

When he woke, the air in the loft was rich with cooking smells. At home, the mornings were frantic as his parents threw themselves together for work and prodded him to get his belt on, get his teeth brushed, get his lunchbox. At camp, they let him be, so he didn't get up yet, resting happily and listening to the breakfast talk. He couldn't hear his Uncle Ray and guessed he'd gone back to town early. Now and then he caught Aunt Hallie through the clatter of the girls' voices, nearly his mother's voice but without the hurry. He rolled over and peered down at her through the railing. They looked alike, too, except his aunt was a runner and kept her hair short as a boy's. She was looking off at the windows now, at the morning light coming in from the lake. She was wrapped in the same blue bathrobe his mother wore, and her arms were folded low at her waist, the way he'd see his mother standing sometimes when he looked up suddenly. . . .

Just then his grandfather came up the steps, stopped for a breath, and squinted through the screen door. Aunt Hallie and the girls looked up at once and their talk skipped a beat. As he made his way into the room, they seemed to part for him. Cousin Gwen got up, stuffing the last wedge of toast into her mouth, and gave him her chair at the dinette.

"How'd you sleep, Dad?" Aunt Hallie asked him.

He waved the question aside. Paul couldn't see his face, only the back of his head where wisps of hair stuck out from the cap and brushed the collar of his wool shirt, light as a dandelion gone to seed.

"Well, I see we have another good day," he said, not to any of them in particular.

"Yes, haven't we been lucky this year?" Aunt Hallie said.

Paul caught the change in her voice—his mother did that, too. He could always tell how well she knew someone by how cheerful her voice got. She saved the plainer darker sound for her family. Funny that Aunt Hallie would talk like that to her own father. Maybe it was because of his hearing.

Then the room froze, as Paul remembered the words he'd overheard in the night, and knew what they meant. Daytime made it worse. Everything was plain to him and he couldn't say these were only terrible thoughts flung at him by the darkness. People died when they got old, he understood that. And afterward, he guessed, they went to heaven. *Your family'll all be waiting for you,* his friend Lynette told him over Monopoly one afternoon. *I mean everybody way way back.* She made it sound like a holiday dinner, all these relations arranged around a long table with candles and the best dishes and no empty chairs except the one he'd come to fill. Lynette acted comfortable with the idea, but Paul wasn't sure, not at all. He could only see himself as the boy he was now, and feel his legs squirming inside his good pants.

"You'd know all this if you went to Sunday school like you were supposed to," Lynette said.

Paul said they didn't do that in his family. Sundays they slept late. His father wore old clothes all day—he watched baseball or worked on the garden or split wood; once in a while he got up before anyone and went into the mountains with his friends. But sometimes Paul's mother took him inside one of the churches to hear a concert, and Paul saw right away that she knew how to act there. And the night the two of them walked through the snow to a candlelight service to sing carols, Paul studied her while everyone prayed, and saw how she looked, respectful and wide awake.

A few days after his talk with Lynette, he'd gone to his mother about what she'd said. They were out at the picnic table under the willow . . . she looked right into his face and told him: *No one knows.* And when she said it this way, she made it sound mysterious and not to be feared. "Don't you think there's more going on than we can see?" she said, and before Paul could wonder if he did, she went on, in another voice. "Besides, Paulie, look how young you are, I don't want to think of you worrying yourself about all that." He remembered how she sat with him, not growing impatient, and how the gold light struck her face and how her hair streamed down in harmony with the willow branches.

His grandfather *was* old, but not old like the old people he saw going in to eat at the cafe near his house, or like Lynette's great-grandmother who stayed with them next door part of the year, who was born in the 1800s. Paul felt his face burning. *His parents really didn't know,* he thought. He felt himself plummeting and grabbed the bars of the railing and squeezed them hard. He locked his eyes on his grandfather's figure below and imagined that he turned his face and smiled up at him, raising one of his freckled hands in a greeting. *Come along, Paulie, you're one of us.*

But no, the room was alive and loud again. His grandfather was stirring his coffee listlessly, and Aunt Hallie was saying, "Our girls are walking down to the barrens this morning . . . Paulie, too, I guess."

"No!" Paul burst out, though he'd only meant to think it.

Everyone turned and stared up at him. Aunt Hallie's mouth drooped open. "Paulie," she said. "Well, good morning." Her composure gathered again. "You don't have to go if you don't want to," she said. "But why don't you?"

Of course, Paul hadn't meant he wouldn't go walking with them, but now that he thought about it, he knew he didn't want to. He didn't want to do anything.

"There's nothing to be afraid of," Billie said.

"You can look for arrowheads," Gwen said.

Paul could hardly talk. He'd gone numb. He dug under the sleeping bag for his clothes and slipped back out of sight to put them on. In a moment, the talk below resumed, as though he'd never broken it.

Aunt Hallie lifted the big teakettle two-handed and poured steaming water over the breakfast dishes. Everyone had gone.

Paul sat by the Franklin stove, paging through old *Field and Streams,* waiting for a break in her work. But she moved from job to job so smoothly that Paul finally went and stood by her as she drove the fine sand from the rag rug to the linoleum and out the door.

"It's a wonder we have a beach anymore," she said, an old camp joke.

"What's wrong with Grampa Paul?" Paul asked.

He had no idea what she'd say. Some things, his mother reminded him constantly, weren't any of his business.

"Here, Paulie," Aunt Hallie said. "Give this a shake for me."

Paul took the mat she handed him and followed her to the porch. He held it over the edge and shook and the dirty sand showered the ivy below. As he finished, he saw she was watching him, so he gave it another little shake.

"That's good," she said, but didn't take it back from him. Her eyes had shifted to the lake. Through the pine branches, Paul saw the hazy sheen of the water and down by the lake's outlet the glint of a boat at anchor.

"Somebody said something, sounds like," Aunt Hallie said, back with him again. "Haven't they?" She walked to the edge of the porch and patted a plank beside her for him to sit, and he did.

"Honey," Aunt Hallie said. "Your grandfather has a kind of cancer. Do you know about that?"

Paul nodded, hoping desperately that she wouldn't ask him to say what he knew.

"Your mother didn't tell you anything?"

"No."

"Just as well," Aunt Hallie said. She was quiet for another moment. "The truth is," she said, "we just don't expect he'll be here when you come again next summer."

"Oh . . ."

"We'll miss him terribly, won't we?"

Paul felt that numbing in his chest again, but then Aunt Hallie put her hand to his forehead and smoothed back his hair, exactly what his mother would've done. He didn't know what in the world he should say.

"Be nice to him, Paulie," she said.

Everyone knew his grandfather's routine at camp—even now it wasn't much changed. He woke early and took the boat out, alone. The chug of a far-off motor was the first sound people would notice as they lay in bed. If he kept any fish—northerns or walleyes (rock bass he said ruined the lake and these he stuck through the gills with his penknife and threw back to die)—he cleaned them on a board grown between two maples by the water, a few of the younger cousins crowding around. He took his time, now and then picking off one of the questions pitched at him, letting most of what they said fly past. But often he took no fish. After beaching the boat, he'd make the rounds of his children's cabins, then shut himself in the workroom, where he oiled and sharpened the tools, or fixed things that broke around camp, or where he just sat and read whatever newspaper he found in one of the outhouses, back to front, until he retired to The Folly and treated himself to deviled ham on Ry-Crisp, some black tea, and his medications, then shooed out any remaining cousins, drew the bamboo shades and slept.

After his aunt went back to her work, Paul drifted down the path toward Grampa Paul's. The day was getting hot. The lake was flat; nothing seemed to move. Someone called to him from inside Aunt Leah's, one of the girl cousins, but he skipped down the hill past the tangle of rosehips, as if he hadn't heard. A lantern was burning in the workroom. Paul veered off the trail and came around the shaded side and sat on the chopping block and waited for his grandfather to come outside. He didn't, though. After a while Paul climbed on the pile of birch rounds below the high screened window and tried to listen. All he heard were the jays fighting up in the hardwoods. He let himself down finally, then stood just to the side of the door, thinking how the others would barge straight in, until he couldn't stand it anymore and edged away.

It was too late to catch Gwen and Billie even if he wanted to. He crossed the strip of road behind the cabins and started running down the wide footpath through Uncle Mac's swath of thinned-out woods, called The Pinery, which lead a quarter mile to Lake Superior . . . and by the time the trail opened out above the rusty sandstone bluffs, he was crying and coughing and trying to get his breath. He went to his knees and covered his face from the glare of the bay, and before long the spasm began to ease. Leaning back into the roots of a cedar, he heard Aunt Hallie's voice again, and somehow the sound of it outweighed what she'd told him. He took a few deep breaths and gradually his hands unclenched. He sat up and stared out at the big lake. Miles out, an ore boat crept along the horizon, above it a wash of bright clouds, too far away to look like anything.

Before supper, everyone gathered on the porch of The Folly for happy hour—Uncle Ray and Aunt Hallie, Uncle Duff, Uncle Mac, and all the others. His grandfather sat in a high-backed wicker chair, and slats of light crossed his shirt, rippling down onto his folded hands. Paul walked through to the table and grabbed a handful of cashews and looked for a place to sit, but all the chairs and even the bench under the window were taken, so he backed against the wall and tried to be invisible.

"How's the boy?" Uncle Ray asked. Paul smiled blankly. It was all the answer his uncle seemed to want.

The talk was about electricity. One of the original land owners across the lake had brought in power and had a TV in his cabin. The road was still dug up in spots and even Uncle Ray complained.

Uncle Duff drank down the last of his beer and snapped the aluminum sharply between his fingers.

"What're you all afraid of?" he said. "What's going to happen is going to happen."

"It's better than listening to that god-awful generator of his," Aunt Leah said.

"I'll tell you, they don't even make gas iceboxes anymore," Uncle Duff added.

Uncle Mac gave them both a stare. He was oldest of the five, the most like Paul's grandfather, everyone said. "We all *agreed* about this, as I remember it," he said stiffly.

Uncle Duff was known as the family hothead, and Paul could see for himself he was itching to let loose with something more. But another look flew between the brothers, accompanied by the slightest nod toward their father. It was the same kind of thing that'd happened at breakfast that day. They *did* have an agreement . . . but it was about more than electricity, about more than not changing things at camp. They were all going to get along for a while, and they were all going to be nice to him.

The porch fell to silence.

Paul looked at his grandfather. He wondered how the sickness could be inside him and not show. Maybe everyone else knew what to look for, he thought. They acted as if they could see it, as if they felt it in the room with them, breathing and growing. Aunt Hallie came out from the kitchen and brought his glass back, filled mostly with ice, and fit it into his hand. "There now," she said. Paul saw his eyes flick from the glass up to her face, lingering just a second, then out to the rest of them fanned before him—all his family—and then saw the slow, tired-looking shake of his head.

After supper, Paul slipped away from his aunt and uncle and the cousins and sat on the dock by The Folly. The evening birds came out, the swallows like scraps of shadow, then the loons and others he didn't know the names of. Far off, he heard a woman's voice calling, but it only made the lake seem quieter, farther from the rest of the world . . . then his grandfather was standing beside him. Without talking, they made the boat ready, loaded the cushions, the poles, the tackle box. Paul dropped into the bow. His grandfather shoved them off and rowed out much farther than he had the night before, both of them looking back at the slice of cleared land where the cabins were, a few lights just now coming to the windows. Finally he primed the engine and started it. Paul turned and faced into the wind and watched the black choppy water separate before the bow, letting the rush of air scour his thoughts.

Near the far shore, his grandfather eased the engine back to a slow chug, then let it die, though they were still a ways out in deep water. From the corner of the sky, Paul saw the great heron again, just as it thrust down its long wings and braced itself to land.

"*There!*" he said, but his grandfather had already seen it.

Paul looked down at the fishing things and could barely think what they were for. He wanted to keep talking now, before his voice froze, though he couldn't think of what to say.

"I'll miss you terribly," he blurted—then gulped, felt his face flush. That was what Aunt Hallie had said, not his words at all. His grandfather was still watching the heron.

"After you go home?"

"Yes," Paul said. "And after that, I mean. . . ."

"Don't you think you'll be seeing me again?"

"No," Paul said. "Not really."

His grandfather thumbed up the bill of his cap and studied him, as if he hadn't taken a full reckoning of him until this instant. "Maybe you won't at that," he said.

His hands stirred on the oargrips, the calluses squeaking lightly.

"Hardly seems fair, does it?"

Paul struggled to look straight across at him, but when he brought himself to do it, his grandfather was looking off, his eyes following the tree line around the lake, taking the same slow route the heron had.

"When I was a little older than you, twelve maybe," his grandfather said in a minute, "a couple of men my father knew drowned over there. In that water off the point."

Paul shot a look back over his shoulder, though he knew there'd be nothing to see.

"There wasn't any settlement up here yet, just an old homesteader's place where Uncle Mac's is now. It had pretty much gone to ruin and my father had decided it should come down—that's what we were busy with that day. I suppose your mother's told you that my father was a doctor . . ."

Paul shook his head.

"He and another doctor named Hollings had bought this land together and it was the two of them tearing down the cabin, and I was supposed to be helping, but I think I spent most of the day by the fire. It was early November, a Sunday . . . there was just a fringe of ice along in the cattails.

"These other men were older, people Dr. Hollings knew from Negaunee. They were going across to hunt deer in this part of the woods over where we are now. Big stocky men, all weighted down with wool, heavy lace-up boots . . ."

"What happened?" Paul asked.

His grandfather took a while to answer. "The weather wasn't so bad," he said. "Not a great deal of wind. The sun wasn't really out, still it wasn't a terribly dark day. Something must have happened in the boat, an argument maybe, or just . . . I don't know, Paulie. I really don't have any idea. Here my father and his friend were both doctors but it didn't make any difference at all. I was the first one to see the boat—it had drifted over toward the outlet, upside down.

"Dr. Hollings had to drive their truck back to town. We followed him in our car, my father and I. There wasn't much of a road then—some stretches of it were nothing more than grades the logging company had left years before. It was night now. My father stayed close behind the truck so our head-lights shone on the bed where the men were, rolled up in a canvas tarp. But the road was so uneven, finally we had to stop and get out and tie them down with rope. I can remember them standing in the woods doing it, passing the rope back and forth."

Then his grandfather was quiet again.

Paul tried listening to the water against the side of the boat, but found himself thinking about those long-ago men trying to swim in the freezing water, about all the things in the boat falling out and sinking. He thought about the guns still lying at the bottom of the water, lost under generations of leaves.

His grandfather finally looked up again, offering Paul a brief smile in the creases of his eyes.

"You ever hear them call this God's country?" he said.

Paul couldn't tell if this was a question he had to answer, but he nodded.

"There's not another place so lovely, Paulie, so full of all of us, I know there isn't . . . *but God's country?*"

His gaze came suddenly back and fixed hugely on Paul. "Paulie, can I tell you something? I'm not sure that God has a country."

"Me either," Paul murmured.

"Nor anyone," his grandfather said. He let go of the oars and let them drift back along the hull. *"Nor any living thing, Paulie."*

The heron lifted its beak toward the sky. A harsh rattle escaped from its throat, echoing across the open water. The blue air deepened quickly, speckled by the dark shapes of insects, then by stars. A fish jumped near the boat, but neither Paul nor his grandfather made a move toward the tackle. They'd come out too late and pretty soon they'd need to turn around and go back, but for a few minutes more they sat in the boat together, watching the heron as it disappeared into the darkness of the reeds.

ᏋᏋᏋ Compensation

"I don't want to see it," I tell him.

This late, the Stockholm's dead, the air's gone out of the meringue, the drunks are still out drinking. We've got a boy and girl tucked elbow to elbow in the last booth, feeding each other fries. Except for Mitch, that's it, everybody's slunked off home. This girl's maybe seventeen. Hours and hours ago it was hot enough for that gauzy thing you can see her tan through. It's too far gone in the year for that stuff. Out in the kitchen, Yvonne has her nose in a romance when she ought to be running potatoes through the shredder, but Yvonne's not my number-one problem tonight.

"Anyway," I tell Mitch, "you're an idiot if you carry it around with you."

"C'mon, Patsy . . ." he says, so disappointed in me.

Back when he was brakeman for the BN, he wore his face full of curly hair, rusty in the sideburns when the light was right. And a company hat, shot back so you could see his eyes, friendly ones, big as quarters. We'd go out north to the Blue Moon and dance if I had a night off. He could go and go in those days—people gave us room. I'd roll across his back, the lights would spin, his hands would shift and grab me. In the truck he'd get to fiddling with the radio while I drove, trying to bring in some far-out station . . . he never could stand to listen to just anything. He'd bring me home things, plants for the trailer, little gizmos from the Coast to Coast. He'd lie out on the picnic table after dark and play his harmonica up at the clouds. "Where'd you learn that one?" I'd ask him. He'd say, "That song? I always knew that one." Sometimes I'd get to thinking, *Girl, you're not so far off this time.*

You can believe it takes a strong memory to remember that Mitch.

On the railroad, they call what happened to him a slack action, where they let the cars hammer together *bam, bam, bam.* Up near Marias Pass, the middle of a blizzard. Which destroyed his back. Which wiped that cheery look off his face. Then his lawyers tell him, *Better get rid of the beard, Mr. Kraebel,* so he shaves it right off, no questions asked, and God, didn't he look strange then? Pinched up like an old guy when he's not even forty. You could see how much hair he'd lost . . . there's more gone now, more weight, too. The skin's stretched so tight I could read the serial number on his skull.

He picks the check from his shirt pocket anyway, smoothes out the creases on the edge of the counter, but he can just skip it. He won't catch me gawking at those zeroes.

I don't know where he was all summer. There wasn't so much as a rumor out of him since the calls stopped. Quarter to three in the A.M. and I'd be just dropping off. *I'm better,* he'd swear. But he wasn't, you could hear how beat his voice was. If I didn't get back to sleep before the sparrows started in, I'd have to get dressed and go for a drive. Being in the trailer alone would spook me if I let myself think about it. The dawn always helped. It was nothing like around Havre, where you saw it coming forever across the flat, treating everyone equal. Here it finds the chinks in the mountains first and blasts into the valley. One morning I pulled the truck over, up by the mint farm, and watched this huge crow take off from a phone pole and fly up until the light hit him. He turned to gold all at once. God, it was something how he flapped around in a circle and wouldn't come down.

That was early June.

"Well, here it is anyway," Mitch says. "The waiting's over."

"It's *been* over for me," I tell him. We've been through all this. I was done waiting last winter.

"I hate to be the one to tell you," he says, "but, you know, the thing is, Patsy, you don't have any patience."

"You keep your voice down!" I say. Yvonne wouldn't notice if the earth moved. But still.

"It's true," he says, lower.

"What's true is, I used it up on you," I say. "I had all kinds of patience before all this."

I could wait with the best of them, even Mama said so. I waited with her every Friday night for Sonny Diehl to bring the truck back from Plentywood or Cut Bank. I waited on those long benches in church, watching the choir ladies, wondering what they had their minds on between hymns when they looked so bored. I waited through every single day of Havre High School, home of the Blue Ponies, waited the fat part of another two years, working at the Arctic Circle, seeing Mark Rupp, my old general-science teacher . . . Thursday nights when he was supposed to be down in the Bear Paws measuring faults.

Afternoons, I'd look out the window of the drive-in and wonder who it was going to be that'd get me out of Havre. The wind never stopped for a second. It blew trash and wore the hills down and shoved the heat or cold in the door behind people, but it never had *my* name on its tongue. Until she rooted down here, Mama's family'd all been movers, and even my brothers were long gone, nomads to the wheat harvest. So what was stopping me from climbing on the next Intermountain that came through town? Why did I think something had to *happen* first?

It's a stumper.

"I dumped that schmo, Winkler," Mitch says.

His Sperry County lawyer.

"I got connected with an outfit out of Minneapolis does nothing but train cases. That's when we got results. You ought to see those guys operate, Pats. C'mon here and look at this."

Last winter's when it got bad. A whole year after the accident. Mitch cried all the time. A man can cry, I don't mean that. Mitch cried like he had the angel of tears planted on his shoulders. In bed, I'd hear him hitching his breath, ready to explode. If I didn't touch him or say something, if I managed to get myself back to sleep, he'd hoist himself up and walk back and forth on the bad place in the floor until I was awake.

"Mitch," I'd have to say, that special way. He'd be shaking against my back by now. "You'll feel better by spring," I'd say. "Your back won't be a hundred percent, but I mean the rest of you. When the weather gets nice, you'll come around. Really truly." We made love more than normal, with me on top doing the lion's share, or sometimes it soothed him if I did him with my mouth . . . even so, I'd have to get up later and bring him a pill.

Every test they could think of, he'd had already, and some of them more than once—myelogram, CAT scan, EMG, which is the freakiest of the bunch, where they put needles in your spine. "If it was *my* back," I'd start to say, but Mitch would glare at me, just hateful. He'd tell me, "Honey, one thing it isn't, is your back, OK?"

"God, Mitch," I'd say. "I'm with you," but that wasn't enough.

Or maybe it was too much.

We talked it around and around, and he went ahead with the operation, the laminectomy, but there wasn't any real choice about it. The pain down his leg got better like they said, but he didn't move right.

It was more than being lame. I'd never know when I'd find him in his pj's, out at the kitchen table, coffee cup loaded with Early Times. The TV'd be on. He'd have this yellow pad out and some red marking pens . . . his printing was like a fifth grader's. TAKE A CLASS, it would say on the pad, which was something I was on him to at least check out. He was always a smart-enough guy, Mitch.

When I first got to Sperry, when we first started going out, he'd swear up and down he was quitting the railroad and going into business for himself.

Nothing you could say would spoil it for him.

But this was now. We'd be out in the kitchen. "They ruined me," he'd say.

"Look at me!" I'd say. "You're *not* ruined."
That was in February.

He straightens up on his elbows, slow-motion, the way he does anymore. If you didn't know, you'd think it was just about sexy. He looks right at me.

"This whole thing's been a lesson to me, Patsy," he says.

"You haven't touched your pie," I say. I gave him the last wedge of lemon out of the case. You can't just sit at the counter with nothing in front of you.

"A lesson in persevering. It's like they say, you have to hang in there," he says. "Sooner or later you get what's yours."

He swivels the check around so it's glowing up at me.

"Why don't you quit this place," he says.

"Lord, Mitch, will you put that thing *away.*"

"You can get rid of that miserable trailer," he says. "You don't want to spend another winter in that thing. Once they leak they're pretty well shot—I mean, you can climb up and slap tar on them, but it doesn't really fix anything."

"I already sold the trailer," I say.

Here's something that hasn't crossed his mind once, you can just tell.

"What'd you get for it?" he asks.

"What do you care?" I say. "It was fair."

"No, I'm interested," he says, but he isn't really. After a minute he gets up the nerve to ask, "You living with someone, that why?"

His voice isn't mean or hopeless, I'll give him that.

"I got a place," I say finally.

He works off the corner of his pie, nodding, giving this some thought.

"Got a black Lab," I go on. "I had a string of tomato plants before the frost."

"Still got the truck?" he says.

He knows I do. It's parked out by the dumpsters.

"I bet you never got it rebuilt," he says. "I bet it's still got shit for compression."

"I had the guy down at the Cenex give it a look," I tell him.

"They should put it in a truck museum," Mitch says. "How'd you like it if I bought you a new four-by-four? Or a TransAm, for that matter? Real leather? Sound system that wouldn't keep going out on you?"

Don't panic, I'm thinking, but I haven't seen a smile on him in so long. Nothing like one.

"I'd get you that new John Cougar," he says.

"Mitch," I say, "where'm I gonna go in a new truck?"

I was still in Havre, twenty years old, when Mama finally married Sonny Diehl. Your basic quick job at the courthouse, no fanfare, no bouquets to grab out of the air. She didn't tell me things anymore, but I knew she didn't give much of a hoot one way or the other, except Sonny'd convinced her the finances worked out better if they did. He was a big guy, Sonny, solid-packed as a bag of Portland cement, topped off with a crewcut the color of a new sidewalk. He was an independent, had a Kenworth three-quarters paid off, blue with silver script on the door—I'll tell you, that truck was his own personal be-all and end-all.

But the night they were killed they had Mama's car, the Fairlane wagon, pointed north toward the border on 232. It was a Saturday night late, cold, fingernail moon, no snow yet. I hadn't set eyes on her for two weeks, which is just what I told the sheriff, then Morgan and Eddie, my brothers, when they found out. Everybody wanted to know what the deal was. Everybody acted like I ought to know. *You tell me,* I said. *You tell me what they were doing out there, Mama driving when she hates to drive, the border not even open that late for Christ's sake, no bags, no cold-weather gear. You tell me why people do things.*

Sonny'd been drinking, no dispute there. But Mama was sober enough she could've waltzed through the breathalizer. Maybe she thought she saw something, some flash across the highway. The car took off through the left lane, dove down into the borrow pit, and came out rolling, six, eight times, who knows, stopping right-side to, seventy yards out in the winter wheat. It wasn't until first light a rancher down from Simpson saw them.

Mama'd gotten awful tight with her words . . . I didn't have the foggiest notion what she was thinking most times. But before Sonny we got on fine enough. You knew she was lonely, but she didn't go acting like it was *my* fault. Then, one afternoon after Sonny'd been with us about a year, when Mama was down at the Eagles helping with the blood drawing, he got me alone in my bedroom. This was junior year and I'd been to bed with Glen Esterhaus maybe three times by then, so I wasn't exactly in the dark when Sonny started buttering me up. I tried to be cool about it at first. Weren't the high-school boys buzzing around me like hornets? Sonny wanted to know. Weren't they trying to stick their greedy little hands *here?* So, all right, that part didn't last long, you can imagine. Next thing, Sonny's saying I'd been egging him on, which was worse than silly. Then he got me by the arms.

All that week you could see where his fingers had been, two neat rows, purple then yellowish, but only the bottom one showed past my sleeve, so it looked like I'd only banged myself on the cooler again.

By last winter, right in the middle of Mitch's trouble, Mama'd been dead almost seven years, and I'd never felt anything that big about losing her, which shames me to say. Sometimes I got twinges about not having gone over to see her that week before it happened. Sometimes I even wondered how she'd've felt if it was me that rolled the car and ran my face through the windshield, but I didn't dig around in it. I'd tell people, *After Mama's accident, that's when I got out of Havre, that's what it took* . . . and leave it at that.

So there I was, getting off shift, the middle of one night. The heat was down to nothing in the trailer. Mitch and his back brace were smothered in pillows in the other room. I smoked a litle dope and tried relaxing with the radio, but it wasn't a comfort. The music didn't take hold at all. Before I knew it, I was shivering, starting with my shoulders then shooting out to the tips of my fingers. My pullover didn't help

and neither did running hot water over my hands in the sink.
I built up the fire, got the wood snapping and burning like
crazy, but by then I was in tears myself.

I didn't know *what* was going on. Of course, I knew how
tense it was living like that, everything so up in the air about
Mitch's recuperation. I knew something had to give and I
thought, *OK honey, here's your nerves going.*

I sure wasn't ready for it to be about Mama.

All of a sudden, I'm remembering us back in Havre, that
night after Sonny came unglued. We were down in their
room. Sonny'd gone out. The bed was full of laundry, towels
all over, Sonny's shirts, but she wasn't folding anything. She
was just sitting with her glasses in her lap.

How would I know she'd take his side, Sonny's side?

"If you got a problem with Sonny, then you stay clear of
him," that's what she said.

All right, I was seventeen, I didn't know much. I was
dumb enough to think she'd stand up to Sonny. Maybe I saw
the three of us parked around the kitchen table, getting everything straightened out. The least she could've done was act
surprised. Her only daughter, it's not that much to ask.

Sonny never got to me again, but so what? I'd smell him
in the bathroom, in the car. I'd try to read a magazine in my
room, then I'd wonder if he'd come in and run his hands over
my things. I'd hear him clomping down the hall even when
he wasn't there. Even so, it was a couple more years before
I could get a place of my own.

Well, Mitch woke up finally . . . I was making a terrible
noise by this time. I felt bad about getting him up, but God,
something was *happening* to me. Anyway, hadn't I lost sleep
with him, hadn't I stroked *his* head in the middle of the night?
Well, he wasn't ready to see me like that. He was stiff as
boards, and I don't mean his back. If I'd been smart, I
would've dried up right then and sent myself to bed, but I
wasn't thinking on that wavelength, not by a long shot.

I couldn't stop myself, I told Mitch all that stuff about
Mama, right down to the burn Sonny's whiskers left on my
cheek, and how I'd seen her steal a quick look down at my

breasts before she walked out on me.

But once I'd said it, I didn't care what she'd done to me or what she didn't do. It was all cleaned away and I missed her. I didn't want her dead out in some field. It was awful, I couldn't get my breath.

Mitch stood looking at me. "Where's the Flexeril?" he said. Flexeril's what he used to take for the spasms. He used to eat them like mints if I left them out.

I didn't do anything. I just sat at the table feeling how I was feeling. Mitch went over by the firebox and warmed his backside, and God knows what he was thinking.

Pretty soon he stopped rocking on his heels and turned to fiddle with the stove damper. Then he said, "I sure wish you wouldn't get this all roaring when you're only going to come to bed. Wood doesn't grow on trees."

He actually said that.

Maybe if it'd been summer, I'd have just walked out-doors, down the lane to the river, and found a quiet place to think about Mama. Sometimes that's all it takes, some water that's moving, some air. Like it was, I had to ask him to leave. Not that night, or the next morning, but pretty soon. Before spring.

That couple in the last booth stand up to go. The girl drifts toward the door, not half so perky any more. She stares off at the cars. She's so thin—nothing's had time to build up on her. *Go home* . . . I almost say it out loud. *Do yourself a favor tonight.* The boy digs around in his Levi's, pries out a wallet, and pushes money in my hand. Then he scuffs over to the girl, throws a beefy arm around her, and they're out the door.

Mitch was watching them too. Now he shifts back my way.

"What'd you do to your hair?" he says.

"Nothing," I say. "Stopped cutting it."

"No, I mean where it curls."

"It does that if I leave it alone."

"How come you didn't let it grow out when we were together?"

"I don't know, Mitch," I say. "Dried faster, I guess. I guess I didn't have the time for it."

He's giving me a wide-open, naked look. He can feel his fingers messing around in it, lost in it. He can feel it falling all over him, like syrup.

"I'll tell you something," he says. "I didn't just get the check today. I didn't just tear over here with it."

"No?"

"I could've gone anyplace with this," he says.

It's so quiet—I get this idea Yvonne's snuck out the back way and run off . . . all I can hear's ice cracking in the freezer, the milk machine humming, a little air leaking through the windows. Nobody's going to come in here now. They'll drive by and see a big blank place where the Stockholm's always been.

"I looked at some land," Mitch says. "Up Patrick Creek. Ten acres, option on ten more."

"Aw, Mitch," I say. "No."

"Timbered for the most part," he goes right on. "Kind of side hill, but not real steep. Southwest-facing. There's a break in the trees, looks like someone got in there once and cleared it, then never did anything, just punked out on it. I figure you could slip in an A-frame easy enough, not disturb things too much. Or maybe logs. . . ."

He shakes his head.

"You know, Patsy, I never pictured it coming to where somebody else would have to cut my logs for me. It still feels real funny—you know what I'm saying?"

When I don't answer he shrugs and goes on. "I walked out there all afternoon," he says. "Just . . . looking it over. Some of the aspen are turned already, way at the top, some of the larch. Everything was so played-out looking, dusty, but pretty as hell, you know? I couldn't believe it, I felt like I already had the papers in my pocket. I could see the way it was going to shape up, how the light would hit it . . . woodpile over here, maybe some chickens fenced in over there. And I could see you out on the steps . . . you were leaning back on your elbows in that Mexican shirt of yours, looking down toward the creek like you'd had a real long day but it was over and things were basically OK."

He's dropped down to a whisper now, but I hear him like he's inside my head.

"You didn't think any of this would pan out, did you?" he says. "You thought I was going straight downhill and you didn't want another thing to do with me."

"Mitch, God, you can't just come in here, quarter to midnight . . ."

"You gave up on me," he says.

"That's not true," I say.

But of course it is.

"Mitch," I say. "You get to a point. You see where things are headed."

If this was before, he'd be all to pieces now, his head would be in his hands.

"Maybe you don't know it but I think about that night," he says. "Out at the trailer, that night. You think I don't know you had your own . . . that you were going through something? You think I don't know that? All I had to do was go over and take care of you a little . . ."

"You were in another world," I tell him.

"Everybody's in another world," he says. "You know what I'm saying?"

He clamps his hands on the edge of the counter and gets to his feet.

"That was the worst winter," he says. "Sky's like ashes, one day after another. This place on the roof keeps catching the wind. I'm lying there telling you any goddamn thing in the world. I don't know where it comes from. I'm lying there, Patsy, I'm thinking, OK, this is the rest of my life, this here. Everybody's telling me, *Cool out, Mitch, the back's gonna heal*— all I got to do is do what they tell me, take the medicine, and I start out having some faith in that, you know? I did. But they don't say a *word* about the other thing, the one that's actually *killing* me, this black goddamn thing . . . and I don't see it coming any better than I saw those loose cars coming at me."

He stops himself short.

"Well, OK. That wasn't the best part of me, Patsy," he says.

"No kidding."

"But the way it seems to me, don't we go back some before all that?"

Who's got that good a memory?

I almost shout it straight in his face. But then I don't. It's too late in here for shouting. Anyway, that's not what I mean. There's not a thing wrong with my memory, it's sharp as glass.

We stand there, looking, just this strip of formica between us.

"It doesn't always keep getting worse and worse. That's all of it, that's what I had to say, Patsy . . . it comes back on the good side."

And what if that other starts in again? What if I need you a whole lot more sometime?

God knows, it's moments like now you try to get back to and fix all the rest of your life.

I reach my hand out and touch the side of his head. I expect a little flinch, a little covering up, but his skin's cool and quiet.

I pick the check up. I fold it and slide it back where it came from and push the snap till it gives a click against his chest. Here's to the good side, Mitch. I reach around me, undo the apron and loop it over my head, then turn and fluff my hair a little in the mirror.

 *Solstice*

Longest night of the year, Reuben thinks, could be the coldest, twenty-two below, with a killing wind. The winter wheat's like eight-penny nails pounded on the slant, ten thousand acres in any direction, broken by fallow. The stars are prickling overhead. Too cold for new snow. Too cold to be sitting in a truck on the county road. Too cold to be out looking for your wife.

Their pickups are idling side by side, Reuben's lights pointed east, Teddy Burnham's shooting out west, hi-beam, hitting nothing. The drivers' windows are half-mast, but Reuben's not got a lot to say. He said it before, yelled it between the cabs, his breath whipping away. *I come home and she's not there. Place is dark. Swear to God there was ice in the toilet. She musta got down and cut the pilot off.*

"So whatcha figure?" Teddy asks.

"What's she think?" Reuben says. "I'm going to chase after her, a night like this?"

Teddy nods. He's a big man, a head taller than Reuben, Reuben's oldest friend. Blocked for him the year they went to district. 1962. Would've been Reuben's best man, too, except he was overseas, working graders and backhoes in Bamberg, Germany, compliments of Uncle Sam. He's known Estelle as long as Reuben Lejeune has, longer if you count a few afternoons at the Tasty Whip, junior year. About football and playing with Reuben, he remembers nothing in particular, no single spectacular instants where he sees them together —only the grunting, the clacking of pads, the endless-seeming walk back from the practice field. But Estelle's still bright in his memory, from that time before she married Reuben and shortly after—tall, outfitted in sharp clothes, with something nervy to tack onto whatever you said, undercut by a shy sidelong smile. The truth is (he wouldn't say it to Reuben's face) he'd rather think about Estelle like she was, not how she's become.

Back then she was best friends with Teddy's wife, Paulette—that was years before he and Paulette linked up. They don't see so much of each other anymore, Paulette and Estelle. Part of it's that Paulette works in town at the credit union, the first woman officer they ever had. Another part, Teddy's forced to admit, is that Paulette's never liked Lejeune. Made it clear she didn't like his pushiness or the things he thought were funny or the way he flaunted Estelle like a mare he'd broke. And she hasn't much mellowed on the subject of Reuben over time, so Teddy's caught in the middle all right, his loyalties stretched taut. He's done his best just to keep things sociable.

"All right, Lejeune," Teddy says. "Just, you can count on me, OK?"

"Sure," Reuben yells.

He snugs his window. Teddy's big face glows at him through the glass, the cheeks red and slick from a ruthless shaving and then the wind.

Teddy cranks down his window again. "You tried in town?" he asks.

"Yeah, she could be in town," Reuben admits. "Probably that's all this is."

Teddy finally lifts his hand, puts her in gear and pulls away. Reuben stares after him in the rearview. It's a good rig Teddy has, four-wheel, sweet off the road. Reuben's own needs work, needs real money poured into it, but he's been holding off. Since Magritte sold out his share of the elevator, everything's been shaky. Reuben's held on a couple years now, but these new men they shipped from out East are a constant pain, so how can you plan, how can you get your friggin' ducks in a row? But it's too cold to dwell on that. It's come time to back around and head out to the house, or go into town, or do *something.* Instead he stays there, idling in the middle of God's own straightaway, with the engine rumbling and the heater blowing a feeble stream, wondering how long a man would last outdoors, on foot. Suppose you just broke down, suppose you just couldn't go any farther?

"What do you know, Reuben?" someone asks as he walks into the Stockman's. Cutler's decked the backbar out with a gaudy display of Christmas gear, all of it twinkling to beat the band. Reuben checks the eyes down the mirror.

"Nothing," he answers.

There's Grange, Billy Q., a few others. Poor showing for a Thursday, but cold keeps the ranchers occupied.

Marge is looking up into the TV and just before Reuben squeezes her shoulder she says, "Evening, Lejeune." Eyes in the back of her head.

"What you got going tonight, Marge?"

There's a ballet on the TV, white flashing skirts and leotards. The reception is terrific.

"Cutler popped for a satellite dish," Marge says. "You know him and gadgets. A hundred something stations—ninety percent of it's the same mushola. He had on the wrist-wrestling championships when I came to work, but nobody was paying it no mind at all. Too damn cold. Look at them."

Her eyes stray down the bar. Almost seventy degrees in here and the men are still hunched over, fleece collars smothering their necks. Some of the beer drinkers have gone to small glasses of liquor.

"I was wondering if Estelle come through here."

"About when?" Marge says.

"Beats me," Reuben says.

Marge watches the dancers. They blow across like snowflakes.

"What can I get you, Lejeune?" she asks after a minute.

"I don't know, a shot." He's been sober a while—the second of two pint bottles under the truck seat gave out yesterday. He wasn't going to have anything, but now it seems like a good idea. "A little antifreeze," he says.

She makes a lovely long pour, Marge, not quick and tight to the line. Even when Cutler's around.

"Your wife run off?" Marge says.

"Hey," Reuben says. "I was supposed to meet her." His face bunches with concern. "I was worried about if she had trouble with the car or something."

Marge frowns. "Grange," she says. "You seen Estelle?"

Reuben knows Grange from around the elevator, and from softball. Used to be a singles hitter, a real slasher, on base all the time, then he just quit, the middle of one season. A while later Estelle said she'd heard his wife died of cancer over at St. Jude's. That was five years ago at least.

"Estelle?"

"Yeah," Reuben says.

"Sure, I seen her," Grange says. "I seen her riding around in Billy Q.'s four-by-four."

Billy Q., born William Quick, hears this late, looks up, his long doughboy face accumulating a sheepish smile. Not in a million years would he have thought of Estelle Lejeune so much as *sitting* in his rig. It takes him a while to work it through. Such a good-looking woman, so high-bred. Everybody at the Stock's knows how the finance company came and drove away Billy's new Blazer. It was a joke him thinking he'd keep it, a dream. The beater he drives now succumbed to cold over the weekend.

Reuben tosses off his drink and Marge gives him another before he can think what's what. It was a mistake coming here, that much is plain.

"Sorry for the cheap shot, Lejeune," she says. "I'll buy this one."

"I should've known," Reuben says.

"That's a fact," Marge says, giving the TV a quick check over her shoulder. What Reuben meant was he should've known straight talk wasn't the legal tender around the Stock's tonight. But he gets the idea that wasn't what Marge meant. The thing about Estelle riding with Billy Q., that's too silly on the surface of it to get worked up over, still it makes him itchy. It's hard to even stay put on the stool.

"So you haven't seen her," he says.

"I haven't seen Estelle in ages," Marge says. "I can't hardly think what she looks like."

Reuben nods.

"Where she been keeping herself? She got a job or anything?"

"No, she ain't working," Reuben says. "You kidding?"

"Some people don't mind it, Lejeune," she says.

"Show me one," Reuben says.

Marge doesn't answer him, just swivels toward the TV screen. So Reuben has to look too, finally.

It's a single dancer up there now, leaping and twirling like a madwoman.

On the way home, on county road 406, he passes the Magrittes' old place, the house where Estelle grew up. Buried somewhere in Reuben's memory is the reflex to turn in at the cattle guard and cruise that long slowly rising strip of road to the house, accelerating with pleasure at the dips, feeling the truck buck to the spring load and down again, then pulling up sharp in the pea stones by the porch, and getting out and straightening himself up to face that house full of Magrittes and its pride, the youngest daughter, Estelle.

It's not full of Magrittes anymore. The sign reads Tronstad in daylight. Magritte and his wife live in Tucson, in a condo, and Magritte has taken up golf. Reuben can't bring himself to picture Magritte's rock-solemn Huguenot features fretting over a golf ball. Reuben himself has never been to Tucson, never played golf, and never intends to do either.

The whole thing's a betrayal of some kind—the sale of the elevator, Magritte's escape from Cobolt, from winter. Not that he and Magritte were ever buddy-buddy—far from it, but there'd been some level of understanding, otherwise Magritte surely wouldn't have sanctioned the marriage or hired Reuben to work under him. Once, Magritte told a table of Masons that Reuben reminded him of himself when he was a young guy, and this got back to Reuben in a few days, and Reuben took it as money in the bank. In fact, for a while there, Reuben used to kid with Teddy Burnham about how quick he'd come up in the world. But later on Magritte seemed to lose interest. Just gave up on him for no stated reason, the bastard. Reuben roars by in the dark now and even feeling like he does, he can't help turning his head. Outlined all in blue Christmas lights, the place seems to hover like a spaceship.

Their place, his and Estelle's, is seven miles out, which can take as little as five and a half minutes on dry pavement, about one long ballad's worth, somewhat longer on black ice, long enough to let his mind wander in earnest.

Like the Magrittes', it's all alone, a solitary outpost, but there the resemblance stops. Reuben watches the truck lights rattle down the storm fencing and sweep over the frozen yard and come to rest on the garage wall. Magritte had stationed his family seat where he could see in one gulp the whole cluster of houses and bars and dealerships that make up Co-bolt as he stood in the bay window with his morning allotment of juice, and where, elevated as he was, the town could see him if it bothered to look, which it still did upon occasion. The Lejeunes' place sits down out of the wind, a two-bedroom ranch style with pale green siding pressed to look like wood —Estelle's choosing. At one time Reuben hated it, though it's not a thing he notices anymore.

The house is every bit as dark as when he'd come home from work the first time. The truck door slams like a rifle shot. This cold, things sound wrong. The snow underfoot, which would wince and squeal up around zero, only prickles now.

Another thing about the house—no cellar underneath, just a crawl space. Reuben flicks on the kitchen lights, then immediately tries the cold-water faucet and nothing comes out. The meagerest trickle is all it takes to keep it from freezing. But what with the skiff of ice in the toilet bowl, this doesn't look like negligence. Since six he's gotten the house up near fifty degrees—still it could be a hundred and not warm things down where the pipes are.

One hand still on the faucet, he tries to remember why in hell he never insulated the skirt around the west side of the house, or put up heat tape . . . then he's remembering Estelle standing at the sink with water gushing out over potatoes in a colander, the fat part of some summer, the barbecue going outside, hours of sun to spare. In that gold light her face doesn't look any older, her body any more gravity-beaten than it did when he used to leave Magritte's with her warming the seat next to him, when they'd drive the access road along the Milk River making their plans, then pull off by the cutbanks and slide the truck seat out and lie together in the open air. She lets the water run, lopping the bad parts off the potatoes with a paring knife. Reuben comes up behind her, feeling himself harden against her backside. What does she say, what encouragement? It's gone.

He swings around suddenly, uneasy at the rest of the dark house leering over his shoulder. He flips on more lights and things look just as empty of her as they did four hours ago.

He puts his hood up again and walks out to the garage to locate the Benz-o-matic. Some luck, it's right where it should be and the tank's only half-empty. He lights it and the flame leaps out a good six inches. He carries it outside with him—it feels good in his gloved hand, emitting a blue hiss against the cold. At the far side of the house he kicks the ice off the hatch to the crawl space and stoops in. The aluminum ladder's under there and the old TV antenna and his duck boat and some long strips of fir he was going to trim the garage roof with. The pipes are clear down the other end. Squatting cuts off his wind so he has to go on all fours.

The cold's more concentrated under the house, more perverse for being undisturbed. He kneels by the pipes and applies the torch. If he's caught it in time, he can melt the length from ground to floor joists in a few minutes. If not, it's probably frozen halfway to the pump already. At least, it occurs to him, the place is old enough not to have plastic pipes, no small blessing.

He's been under the house fifteen or twenty minutes, massaging the copper tubing with flame, when he hears the telephone. It's rung maybe three times before he lowers the torch to be sure. He calculates five rings to get outdoors, another four to get to the kitchen. It rings twice more before he starts to crawl back through the frozen litter, that double ring of theirs on the party line, muffled by the carpet backing. *Crink, crink,* it sounds like. Then he just stops crawling. His breath crowds around his face. He'll never make it, he doesn't stand a snowball's chance. So he makes his way back to the light, telling himself to *under no circumstances* wonder where the sweet Jesus she's calling from or what ugliness she's going to fling at him. But the ringing keeps on, eighteen rings at least, twenty maybe, who knows? He could have slithered the whole way on his belly.

Upstairs, he does what he was too cold to do when he first got home from the elevator, namely, take a decent inventory. In their bedroom, his softball stuff's in a heap by the vanity—the blue nylon duffle's gone, that's the first thing. Otherwise the room's intact. No sign of temper, nothing shredded or slammed around. Sitting on the edge of the water bed, though, he notices that she unplugged the timer for the heater. The water slides around under him like bearing butter.

He looks in the drawers that are hers and in her end of the closet and he can't tell what's missing. Old jumpers and corduroy slacks and underwear with ruined elastic—he can't remember seeing *any* of this before. He grabs out a swimsuit and holds it up to the light. It's blue and stretchy, so sheer she would've shown through, wide bumpy nipples and all the rest. No way she could parade a thing like that around, no way he'd condone it. The suit fits entirely inside his fist, feels like squeezing a handful of butterfly wings.

OK, Estelle, he thinks, what about money, what about that? One time Reuben almost got himself talked around to applying for a VISA card, or one of those, but at the last minute he thought what did he need crap like that for, so, thank God, he doesn't have any credit cards to try and lay hands on. The checkbook is right there under the phone where he left it, all in sequence, and the savings book is still where he kept it hid, tucked inside the Book of Deuteronomy up by the almanacs. So what she's doing for money is another mystery.

The rest of the house looks the same. He always pretty much thought of it as *her* place on the inside. He was working all the time, she was the one who stirred around here all day and said they needed a new sofa or whatever, and went down and picked out the material and all that, curtains to match, and he was the one who made the payments. There'd never been any money from Magritte, except wages, never would be. Unless there was some private channel, maybe an account over at Paulette's credit union he didn't know about.

Anyway, he thinks, here she's gotten the house set up like she always wanted, then just left it. The Estelle Lejeune Museum. Except, he gets this idea walking through it, dragging his fingers on the cold veneer: there's really not that much of her in it, no classy hand-me-down stuff from the Magrittes, not even anything that said it was Christmas. Mostly it's just pieces from the merc, or from the Sears in Great Falls. Their high-school pictures used to be out on the highboy along with some end-of-the-season shots of the Stockman's team, but he hasn't seen them in a while. There's a drawer in the junk room with three or four albums filled piecemeal, backyard parties and old float trips with Teddy and Paulette before they had kids. He kind of hates to even check if they're still there.

Actually, the duffle wasn't the first thing. The Plymouth was the first thing, which he saw was missing on his first trip home. He's back in the kitchen now, directly over the furnace. He takes down a bottle from up by the breakfast cereal and splashes some in a coffee mug. The garage was built to hold two rigs, but it's filled with enough junk that only one fits now, Reuben's truck, of course, which he needs to get to work in. The Plymouth sits out—even with a block heater it didn't start yesterday, and although he didn't actually try, there's every reason to believe it wouldn't start again today.

But then, OK, a fact's a fact—she'd gotten it running somehow.

If she goes west, she crosses the reservation and the road starts winding through mountains, then breaks out into the valley at Sperry Canyon, but far as he knows, she doesn't have a single contact in Sperry. East, there's just more of the state. Hours and hours of it, then Williston, Minot, Devils Lake, Grand Forks, eventually Minneapolis–St. Paul, where they saw a Vikings game once and Estelle did some shopping and Reuben got into a fracas with a maître d' over some bum steaks.

It's not so hard to picture the car zipping through the night, and her behind the wheel, bolt upright, the radio switched off, the ashtray spilling over, but he can't see into her thoughts. If somebody made it simple as roulette, red or black, east or west, he still couldn't say which. But in his mind, the car's so small he can reach out and pick it up between two fingers and tweeze it back.

Now he hears her voice, not from recently, but from maybe five years back, near the time they officially stopped trying to have kids. The two of them are out by the river and it's a nice night, the cottonwood giving endless bars of shadow, a trace of sweet smoke in the air, some fireworks far-off. But something's gone wrong, something that escapes him now—all but the frustration of it. The flat of his hand's still burning and she's gone to one knee and is coming back at him straight, saying, *Don't you ever, ever, ever, ever* . . . the words not so much chewed off and spit out at him like on TV, as launched into his future, so he picks them up in bed at night like a distant radio signal.

And he hasn't ever again hit her. Not one single time after that. Not even drunk when it would've been easy to let himself go, or when she cranked up the Magritte in her voice, when she brought up things she knew better than to bring up, then took a stroll and wouldn't let him get back to zero no matter what. Not any of those times.

But right now he can't hear anything but this *ever, ever.* What happened last night? They sat right here in the living room and watched M*A*S*H, the one where Hawkeye and Margaret get trapped by a sniper and end up sleeping together. After that there was a movie with one of Charlie's Angels in it, but Reuben went to bed before it was half over. As he lay there, his feet still icy, he heard the shower going and thought Estelle would be in to bed pretty soon, and he could almost smell the dull perfume her hair gave off and the lotion she rubbed into her legs . . . but next thing he knew, music was pouring out of the clock radio and it said 6:46 and he didn't know what she'd decided on, coming to bed, staying up, or whatever.

And when was the last time they got it on in bed? Saturday was their night, as a rule, but not this past Saturday, and why was that? Well, sometimes they just didn't. Maybe he used to make demands, but no more. No way is it worth it. He tries a comforting picture, Estelle in bed, the frosted hair streaming down onto his chest like electricity. This is from a long time back, he realizes, before she had it chopped off— and before she started wanting the lights off. He tries hearing the little sounds she makes but he can't quite. All he sees is her in that blue swimsuit.

Now the phone starts ringing again. This time it's only an arm's length away and the two rings are sharp, two little dabs of antiseptic on a cut.

"It's me," Teddy Burnham says.

"*God,*" Reuben sighs. He can feel all his weight crash down against his belt.

"You're not drunk, are you?" Teddy says.

"What's the story?" Reuben answers.

"No story," Teddy says. "I think you ought to let her go." His voice sounds serious and foreign.

Reuben sits down on the dinette, his feet on the chair, still wearing the felt liners from his Sorels. "I thought you were helping me."

"Let her go if she wants, that's how I can help."

"Look," Reuben says. "She's not over there, is she? Estelle?"

"What're you talking about, Lejeune?"

"I don't know . . . her and Paulette."

"What's wrong with you?"

"I just, I don't know. Listen, is Paulette around?"

"She can't come to the phone," Teddy says. "She's getting ready for bed."

"No, put her on, willya?"

"Lejeune . . ." Teddy's paw goes over the receiver, stays there a while. Pretty soon somebody on the party line breaks in and Reuben says, "Paulette?" Whoever it is hangs up. Who are these people? Reuben can't ever bring himself to eavesdrop, but he knows *they* do—all day long they sneak their fingers off the button and listen in. Probably they all know about him and Estelle—he should be asking them.

Finally Paulette does come on.

"You in the bedroom?" Reuben asks, knowing she must be. It's a huge room, two of theirs easily—Navajo rugs and oak furniture and all that, passed down by the older Burnhams, while Reuben hasn't gotten so much as a water glass from anyone.

"I'm sorry about this, Reuben," Paulette says. Where Estelle's voice is low and smoky, Paulette's is high and sharp as a hook. And here she's half Teddy's size.

"She talk to you the last day or two?" Reuben asks.

Paulette doesn't answer right away, which worries Reuben, so he blasts ahead. "I don't . . . what's this all about?"

"You know as much as I do."

"I don't know anything," Reuben says.

"Well, what else is new?"

"You help her get her car going?" Reuben says. "You know, I left this morning it was frozen, wouldn't crank over one crank's worth. I know because I tried it. And to tell you the truth, Paulette, I don't see her out there in the goddamn freezing cold with a torch on the oil pan. I just can't picture it."

"You never know," Paulette says.

"*I* know," Reuben says. "I'm telling you."

"Why ask me if you've got it figured?"

Aw, Jesus, Reuben thinks. From over his shoulder he can

hear the trickle leaking out of the cold-water faucet, thin as tinsel.

"OK," Reuben says. "It's just I'm sitting here and what am I supposed to do?"

Paulette's so quiet on the other end Reuben asks if she's still there.

"I got to go," she says.

"Don't you do this to me, Paulette."

"Reuben, I've got to go to work in the morning."

"Look, Paulette, what did I do? Is it my fault Magritte sold out to some morons from Chicago who don't know wheat from quack grass? Is it my fault I'm not Magritte by now? These aren't the good old days, you know what I'm saying?"

"Oh, Reuben," she says. "It's not the money."

"There's just things I can't help," Reuben says.

"Believe me, it's not about money. It doesn't begin to be about money."

He hears her muffle some words to Teddy. He can picture Teddy parked in the doorway like a stuffed bear while his wife gives Reuben more flak. His old pal, his old blocker. Or maybe it's not Teddy, maybe it's Estelle sitting next to her on the bed, her head tipped to the earpiece. Maybe Teddy put the Plymouth out in his barn, maybe the keys are warm in his pocket.

"Where is she?" Reuben barks.

"There's nothing to bully out of me," Paulette says. "If she took off on you, then all right, that's what she did, and more power to her, but she *didn't tell me."*

"Is it my fault . . ." Reuben starts in again, hoping this time the blame gets assigned where it belongs, but Paulette deadens the line.

When he tries again, the line's busy and still is fifteen minutes later. He hasn't budged from the table. He should've known he couldn't pry anything out of Paulette. What he needs is to talk to Teddy again. He ought to simply drive over there and get it straightened out. Another drink would be good, an inch or so to keep his blood moving, but the bottle's clear over by the sink. His shoulders have started aching and the rest of him feels like it's setting up. He tries out this picture of Estelle padding barefoot down the hall over at Teddy's, climbing in the guest-room bed, burying her head. He wonders how it would be coming face-to-face with Teddy at the front door, middle of the night, which is a way people get killed. He remembers how it felt sitting in the truck earlier, the head-lights glaring down the empty road, the dry snow blowing by, filling in the hollows, the endless supply of cold pouring out of Alberta with no regard for people or their troubles. He hears the furnace shut off, then the little *tings* the baffles make cooling inside the ductwork, then for the longest time, nothing at all.

V-E Day

The girl was dappled through the screen door, church-dressed though it was Tuesday. Mrs. Wheelis considered whether she could bear another kind offer of sympathy. She'd only meant to let some air in. May had exploded in Sperry Canyon, as if the spring of 1945 had been unnaturally pent up. The rooms were stricken with light. Her weight sagged inside her housedress and pain thrummed behind her eyes—notice that today would be only a shade more tolerable than the week past, which she'd spent, intermittently, with heat on her stomach and ice on her head, thinking, *How can I go on,* but going on, of course, for Jack's sake at least, not failing to hoist herself up and set a decent noon meal before him. The Reverend Herbig had been over twice and offered a prayer for Cal. Buddy'd been there too—he'd come from over the mountains as soon as Jack telephoned—and he'd told her, despite his hangdog face, that the prayer was the most beautiful thing he'd ever heard. This helped her as much as anything: knowing that her next oldest hadn't lost his faith, something she worried over no little bit. She drew in a deep breath, gathered her forces, and squinted through the mesh.

"Mrs. Wheelis . . ." the girl said. She was holding yesterday's *Daily Inter Lake,* and Mrs. Wheelis wondered for an instant if she'd anything to do with the paper. But no, that was wrong, they'd only forgotten to pick it up off the porch last evening. She seemed a good height, but had an unsettled, undernourished look to her, Mrs. Wheelis thought. Her arms were white as peeled switches.

"I couldn't sleep once I knew I'd be coming here. I'm sorry, I see it's too early yet . . . my landlord gave me some gas coupons."

"You've driven . . . to see me?"

"From Missoula. You don't recognize me, do you?"

"Forgive me," Mrs. Wheelis said. "If you knew all the kind souls we've had in this week. It's been a feast of commiseration."

"Loraine . . . *Cahill?*"

Mrs. Wheelis fought the desire to retreat into the front room and let the girl's name flutter away. Such was her estate as Sperry Canyon's latest Gold Star mother.

"My father's Judge Cahill, the J.P.?"

Mrs. Wheelis felt unspeakably heavy. She sensed the perspiration collecting along her scalp. She could not be expected to stand in the doorway like this any longer. The girl reached for the handle as if it might be electrified. Mrs. Wheelis bit her lip, stepped back, and let her in. Truly she could be no worse than the Percivals and their blessed Christian Science. . . . *What if it had been one of their boys, what kind of line would they have then?*

The girl surrendered her paper and set herself down across the room on the edge of the grandfather chair—Jack's spot; but *he* filled it solidly, his straight back pressed to its own, his head inclined a notch to the south as he listened to her approvingly, smoothing down first one side of his white mustache with the back of his finger, then the other. Not that there was a thing to say now.

Mrs. Wheelis made her way to the sofa in her slippers. Her fingers were swollen around her rings, and her ankles were worse. She put off squeezing them into proper shoes as long as she could get away with it, and now she'd been caught. These visitations . . . they pinned her and Jack to the front room like specimens. May the Lord forgive her for wearying of all the talk. Cal was at peace now, they all said. Of course, yes, he was at peace. But the word rankled: it sounded inglorious, pale as ether.

The girl was still arranging herself, craning her neck at the furnishings. The judge's house would no doubt be more splendiferous; still, there was enough to be proud of here, and all of it hard-earned. Mrs. Wheelis's eyes fell on the paper. WAR IN EUROPE FINISHED / TUESDAY LIKELY TO BE V-E DAY. Beneath that a small box read, *"Best News in a Long Time," Says Montana Gov. Ford.* Beyond that she could not see, having left her reading glasses upstairs on the nightstand. She looked away. Hitler done in finally . . . and everywhere one turned this awful talk of peace.

"My sister sent me the clipping about Cal," the girl said. She actually picked it out of her bag and laid it across her lap. It was flag-shaped, Cal's commission-day photo flying out to one side of the column of print.

"You must have known him from school, did you?"

"I was in Buddy's class, Mrs. Wheelis, but Cal . . . everybody knew Cal. There was a cookout you had once, in back, with Cal's piano under a striped awning. The peonies were out and your husband sang."

"Before the war . . ." Mrs. Wheelis said automatically. How often one turned to that phrase, and how tired it had gotten. "I don't believe I would have thought of that day again. Forgive me if I don't recall you, I hold onto things so poorly now."

"Oh, Mrs. Wheelis, I wasn't the kind of girl anyone'd notice especially. I came with my sister, she . . . well, I was just a tagalong. But how I admired your husband with his rolled-up cuffs and his voice so high and sunny—nothing like what our daddy would've thought of doing. *He* always has his decorum to think of, being in the public eye, you know. Mr. Wheelis leaned on Cal's shoulder as he played . . . they were just two of a kind, I thought. Well, excuse me for running off at the mouth, but anyway, you wouldn't remember me is all I mean to say."

As the girl spoke, Mrs. Wheelis did make a modest, unfruitful effort to place her. She supposed the girl's free-falling hair with its swooping curls was the way they wore it in the movies now, but she and Jack hadn't sat through a whole show since Mary Pickford retired. She probably smoked cigarettes, too, but not in the Wheelis parlor she wouldn't. What would she be if she was in Buddy's class . . . twenty-four? And no sign of a ring?

"I know the people must have worn you out talking about Cal. I argued with myself about if I should come up at all."

Mrs. Wheelis could not help the sigh that issued from her lips. "They mean well," she said. "For the most part. You do hear from the German sympathizers. . . ."

"Of course, people aren't sure what all to say," the girl offered. "Running into a tragedy like this."

"When I think of all the families going through what we are, the Bartletts and the Salanskys right off the bat, and poor Mrs. Fetter. And all for what, will you please tell me that?"

"I'm sure I can't," Loraine said.

"I should offer you some coffee," Mrs. Wheelis said.

"I won't tarry, Mrs. Wheelis," the girl said, but didn't stir from the chair.

So Mrs. Wheelis rose. "I sent Mr. Wheelis to the lumber-yard this morning finally," she said. "Buddy went down and helped out for a while so his father could stay with me, but he had to go back east of the mountains. No use for the both of us sitting and feeling sorry, so I sent him back to work. Labor sustaineth the grieving mind, don't you know."

She headed for the kitchen. The sun had not yet come around the house—compared with the funeral atmosphere of the front rooms, the kitchen was cool and undemanding. The Boston ivy had leafed out with the sudden heat, casting a shimmering green across the porcelain. Beyond this frame, their trees—the mountain ash, the cherry, the two willows— were variously dense with new growth. Through them she could still make out the bright wings of snow on the peaks to the north.

Jack had left coffee on the back burner, but she dumped it and began to make fresh. She reached to the tin for a match

and scratched it across the striker, and as had happened before
—first with the February telegram branding Cal *Missing in
Action,* then more brutally now that they knew he'd been dead
since January—she saw him: the brazen way he flicked the
match on his zipper before touching it to his Lucky Strike,
there in the kitchen, tall, winsome, pleased with himself, one
eye squinted against the smoke . . . and always a conspiratorial
squeeze for her.

The girl had trailed into the kitchen and taken refuge at
the table by the long row of windows. When they'd all eaten
breakfast together, it had run the full length of that space: she
and Jack at the ends; on the sides, Walter, the oldest, now an
attorney for the War Department in Washington; Annabelle
next, married and living in San Jose; then the two younger
boys, Buddy and Cal, almost a second family. Now the leaves
had been dropped, and it was almost too intimate for her and
Jack. The girl's fingers smoothed at the oilcloth absently. Mrs.
Wheelis felt lightly intruded upon and didn't quite know what
to make of it.

"Mrs. Wheelis, I . . . what it says in the paper is so
wretched and all, but it doesn't say what *happened.*"

Mrs. Wheelis stopped in the midst of tying her apron
strings. "He was shot, that's all," she said flatly. "Those vi-
pers." She'd repeated this much of it so often that the words
conjured nothing for her now but the expectation of a little
comfort, unbuttressing her features into a flurry of sobs. But
it'd had no effect whatsoever on the girl. She was still waiting,
her eyes upcast and bold as buds.

Mrs. Wheelis had, of course, broached nothing more
with anyone—even Jack or Buddy or Annabelle who called
long distance. They'd all read Walter's letter, their copies of
the ten pages of close typing, the whole business laid out
. . . so why go through it aloud? Nor had she followed
Walter's directions over to the atlas—*Hatten,* he'd written, *a
town roughly 15 blocks long, 25 mi. E.N.E. of Strasbourg, within
sight of the Rhine.* But to the girl she went on, despite herself,
"The weather was so bitter, and not a chance to defend themselves."

"It was the ninth?"

This lacked the force of a question—the paper had said as much. Mrs. Wheelis reached for the breakfast cups in the drainboard, but hesitated and stepped around to the hutch for the hand-painted china. There was nothing presentable in the breadbox, but she swung the door open and shut anyway, confident the girl couldn't see.

"And he'd only been over there since late November . . . just a handful of days, really."

Mrs. Wheelis attended to the cups, her back turned. They were finely scalloped, so thin they let light through.

"And all this time nobody knew anything."

With Walter commissioned straight out of law school and stationed at the Pentagon, she and Jack had felt, for a time, less cut off from inquiry than some, but what good was it? In March a letter had arrived from the division's commanding officer. *My dear Mrs. Wheelis,* he'd begun, *I appreciate the anxiety you must feel about your son.* He apprised her of the problems the International Red Cross had getting word back to the States during the closing days of the war. She'd never be used to seeing Cal called Lt. Wheelis. *It is my personal hope,* he had closed, *that the loss of your son is only a temporary one. Though there will be long days and lonely nights until definite word is received from him, we must keep our faith so that we will never fail that courage which he showed by his deeds. . . .*

Mrs. Wheelis poured the coffee. "I thought it was more burden than I could shoulder. They'll tell you not knowing is the worst, but believe me . . ." she groped for the proper thing to call the girl, settled on *Miss Cahill,* and went on, "it can't compare to the truth."

"Oh, yes," said Loraine softly. "I agree."

Mrs. Wheelis took her husband's spot across from the girl. "It just isn't understandable to me," she said, "why a young man like Cal should be taken when the Lord lets so many others live. You take the boy in the old Humphries house—he's maybe five or six and a total imbecile, nothing but a terrible worry to his parents, will never do more than feed himself, if that, when boys like Cal would have been a credit to all of us. He and Buddy had such plans . . . and here's this perfect monstrosity."

"Mrs. Wheelis . . ."

"I know," she said. "He works in unfathomable ways. Reverend Herbig says don't rationalize—the world turns haywire in wartime. I don't know, I must be a pretty poor Christian."

"Mrs. Wheelis," she began again. "I loved Cal."

"Oh, but we all did," Mrs. Wheelis blurted out before she'd heard what the girl meant.

That this nervous bird perched across from her thought she was a girlfriend of Cal's had not crossed her mind. Still it didn't surprise her greatly. Of the three boys, it was Cal they flocked to—but he'd not made attachments. Before the war, he'd moved among their attentions with a breezy, courteous, self-absorbed air they misread as sophistication. He leaned over the keyboard, his shoulders bunched, playing "You're My Everything" or "Moonglow" or "Rosalie." He may have ignited their hopes, but he wasn't playing for any of them, of this she was certain. And at the university, and at officers' school . . . she didn't know, of course, but he wasn't a boy to keep secrets.

Cal was the most transparent, the most an open record. Stubborn and high-principled with the older two, and a bit less so with Buddy, she'd dropped her guard totally with Cal. Perhaps she was simply too old. She could summon no fastidious anger with him. To him she confessed things she'd tell no one else on earth, even Jack. And Cal . . . hadn't he known their bond was special, hadn't he taken on so much of the business of raising himself? And hadn't . . . but no, it was this, thinking of him as a gap-toothed boy, that she must avoid. How ferociously it broke her! There were limits to people's tolerance, after all.

"I imagine you did," she said.

"Mrs. Wheelis, do you remember Lester Parmelee?" the girl asked, and paused not nearly long enough for Mrs. Wheelis to consider who he might have been. "His father was a county commissioner for a time. I think he went to school with Walter, or maybe Annabelle—he was older, anyway. Well, I did the most foolish thing: I married him. Out of the clear blue. We drove down to Jackpot to a J.P. one Friday . . . you can imagine what my daddy had to say about that! I used to think it was the war being in the air, feeling like we should go out and do something, you know, but I guess it was really just me. Well, I'd rather if we didn't go into all the particulars, Mrs. Wheelis, but it didn't work out at all, not from the first instant. He made me feel just dead. I'm sorry to have to say it like that, but it's true. Please don't think I'm awful, but I left him. I thought if I went to school I could be a teacher and support myself, but that didn't pan out either. Then Lester wouldn't give me a divorce. He said there wasn't a thing I could do about it . . . he wasn't insane or cruel or adulterous—you should've just heard him tick off all the things he wasn't."

Mrs. Wheelis began earnestly to regret inviting her in. Well, she hadn't done that outright, had she? Invited the girl in? She recalled some distant kitchen talk, some tarnish on the Cahill name, perhaps a rumor of this trouble. But there were so many intrusions into Sperry's life now that she could hardly be held accountable for keeping track. And as for approving of the way they went headlong at their affairs, she'd be charitable and reserve judgment.

"You see, I found Cal again in Missoula, by accident really. He was playing at the Florence with Tommy and Floyd Valentine. That would be almost three years ago, and then, well, in July he had to leave for Camp Roberts, of course, and then Camp Gruber. . . ."

She broke off and scanned the kitchen, looking everywhere but at Mrs. Wheelis, who, having failed for the moment at finding a way to call a halt to the girl's storytelling, had gotten to her feet to dole out more coffee. But at the mention of Camp Roberts came a full-blown remembrance of Cal and Jack and herself on the screened porch the evening before his train. There'd been a wire from Walter, something a bit sententious about manhood they'd all laughed over. "Don't you just love the way Walter puts things," Cal had said. How wistful and silent Jack had gotten then. But Cal had not seemed at all afraid, not at all overmatched by the task.

"We wrote," the girl raced on. "Frankly, Mrs. Wheelis, I couldn't picture Cal in the service in the first place, but then, being an officer . . . it seemed so unlike him in a way, but then I guess you never know. Just think if he could've kept his band together, though, and helped people get their minds off the news. But anyway, we wrote, or I wrote, and I thought he's got no reason to write me back, a messed-up girl like I was then, but yes, he did write, a lot, and I saw him one time after he was commissioned, on that leave, though I felt queer about it. I didn't know what would come of it, and he didn't either, I don't imagine . . . he called me *Lorrie*—nobody'd ever bothered to call me anything but *Loraine*— the full thing, you know, not even Lester. But it seemed right for him to spend his leave with you and your husband. I caught the bus up here one night—I hadn't been home since leaving Lester and there was still a certain amount of ill will, you might say. All we had time to do was walk by the river."

That leave. How blithely it rattled off her tongue! It was only the last time Mrs. Wheelis had seen him. He'd come home a first lieutenant in the Rainbow Division, fifteen pounds firmer, bringing extra points from the ration board and sixty-five gallons of gasoline, his little-boy smile crystallized and radiant. It was a reunion, a holiday. She'd gotten a ham from some people in Creston. Cal's sister had come up from the coast, and friends had banged in and out all week. When in this cache of hours had he not been with them . . . when had he gone to the river with her? Nowhere in any of this could she find a shadow or a flicker of the girl. His heart had been with them fully.

Mrs. Wheelis stiffened suddenly at the thought, and the girl reached out for her arm. In her embarrassment, Mrs. Wheelis let the moist fingers light on her skin.

"I'm not one to carry a torch or anything, Mrs. Wheelis. Believe me, I couldn't help it."

"I'm sure you've had a hard time of it," Mrs. Wheelis said. "Now it's been kind of you to come by."

Finally the girl stood, but not apparently to go. She brought her eyes up close to the window glass. "I can't picture it being spring," she said. The yellow bow in the back of her dress had come untied. "It seems wrong. Everyone's saying the war's over, even if that Truman hasn't said so yet . . . but I don't feel a thing at all. Look, you've got your marigolds in already."

Need she explain it was only bending and stooping over garden tools that broke her wakefulness? The marigolds, yes, and the bulbs pushed deep with her thumbs, and the sweet peas and the onions and everything else she always planted.

"Mrs. Wheelis, couldn't I call you Rose? Would that be too offensive? I'm sorry I just can't tell, Rose . . . Cal always said . . . no, well, oh *damn, damn.* I came all the way up here this morning . . . because they told you *everything.* You see, you had the rights and what did I have—I had nothing at all."

Why wouldn't she go away? The headache droned in her temples. Why wouldn't they *both* go away?

"Now I've troubled you," Loraine said. "I promised myself that was one thing I wouldn't do. But I have to know what happened to him. I don't know what he was doing, or where he was . . . I mean, *France,* the paper said, Mrs. Wheelis, Rose, that's the moon."

Words had battered her all week. The stinging of her eyes and the woozy roll of her stomach were so familiar she barely acknowledged them, but now she felt herself fly past the moment of tears, and heard her own voice rise. "Oh, it's a privilege, you tell me, to be getting letters and telegrams from the War Department? And those months of hope all come to nothing, and your prayers against something already done and finished, Miss Cahill . . . you can't possibly know. Everyplace you turn in your memory he's running up to you in his different ages. I'm sorry—I thought you'd come like the others."

Loraine cleared the hair back from her face and left her hands idling there at her cheeks. "I've never been much like the others," she said. "Your neighbors, I think they come because they're glad it hasn't been them it's happened to. I should've stayed away and kept my mouth shut, but I'm not so good a person as that, I guess. Anyway, I did come, and yes, when you say it like that, it *is* something being the one they tell. What kind of hopes did I have living all winter in a basement, a dark little box and the pipes dripping? My sister let it slip that she'd heard from Daddy that Cal was missing months ago, but I didn't know whether to believe her or not —that would be just the sort of mean thing she'd say to make me feel worse. Then I thought it was probably beyond even her. But I didn't know . . . I'd lost my judgment. Please, I didn't come here to be rude. I was hoping we might find a way to . . . give each other whatever we had."

The kitchen's blue shadows had thinned, and with them their safety. "It was November," Loraine hurried on. "His letter said he'd gotten his orders."

Mrs. Wheelis remembered that letter—or the one he'd written to *her,* on stationery marked PARACHUTE TROOPS U.S.A., Cal's typing crossing the silver outline of a soldier touching down, rifle in arms, parachute deflating grandly behind. *And whose letter had he sat down to write first?*

"Something got into me, I was just fired up, do you understand, and afraid all at the same time. I took off for Camp Gruber on the bus . . . I didn't tell anyone, and I lost my job at the phone company. It was blistering in Oklahoma and there I was dressed all wrong, but I'd never stopped to think about it, you see. Cal, I got word to him after a while, and he met me at the hotel in Muskogee. Mrs. Wheelis, you should have seen him pull up in his jeep . . . he was beaming, he looked like he was having the time of his life. He was going to Marseilles and I'd only caught him by two days.

"Now, I know this next part, well, strictly speaking I was married to Lester . . ."

"No," Mrs. Wheelis said. "Please, no, haven't you said plenty?"

The girl went abruptly still, as if she'd been carried along by a gust that had blown itself out. Even the thin cloth of her dress seemed to collapse.

"Mrs. Wheelis," she said in a moment. "I lost his baby."

Her voice was so tiny that Mrs. Wheelis thought she'd said she *felt* like a baby, and was about to answer, *The Lord asks us to buck ourselves up.*

But the girl went on. "I took such good care of myself, I ate right, I had good thoughts in my head. I just knew after the war there'd be a way to make it look right. Worse things get explained, don't they, don't they really?"

Mrs. Wheelis heard the clock in the front room catch and hesitate, then strike the half hour. She honestly didn't know if it was 10:30 or 11:30. The sun was bland with haze and nothing stirred. This is what the summer would be, time that crept by without her, a film of clay dust collecting on the sills, on the dark drapes, on the grained walnut of Cal's piano. Mrs. Wheelis let out her breath as if she'd held it to the point of spoilage.

She got once more to her feet and undid the apron and draped it over the chair back and left the kitchen. She climbed through the shadow on the front staircase and slipped into the gabled room she shared with Jack. The bed was still unmade, the covers evenly turned back on his side, strewn apart on hers. The room smelled comfortably of them both—witch hazel and talc and the soft odors of their bedjackets in the open wardrobe. What a . . . refuge it had been. She pulled up the spread and sank to the edge of the bed, and the maple frame gave a thin creak she'd often confused with the stirring of one of her children in the night.

She reached, after a time, for her reading glasses.

When they'd seen Cal off at the station in Stillwater, and distance had stolen him from sight, she'd *known* that she had surrendered him. But that this girl downstairs had *not* abided by his leaving, that she'd *not* called it absolute, that she'd run after him and caught up with him. . . . Her thoughts balked at the sight of them coming together in a hotel room, but before she shut her mind's eye to it, she glimpsed the drawn shade and the gritty mortal light it let in upon them. Oh, she was not the prude the girl would figure her to be—no, nor so God-hardened. What good was age if not to tell between the exception and the rule? It was only this: The girl had touched him last. Mrs. Wheelis found that her condemnation failed her utterly.

When she reappeared in the kitchen, the girl seemed not to notice, but with the rasping of the porch door against the linoleum her face turned up in confusion, shaken not from thought, it seemed, but from a moment's not thinking. Mrs. Wheelis nodded at the open doorway, and the girl rose obediently.

"Here's a better spot for us," Mrs. Wheelis said, pointing with the hand that held the letter toward the wicker chairs. "There's no sense in being cooped up, is there?" The screens were dusty yet, but the breeze seeped through and the new leaves of the lilacs brushed against them peaceably. Mrs. Wheelis drew out the letter and smoothed back the thick folds of the onionskin.

"Walter managed to locate a man from the Rainbow," she began. "He'd just been freed from a German camp. . . . *Frail-looking from the rigors of his captivity,* was how Walter described him. Walter had read about him by chance in the *Baltimore Sun.*"

She paused and glanced up to see if Loraine had settled. From down the hedgerow she heard a meadowlark, the first of the season, and from farther off came the steadying call of the noon whistle. The girl was sitting back. Her hands were at rest, and her eyes had drifted shut as if she were awaiting a story at bedtime.

"*Dear Mother & Dad, Annabelle, and Buddy,*" Mrs. Wheelis read. "*I am writing this letter to you all & using carbons, for it will have in it things in which you will all be equally interested. Of course it is about Cal.*"

&c The Flood of '64

 1

CARL PRUDHOMME

I took over in 1964, the year of the flood, March. The worst of the wind and cold had petered out, but winter hung on like a worry. Bradley'd come through his surgery. I'd left him doped-up at the hospital and driven out to the old house for supper, where my sister Carla lived with her husband Teller Stoltz, surrounded by an eighth-section of winter-burned Scotch pines. She hadn't let on I was coming. Teller'd gotten home sour, a heavy, dull-spirited man. First thing, he started riding Carla for not being there that after- noon when he phoned. "Teller thinks I'm furniture," she said. That was about right. I wished she'd leave him, but she wouldn't. Mother'd done her best to convince Carla she'd never make it on her own. Well, it was hardly the night to fight that battle. I detached myself before the pie and coffee, and Carla followed me to the back door, hanging on my arm. I told her I had to get back.

I'd just muscled through the ruts at the end of their road when the call came through about Bradley. Belinda was on dispatch that night and she was crying.

"I guess that makes you sheriff," she said.

I guessed it did.

The radio crackled. "You aren't one little finger's worth of that man," she told me.

"Damn it now, Belinda," I said, "you can't be talking to me over the air like that."

"I don't care, it's just dreadful."

I flipped off the radio and headed back to town, wondering how everything could go to hell in a couple of hours. It wasn't gunfire or a mangled patrol car, but a bleeding deep in his stomach. Bradley Vaughn had been Sperry County's sheriff/coroner since the New Deal, and he'd been just the ticket: hard as sin on drifters, reasonable in matters of local tomfoolery, starkly outraged by true violations of order. Twice blessed, he'd descended from the Vaughns, who'd traded with the Salish before they'd disappeared from the valley, and the Cripps, who'd migrated west from Fort Benton to start the bank. He was an emblem of the town's own pride in itself, it seemed—the Republicans hadn't bothered fielding a candidate against him since the '40s.

I shouldn't have been sheriff so soon, but the year'd taken its toll on the chain of command. Mitchell had moved south with a sick wife, and Greeling had taken the head job in Libby. Kooser was still around, of course, as rumpled and woebegone as ever, but everyone knew he wouldn't take it. Besides which, Bradley'd taken a special interest in me. I was never sure why that was, for we were nothing alike. Bradley was old-fashioned, ceremonial, dead-sure of himself. I see him heading the color guard's showy passage around the rodeo grounds each August as the fair opens, taller in the saddle than Gary Cooper. Well, being in the public glare about crucified me most of the time, so that was one tradition I did away with. Maybe Bradley thought I'd be a one-foot-in-front-of-the-other kind of guy who wouldn't threaten his reputation, I don't know. He must've had his reasons.

Whatever else he was, or did, he knew what to say to people. I thought over time I'd get the knack of standing between people and their trouble, too, but I never did. Never shook the feeling I was steeped in it.

One winter night, early on, Bradley took me with him to a barn west of town. Two houses stood at the end of the road, separated by a windbreak of Lombardy poplar. Two sets of outbuildings, fields rolling away from each other, two puddles of vapor-white light in the empty driveways. A boy of seventeen came from the barn and met us. He should've been freezing—all he had on was a cotton T-shirt and overalls and a Cenex cap. The breath hovered around his face. He waved us inside. The light was a puny yellow and the air quiet and bitter. From the center beam hung the body of a girl his age.

Her neck hadn't broken in the fall, Bradley whispered. She'd strangulated.

This was his family's farm, the boy told us. The girl came from next door. No one else was at home. They were all in town at the Sons of Norway.

She wore a square-dancing dress, with layers of white ruffles, and a pair of sky-blue Tony Lamas. They were brand new, those boots. The bottoms had a few light crosshatches from the rungs of the ladder. She'd carried them over in the store box, then changed out of her tennis shoes.

"I never seen those boots," the boy said.

He stared up at her, at the dark rafters. He didn't have to tell us how he and the girl had grown up side by side, or about the elaborate hopes the families had held for the two of them together, or how, maybe just lately, they'd begun to believe it themselves. But the boots changed everything. She was a total mystery to him.

Bradley wrapped his arm around the boy and led him out to the patrol car where it was warm, where he could ply his magic. I stood the ladder up and cut the girl down.

Already the air had stolen her body's heat. I laid her on some bales of straw and covered her with a saddle blanket and turned away. I could almost hear Bradley's steady recital out in the car, but the barn was still. In summer, birds would bat among the trusses . . . now there was only the wince of timbers shrinking in the cold. I suddenly knew something: I was like the boy, not Bradley. In his own eyes, Bradley was a keeper of the peace. The boy and I knew we were destined to arrive late and pick up the pieces. The boots were just the start of all we didn't understand.

Bradley's funeral was packed. It was the kind of event Sperry did up royally in those days. If it weren't for being in such bad taste, they'd have hung bunting across Main Street. I stood up in the side altar at the Episcopal Church on Third as a sleeting rain fell outside. I could hardly make out the shepherds and the lambs in the stained glass. People still had their coats on, and the hacking of early spring colds ricocheted off the stone-work. Kooser was up front, dutifully, and there were others I knew, but I didn't look at them. My nerves were lousy and I forgot the notes I'd scribbled. I stared down at Bradley in his box and wished he'd get up and make his own damn speech, for he'd do it right.

I pulled my eyes away from his dress browns and focused on the assembled. "Sheriff Vaughn was like a father to me," I said. My words rang out shamelessly. Who'd let me get away with such claptrap? He was one of them, one of the old valley, and what was I, an interloper, and the best that might be said of me was I hadn't made any major blunders yet. Carla was the only one who'd know what I meant, but she hadn't come. Still, they weren't really listening, so I went on, and what I said was true even if I hadn't meant to say it.

Mother'd brought us to this valley on the train when Carla was just old enough to sleep through the night and I was nine. Our tickets said Seattle, but the trip had worn her down and we got off in Stillwater, Montana, with a woman named Blood. Mother was in a tender state, unready for the woman's hospitality, its richness or its obligations. It soon came out that Mother'd picked Seattle for no better reason than that was where the Empire Builder ended up . . . a long way from Kankakee.

Once Mother'd thrown off the trance that leave-taking had put her in, she told Mrs. Blood that the valley was the loveliest place she'd ever seen.

"Well, *we* like it," Mrs. Blood said. "Of course, there are hardships."

Our mother said, "Yes, aren't there always, but if a person will only persevere . . ."

Mrs. Blood wasn't the sort to beat around the bush for long. What had become of the children's father? Mother'd been vague on this score while we were on the train. It won't do to be telling our life story to just anyone, she'd warned me. But I was only nine and in love with the train itself and not much aware I had a life story.

"Overseas," she told Mrs. Blood now, hinting that he was tied up with the impending war. This was a pure lie, untainted even by calculation, I think, born of believing she'd launched a new life here in Sperry.

I remembered my father, of course, and he was nothing more exotic than an aging Presbyterian who worked in Hoscheid's Hardware. He hadn't run out on Mother so much as retreated from her . . . to a room in the corner of the cellar where, I knew from my rare visits, he had everything under control. There were egg cartons on matching shelves, with tiny screws and brads and hooks of like size in each hollow, and shoeboxes marked in his precise hand *felt, bearings, fuses.* . . . A whole shelf of wood planes set up in descending order like bells. He had a stuffed chair opposite the bench, and on the wall some scrolly writing that said, BUILD THY HOUSE UPON A ROCK.

I remembered his suspendered back disappearing down the narrow steps after dinner. It got so that Mother wouldn't venture down there to get him anymore, but would send me. The rock walls gave off a heavy chill. I squinted through the peephole before I knocked, and saw his face illuminated by the coils of the space heater at his feet.

"Come here," he said.

I came forward despite myself. He took my head and rubbed it with his fingertips. Perhaps he thought it felt good. But his fingers were bony and they pushed my hair the wrong way and my knees ground into the pebbly concrete of the workroom floor.

"Don't let your mother fox you," he said.

"No, sir."

Was it a speech? I'd have listened, pain or no, but that was all he said.

The funny thing was, soon as Mother had said he was in Europe, I began to believe her. The story grew as the war grew, and as it was passed down to Carla and to the world at

large, it overshadowed my feeble recollections. By the time
I was in high school, I didn't blink at all to say my father was
missing in action, and soon after that, it was natural enough
to accept our status as a family deprived of its father by tragic
global events.

Up there at the altar, the sweat was running down the
insides of my uniform. Father Keech caught my eye, extended
a bare wrist from his vestment, and pointed at it. Yes, I was
about done.

"Nobody will miss him more than me," I said and
stepped back out of the light.

If the mourners had been paying attention they'd have
stood up and hooted at me. A few of the better Christians
might have forgiven me my presumption on the grounds that
I was obviously overwhelmed by the position I found myself
in, but none would have figured I meant exactly what I said.

Thus, I stepped through Bradley's memory into 1964 and was
on my own. It was a year of regular troubles: bum checks and
runaway sixteen-year-olds and livestock loose in the borrow
pits. People assaulted each other with fists and bird guns and
filleting knives—once, in a bar up the Trapline, a pair of
Canadians beat each other senseless with a two-pound rainbow trout. Husbands hit on their wives in secret and the
damage sometimes surfaced, but mostly it didn't. Tourists
slipped off rocks in the National Park they had no business
climbing, or capsized their yellow rafts, or got themselves lost
in the backcountry, armed with fancy gear and no common
sense to speak of. The numbers say things were a little worse
than the year before and not so bad as the next.

But none of that matters because that year belongs to the
flood. The flood gave us a *before* and an *after.* It changed
everything—for the people who holed up at the grade schools
while their houses washed away south, for Carla who lost her
husband . . . and for me.

The Democrats were loyal to Bradley and assumed I'd
run in his image and be swept into office again at the regular
election. The truth was, I hadn't yet given that much thought.

The voters had punched Bradley's card so many times I'd ceased to think of the thing as an elected office. But I got a sudden fear they'd come to their senses now and shoot me back where I belonged. If the party regulars had any smarts they had their doubts, too. But that was before the flood.

People take catastrophe different now. They want you to convene a task force to see what scoundrel to blame. Nothing will do but some blood let in public. They think we can keep them from harm. But in '64, after the water had seeped back below the floorboards and retreated from steps and lawns to the river's banks, and the sun finally shone and dried the silt left everywhere like a fine ash, people came out and slapped each other on the back—they'd pulled in harness, they'd kept a tragedy from being awfuler than it was. And all of us the public could point a finger at—the valley's three mayors and three chiefs of police, and me—we were glorified in the press. Soon I was known as Sheriff Prudhomme, the one who'd gotten everybody through the flood. My grace period lasted all summer and into fall, and the party was thrilled to see they had another winner at the polls.

 2

CARLA PRUDHOMME STOLTZ

Teller was home all weekend, fussing in the toolshed, then coming in the back door to the kitchen all greased up. He stood at my sink, his back funny as a feed sack, squirting Joy up either arm and lathering and scratching with his nails, but he never would get clean and white again. He came to bed moldery in the creases, and smelling of hair preservative and the dope for his toenails.

"What's all this mess?" Teller wanted to know.

"Baker's clay," I said, thinking of Mama. I'd rolled it out like her in long snakes, then twisted them into rocking horses with wild-looking manes I did with the end of a paperclip. They were all baked and laid out on waxed paper waiting for their shellac. Teller picked one up and bit at it.

"Not for eating," I said.

Teller squinched his lip and swore at me. His latest declaration was he wasn't going to hit at me anymore, but I didn't bank my heart on it.

"So what're they for?" he asked.

In my own mind I asked *What are you for, Teller Stoltz?* but I kept my tongue.

"With all the real goddamn work there is to be done around this place . . ." he said, and wiped the rain out of his hair with a dish towel.

All day it was like that, in and out, never farther away than the barn, so finally I called Benjamin and said we couldn't. Benjamin said I wasn't trying hard enough.

"Don't you think I want to?" I said.

I watched the window by my dresser smear with rain. The clouds were so close overhead you wouldn't know there was mountains around. It felt like living under a trailer. Mama said spring made her think of Kankakee, her and Tina Spellman yanking off hunks of lilac and prancing down Toulouse Street like a vision. You never knew with Mama, though. She probably just saw some girl do that once and stayed up on the porch swing dreaming.

"Don't you think this rain is killing me?" I said.

Benjamin said, "When're you going to call me?"

I hung up and walked around upstairs. Same news out Carl's window, messy and gloomy. Teller called that room his *office,* but I never broke myself of calling it Carl's, for that's where he slept those years we were growing up here, with the roof angled down sharp over his bed. When he had the nightmares he sat straight up and his head rang on the plaster. Mama tried to make him move it any number of times, but nothing doing for old Carl. He liked that tucked-away feeling. Now I'm on the subject, I saw the whole house like it used to be. Our bedroom was Mama's, the big one facing the Swans where the sun came up, when it did. I could walk through the door with a load of laundry or something, gathering wool, like she said I was always doing, and feel like I was walking in on her, and want to just run back to my own room, but I didn't belong there either. Other times I thought it must be Teller who didn't belong, because Mama never lived there with a man and why should I have to?

Teller set up a folding table in Carl's room, with a type-writer for pecking out his letters to the editor, and next to it a shelf for his treasures. Here's a newspaper picture: Teller giving a calf he didn't want to the 4-H, shaking hands with Earl Perry. He looks like he thought Earl Perry'd found a way of gypping him. That was how Teller looked a lot of the time. Next to that's a picture from our wedding: Mama and Carl and Teller and me. It wasn't the official 8-by-whatever Mama paid for . . . that one I had downstairs where people could see it, but then I got sick of it myself and put some dried flowers there instead and Teller never said a thing about it. Mama looks real good in this one, if you think how soon afterwards her tumor showed up. Her hair's fluffed out and her eyes don't look so awful suspicious. She'd spent most of the reception dodging Teller's relations . . . when nobody was listening she called Teller's father Alley Oop. I wasn't so lucky staying out of their way. Teller's mother cornered me in the bathroom, all schnapps and My Sin. She wanted a promise out of me that I'd be a decent mother, and I said, *We'll see, won't we?* I hadn't thought up the idea of telling Teller I had an infection and couldn't have any, that was later.

Carl was in uniform, of course, and who could tell what he was thinking? Maybe he was just glad to be rid of me. The uniform was Mama's idea. Carl was born to it, she always said, and she thought it would give the wedding some class, but I didn't care one way or the other. Teller has the same look as in the calf picture, like Mama and I'd put something over on him. And there I am, a long-stemmed glass in my left hand and my right stuck straight out with Teller at the end of it, like I'm already holding him off. But that's just reading into it, I guess. I was a little drunk and wasn't thinking about much of anything. I'd done my thinking by then. I'd decided if I couldn't have Benjamin, I'd have his cousin.

Blood family meant something to Teller, but things were sour between him and Benjamin starting way before me. Benjamin thought he was too sharp for the rest of the family, Teller said.

Well, you could understand why. Benjamin had gotten his mother's looks, so his lips were thinner and his chin made a nice angle and his eyes gave off light instead of sucking it in like Teller's. And Teller hated how Benjamin could always talk his way around him. The hunting season of the year they were seniors they got lost together in the woods three days and almost died. After that they hardly spoke. When anyone said Benjamin's name, Teller made them listen to his end of the lost-in-the-woods story, which was that Benjamin wouldn't turn around when the snow got heavy, and later when they both knew they were in trouble, he wouldn't take Teller's word for where the road was. "We wasn't lost till I listened to *him,*" Teller said. And that was all there was to say, too, because nobody had to ask why Benjamin got his way.

Benjamin and I would meet up in Stillwater, where the skiers and the pretty Canadians stayed, instead of in Sperry. Sometimes I felt safe for a little while, when Benjamin locked the door and snugged the pull drapes and came over and lifted me up. He never had the patience to wait until the room warmed the rest of the way up, so the top of me felt good, but if I stretched my foot out the sheets were icy and the shock of it made me remember what I was doing.

You're so good, Benjamin would say. He had long clean fingers and he liked me to suck on them.

When he was finished he'd say, *Why did I ever leave, Carla?* But he wasn't really asking.

I did, though. I'd whisper it in my mind. *Why didn't you stay with me when you could?*

That was one thing I didn't have the right to say out loud. I could say, *What'll happen when Teller finds us out?* Benjamin would only smile in that hateful way and say, *Honey, you actually think I'm worried about Teller? You actually think he's worth thinking about?*

Or I'd ask, *How long can we keep this up?*

All afternoon, he'd say, and then I'd say, *You know what I mean,* but I'd slip over by him again anyway.

Benjamin drove off first every time. I sat in Mama's old Chevrolet letting the radio play and wondering if I should hate myself. How could Benjamin show up after eight years and know I'd take right up with him again like time didn't mean a thing? Eight years of not knowing how he could turn me down and of losing Mama and living under Teller . . . and then first thing I'm ready to hop into bed with him, which is more than ever happened back then, for certain. I don't say a word against him. I don't give Teller a thought at first either, but when I do, he scares me, knowing what kind of misery it would be to him finding out what I was up to. Mama said a woman deserved whatever she could manage for herself, but Mama didn't have men to contend with. When I couldn't stand it anymore I put the car in gear and drove to the market so I'd have a bag of something to come home with.

 3

CARL PRUDHOMME

When Mother was sharp she knew something was wrong with Carla. Carla must have seemed a paler, higher-nerved, less resourceful replica of herself. Carla's teachers complained—she was disruptive, they said, drifty, even foulmouthed. Mother countered, "Carla's just *brash,* she speaks her mind is all. Precisely like I was at her age." But Mother was never brash and she only spoke her mind by accident. Carla wasn't brash either. She was scared and thought she didn't deserve much. She cut a slantways path through adolescence, friendless as a spirit. Mother'd say, "Honey, this is just a backwater, you'll fly out of here and find some real people who appreciate you." Or she'd say, "There's plenty enough going on at home. Don't you give those penny-ante's in town two thoughts."

Mother worked at Penney's then, downstairs in the catalog department. She gabbed at the customers all day without saying anything, and never made friends with the other women. Once in a while some man would play up to her in passing, but she'd act high-bred and make him feel childish for trying. She remained as solitary as Carla. Some nights I'd drive up and find them on the porch stripping furniture, their hair up in blue bandanas, basketball kneepads over their sweatpants. Mother would be humming some lost melody, and Carla'd be grinding a wisp of steel wool around a chair leg with a look that said if no one stopped her she'd worry it down to nothing.

"Oh well, Carl," Mother would say, looking up, "we've found ourselves a project."

She had the instinct for kindness but not the will for carrying through. Over time the cellar cluttered up with their forsaken projects: unglued, uncaned, the handsome grain barely half-salvaged from the brittle white or pink enamel. Once they were married, Teller groused about the mess, but Carla wouldn't go down there anymore, not needing more of a reminder than Teller of how Mother menaced us with her good intentions. Finally one morning I passed Teller chugging along grim-faced down the county road, the back end of his Willys truck piled to a surfeit with the projects, bound for who-knows-where.

One summer evening when Carla was sixteen, Mother and I sat at the table in the back yard after supper. The air was alive with swifts and the fields stretched out from the base of our hill to the mountains in a soft haze. Far off, our neighbor's combine crept through the wheat without a sound. Carla had gathered up the plates and carried them inside. Mother's curls sagged in the residue of the day's heat and the gold light slipped from her face. She looked almost at peace. We'd passed as normal an hour there as I can remember. I'd told her about the training program in Albuquerque I'd just come back from, and she smiled, though she was only half-listening.

At the slap of the screen door, her face shot around to watch Carla make her way toward us with the coffee. How ungainly she was: long freckled arms with no more muscle than willow switches, giraffe neck, the palest red hair that seemed to ignite as she crossed from shadow into sun. Her eyes were fixed on the two cups in her hands as she inched across the shaggy grass, terrified of losing a drop.

"Oh Carl," Mother said when Carla had delivered her cargo and retreated to the house. "You've got to take care of your sister. You've got to see that nothing happens to her." "She'll grow out of . . . whatever this is," I said.

But Mother wouldn't be bought off. *"Carl.* I want you to *promise* me. Carla's going to need you. Promise me you'll take care of her."

"Of course I will," I said.

She seemed satisfied, but beneath that look shone a reflection of Carla's little terror. She started to say something more, then didn't, and we sat together silently until it grew too dark to see.

Maybe she was going to tell me Carla wouldn't ever marry. She'd have been wrong there, of course, for Carla married Teller Stoltz, when she was nineteen, barely three years later, and I was the one who stayed alone. Maybe she was going to embroider on her notion of what troubled Carla, then thought better of it. Maybe she only wanted to say we'd have to go in the house soon. It didn't matter—I'd given my promise. But Mother should've known it had been extracted from me long before, as early as our train ride west, when Carla clung to Mother's shoulder refusing sleep, not crying but tugging at the air over and over, as I hovered nearby, nine years old, swelled with pride as a man-to-be.

The Stoltzes had been in the valley as long as the Vaughns and the Cripps. They'd multiplied but they hadn't prospered. By our time, the phone book had a list of them three fingers wide. I knew a Stoltz in high school, a big shot on the basketball team the year they took state. He was too heavy and angry to make it playing college ball, and the last I heard he was cutting firewood for people and spending too many afternoons in bars around the canyon. That was typical, though—the Stoltzes ran to boys and their fortunes tended to peak about the time they came of age. Some of them must have liked each other—and themselves—but that wasn't the rule.

The first one I really knew was Benjamin, who came home to dinner with Carla. He was tall the way they are, but with a good straightforward face. He looked like he stood a chance.

Mother made her fancy spaghetti for the occasion, her knee-jerk reaction to having an extra mouth to feed.

"This is just excellent," Benjamin said, toying with her linguine.

"Well, it's not that we're Italian," she confided. "The Prudhommes were from *Kwi-beck,* and my own people were just plain American-grown Hoosiers."

"You play basketball?" I asked to make conversation.

Benjamin frowned indulgently, as if I'd uttered something truly asinine.

"Benjamin does debate," Carla said. "They give him any subject and he can talk on it."

"Well, that's a real talent," I said. Still, it wasn't so tough to imagine him wearing a sweaty tank top, with maybe a few pimples on his back, inflamed from running.

It was a quiet meal, unremarkable except for Carla's having dragged someone home. She looked around at us with a hint of pleasure, her gawky neck not bent to the silverware for once, her eyes outlined in black makeup. I dared think maybe it was the start of things turning around for her.

Over sherbet she announced, "Benjamin's going to study law."

"Won't your folks be proud," Mother said.

"They don't think I'll do it," he said.

I kept my mouth shut. It did seem an unlikely outcome for a Stoltz. But the next fall he left Sperry for his undergraduate, out Midwest somewhere, armed with a scholarship. Carla wrote him letters that year, but when he didn't come back over the summer, she seemed to give up her stake in him all at once. She never said his name again in my hearing, and Mother and I assumed he was a first boyfriend and nothing more noteworthy than that.

Benjamin didn't enter my thoughts again until the summer before the flood, when Kooser mentioned bumping into him over at the courthouse. "Now there's a boy with a smart mouth on him," Kooser said, gnawing on a maple bar in my doorway. "Give you odds he washes out."

I tried to remember if I'd liked him, or if I just liked Carla getting some attention. I tried to think what all Carla had said about him back then, the words she used, and if she ever came looking for advice. Then I wondered why in hell I hadn't just gone ahead and given some, just to balance out Mother's chaotic offerings of wisdom.

"No bet," I said.

Still, it didn't surprise me to see him in the valley again. I could figure him hankering to come back where he was raised. He had a point to make, an emblem and membership to hold up to his lessers in the clan. Teller, for one. And I wondered how long it would take Carla to hear he'd come back to make his fame and fortune, and what she'd make of it.

When Teller first came around, we smelled a whiff of the rivalry between the cousins, of course, but it didn't seem so major with Benjamin long gone and having no claim.

"Carla's just got a *thing* about Stoltz boys," Mother said brightly.

What Teller lacked in appeal he made up for in doggedness. He had a decent job at the Feed and Grain, and he came over after work wearing their red-embroidered shirt, the dust combed out of his crewcut and his nails cleaned. He wasn't so peevish then, only slow to talk and solid-seeming. Carla would go riding with him in his truck, or out to eat at the Beaumont, or up north of town to the Blue Moon. At some point his attentions became an offer. Mother made sure Carla took him up on it.

"You know, you can get a grip on a man like that," Mother said.

I couldn't help but think her mind was drifting back to her own husband in Kankakee, insubstantial as a cornstalk.

"Being out-and-out *attracted* to the man isn't so much in the long run of things," she told Carla. "He'll get familiar, don't you think so, Carl?"

Carla looked at me desperately. "Well, hell," I said. "I'm no expert."

Why didn't I raise my voice then—one time was all it needed. Why didn't I tell Mother to lay off and tell Carla if she'd loved once it could come again, and not to settle so quick? A strong word then and I might've missed all of what I did later. They say hindsight's cheaper than a backstreet dog.

 4

CARLA PRUDHOMME STOLTZ

Monday. Teller vacated the house, grumbling. I used to say, *Teller, tuck your belly in, don't look like gravity's got you beat to pieces.* Anymore I only said, *Call me if you're not coming home.* Today I didn't say anything. He was foul. Wouldn't take so much as a cup of coffee. I watched his Willys dipsydoodle down to the county road, mud spinning off the back wheels like the drizzle off a calf's behind. The kitchen was agloom. Seemed like all I ever did was look out the window at rain. So I grabbed a slicker off the peg and went out myself. It wasn't a storm anymore . . . whatever it was we were inside it and everything looked the same. Mama's crocuses were poking out of the bed by the chimney, and those other ones, those spiny things, but they didn't look right. The eaves trough outside Carl's window had come undone again and the water'd busted down and washed away the dirt from around the roots of the rosebushes. I pulled one clear out with my hands, it looked so feeble. The grass and the wood and the air, it all smelled like an old garden hose. I thought I was going to die if I didn't see Benjamin.

I never let him come to the house.

If he came here I knew it would bring Teller home. I don't say Teller had powers, but that's how life works, doesn't it? He'd come home with a headache up his sinuses, cussing every step of the way, and Benjamin's big green Buick would be sitting under the lilacs and *poof,* that would be that. Even if Teller managed to stay away I didn't want Benjamin to see me in this house—where he'd eaten all those dinners and charmed Mama up one side and down the other, and sat up late with me under the afghan, letting me know what a dipshit little pond this valley was. It didn't help a thing to remember how I was then, and I didn't want to see him burning up my mind, either.

When the rain kept up and kept up I made a fire and shut the kitchen curtains and pushed my chair close in, but I couldn't stop the shivers and my mind skipped around like it couldn't get warm either. So, yes, I called him, and it was like I didn't have a will not to, and in the while I was waiting to talk to him I said, *Carla, let him be, don't you be a pushy girl,* but soon as he got on the line I said, *Benjamin, you have got to get out here.*

In a half hour he burst through the back door, streaming. He was sort of laughing and his shoes were muddy and his hair was laid into tracks by the rain. He flung his coat across the oilcloth. No sign of being scared for him, that's what I loved. He was all around me and when he let go something was still funny but I couldn't see what it was.

"Getting bad," he said.

"No," I said. "It'll be OK, it's just this one time, I promise."

"No, I mean out there," he said. "Getting close to Biblical."

"Oh, Benjamin, don't joke with me," I said. "Please just be a good boy."

I'd planned to use the hide-a-bed downstairs. I'd moved out the coffee table and unfolded it and put clean sheets on and put the cushions back before he came. And I'd wanted to put some flowers out in a tall vase but it was the wrong time of the year and all I could think about was the roses, all soggy and full of prickers. Then when I saw Benjamin I wanted him in my own bed.

So I led him up the stairs and down the hall into the big white-painted room and the second he was inside it with me I knew I'd been all wrong about those old Benjamins and Carlas haunting us here. They were dead and gone, as much as Mama whose refuge it was before me.

"Take all the time you want, Benjamin," I whispered.

He was huge and slow and this was all new because the happiness was crackling inside me and it was mine and I owned it. There were beautiful waves in my mind and a roar that wasn't any words for once. I wasn't afraid of Teller or a thing in this world except having it be over, and then it was.

I woke to his shadow blocking the window. He shook his head and the light leaked in around his cheeks.

"Don't get dressed," I said, but already he was making a knot in his tie. He came over and sat on the edge of the bed. I pulled his hand to my mouth but he didn't want it and put it on my shoulder, then it slid back to his lap.

"Carla," he said. "This wasn't bright. Don't ask me to come out here again." He offered up a little smile to show he wasn't being mean, only smart enough to do the thinking for both of us.

So he was already away from me. Already thinking of the next time and the next.

Benjamin!

You know, Mama had a feeling she called *The Light Shining on Her,* but it almost never came to me and I could never call for it to come, but when it did come I'd think, if this would only *last* I could tell her and Carl what ailed me the rest of the time, which they deserved to know.

Benjamin, stay a minute, I thought.

"I'll wait for you downstairs," he said.

I didn't do more than put my robe on finally and go down and there he was in the kitchen holding the rosebush.

What's this? his eyes said.

"Oh well," I said. "It just . . . came loose."

Benjamin made a sad face, then looked around for something to wipe his hands on.

"All right," I said. "You can go now if you want. It was just the rain."

He fastened his coat and edged over toward the door and saw the mud he'd tracked in before. It made him want to say something . . . but if he'd wanted to talk it should've been upstairs when I could maybe say the right things back to him.

So now I just said, "I'll clean it all up," and there wasn't a thing for him left to do but hunch over and kiss me like an old wife and go. For a second time that day I watched one of the Stoltz boys drive off spinning through the mud toward the county road.

CARL PRUDHOMME

Then it was Monday.

A box spring shunted through the meadow by the highway like a bumper car, ridden by a rain-beaten collie dog whose bark you couldn't hear for the rushing water. Chickens were trapped in their coops, rising with the water, all but a few drowning at the roof among each other's flailing wings. Cattle from ranches hidden up the canyon pounded with other debris against the weakening supports of down-stream bridges. And in the narrows of the canyon itself, just below where the two forks join—a third being restrained by a massive concrete dam—everything vanished. Fifteen miles of highway and power poles, the main line of the Great Northern, huckleberries, moss, and topsoil . . . every scrap of it down to bedrock.

Never thought it would get so high, everybody said.

But our job was to know better. It snowed in early May, not a freak spring storm, but heavy snow that laid in, and the rest of May passed for November. The valley acted stunted. People went at getting their gardens ready as always, but hesitantly, the way birds will roost during an eclipse. Then it rained. It rained the 5th of June, and the 6th, and the 7th. Back east in the mountains, tributaries gushed out of control. Understand, it wasn't anyone's *official* job to keep an eye on the tributaries, so all we got were the rumors. We watched the flood gauge at the mouth of the canyon. Monday noon it hit 14 feet, flood stage even. It seemed to hold there, like a child's fever.

No flood had hit the valley since 1948, and before that

1907. People forgot. Even now they say we're safe for a generation or two—it simply takes too much going wrong at once, is what they say. The flood plain's crammed with new houses. Log ones with bubbled Plexiglas in the roof, cedar ones shot full of stained glass, whole tracts of cheaper jobs and trailers where young families live. In the spring, marshes form in the low spots, and gawkers drive out to the Old Steel Bridge to see the churned-up runoff lap a few feet into the parking lot. They don't worry now. But that day in '64 the water broke flood stage in a burst and rose a foot an hour. At dark it stood at 21 feet.

A glacier made this valley, and generally speaking it's flat as a skillet, with mountains butting up to it so sharp they say you can stand with one foot on the floor and the other starting to climb. Even so, there are rises and ridges where the debris piled up. You can see them at a distance, soft humps with apple and cherry trees, and at the center, a house and small barn and sheds and some tall trees to break the wind. It was a place like that Mother rented for us, then bought when Father's money came, though not the land on all sides, which the original owner leased to our neighbor for wheat and oats. After Mother died, Carla and Teller came there to live, and it was up to them to acquire that farmland, in batches, and plant it with Scotch pine to be harvested in seven years for Christmas trees.

Monday morning I called out there. Carla didn't answer and I thought she must've come to town with Teller. At lunchtime I went out with the Rescue Unit and told Belinda to keep trying for me. Midafternoon Belinda caught up with me and said no luck on the calls. "Bet you the lines're out," she offered.

Well, I thought, she was either in town or home. If she was here she'd find me. If she was home she'd be safe enough, even if water cut the roads off around her. All she had to do was stay put.

We were only two weeks shy of the solstice, but still the dark came early and settled on the stirred-up face of the water. All

afternoon the reports came in. A few families got to neighbors' houses, then the water stranded all of them together.
Some we could bring out by boat. Some made it down to an
open section of road and into town, and we sent them to the
grade schools, which the Auxiliary had fitted out with cots and
cauldrons of chili.

In the heart of our confusion, I thought of Bradley
Vaughn, how this should've been *his* flood, how he'd have
called up an extra ration of calm and deployed it among the
deputies and volunteers. And here I was, jumping from hunch
to hunch and all I could tell for gospel sure was it was getting
worse.

And I still hadn't found Carla.

About five, Kooser and I slid into a National Guard
helicopter with a pilot named McPhee who lifted us up into
the murk. Out past Byrum Stage we spotted a caravan of
house trailers creeping out of the lowland like some glowing
long-jointed insect. Beyond that, no lights at all. In a few
minutes we set down in the gravel where Teller's truck usually sat. The barn was shut tight and the house was dark.

"Looks like she stayed in town, Carl," Kooser yelled.

"Most likely," I said. But I went inside anyway.

The kitchen was a mess: mud tracks all over, a rain slicker
lying half in the sink, chairs standing funny, shades drawn. We
never used to pull the shades except in summer when the
dinnertime sun caught our eyes. I shouted into the dark part
of the house. It didn't feel empty. I slipped off my boots and
went through the living room and up the stairs and down the
hall I knew by heart. The bedroom door was bolted.

I put my ear to it. In the background, the chopper's
blades echoed off the face of the barn in soft *whops.*

"Carla?" I said. "It's me, Carl. What in hell?"

Nothing for a moment. Then the latch clicked and she
let me in and scuttled back to the shadows of the bed.

"Leave the light off," she said.

She had that sound of having cried and gotten over it and
being limp.

"What's going on?" I said. "Where's Teller?"

"I can't stand all this water, Carl."

"You're all right," I said. "Kooser and I came out to get you." I lifted the blanket around her shoulders but she let it drop. "Put some things together and you can stay at my place till this thing, till the water goes down."

She didn't budge.

I'd seen her like that too often, near-frozen. Mother used to say, *Carla's on her little island,* and let it go at that. But now Carla *was* on an island and I couldn't risk leaving her there.

"There's lots of scared people," I said. "You're one of the lucky ones. Come on now."

"Carl," she said. "Why are you so good?"

"I'm not good, I'm just taking care of you. Now *please.* You're too big to carry."

"Carl," she said. "Teller's not coming back."

"Nobody's getting through," I told her. "If he was in town he couldn't have made it past Ruperts'. Most likely he went out to his mother's. You know how those boys are. Not to mention the phone lines being out."

Teller, right then, was the least of my worries. Carla fussed and stalled and it was all I could do to get her out of that bedroom and into the helicopter.

Then I let her into my apartment, switched on the lights, and sat her down on the sofa where I could get a decent look at her.

"You all right now?"

"You better just go on," she said.

"You going to make it then?"

She nodded. I had to settle for that. I never knew what would set her off, or how long it would last, but I couldn't stay.

"I'll get back later and see how you're doing," I promised.

But we worked the whole blessed night.

Tuesday morning, the water, which had gone off the gauge at 26 feet, dropped a few inches and bared the first red marker, and kept slipping down. By afternoon we were saying, cautiously, that its back was broken. Still, it would be with us for days, and reckoning the damage would take us longer than we knew. I leaned my head back against the seat of the helicopter and let my eyes close. Since yesterday I'd eaten a bowl of that chili, six or eight glazed doughnuts, and any number of half-cups of burnt coffee. I had a headache and it jangled with every thrum of the engine.

"McPhee," I said. "Get us the hell out of here. Find us some sunlight."

"How's that, sheriff?"

"I said . . ."

But McPhee was banking us sharply now. I opened my eyes. Below us, trapped in a snarl of barbwire and uprooted fenceposts, was Teller's old Willys truck, the windshield and roof stove in, and the back end jutting into the current like riprap. I judged we were better than two miles downriver from the house. There was no place to land. McPhee held us in a tight hover. I thought about letting myself down with a rope, but there wasn't any point in heroics. The cab was empty. There was no telling where he'd hit the river.

 6

CARLA PRUDHOMME STOLTZ

The floor was just dry when the door banged open and Benjamin lumbered in again. For a second I let myself think it was for me.

He was winded and his face was flushed like he'd been out in the car hollering. "The water," he said. "It's over the whole goddamn road. Jesus Jenny, I about stalled out."

"Go out north," I said.

He waved his arm in that direction, and I thought, *Yes, the road dips low there too, down by the mint farm.*

"This is a disaster," he said. "This is a goddamn I don't know what."

What had two hours done? He scuffed back and forth

where I'd cleaned. He was acting like nobody I knew, some strange man come here out of the bad weather like it was the only high ground he could get to.

"Carla," he said. "I can't be here. You realize that."

"Didn't you like it being here a little while ago?" I said. Oh, I wasn't trying to bait him, just to . . . but his eyes dodged around and he made that same look Teller makes two blinks before he grabs my shirt and starts to slap.

I couldn't help it, I threw my hands up in front of my face. Then when nothing came I let them fall and was so ashamed of myself. Benjamin just glared at me.

"Who do you think I am, Teller?" he said.

I didn't know who he was. He wasn't the man who'd just now held me above him, smiling with his eyes shut, letting out little breaths saying *Car-la, Car-la,* so it sounded like the *Dar-ling, Dar-ling* I always wanted to hear. Somewhere down under his suit *he* wanted to hit me, too. It was my fault that he'd be stuck here, because it couldn't be his fault.

"There's a back way," I said. "Through the orchard."

"A regular road?"

I didn't want to look at him. "Enough of one," I said.

You've even been on it, I thought. *One of those nights you let Mama beat you at cribbage and pretended to drive off, then parked down past the cattle guard and came back for me and took me walking. But you didn't know where you were. It was just night and you wanted to kiss me.*

"OK," Benjamin said. "I'm going to call my office, just in case."

He went around the corner and hunched over the phone and all I could see was his two elbows sticking out past the doorjamb like wings.

"Shit," he said, clunking it down. "Dead as a friggin' goose."

He marched back across the kitchen and I said, "Why don't you just say I called you because I got scared and Teller wasn't around, or Carl . . ." but he didn't stop to listen. Bang, out the back door again, and out I went after him. "So just leave me here," I yelled. The car door was already slamming.

He backed around in the mud near the shop and took off past the barn and that was all I saw.

So he was gone again. I sat on the steps and for a few minutes everything ran together. The boy he'd been. The girl I'd been. My wanting him. I clamped my hands between my knees and tried to think what was what. I wanted to get on a plane and fly out of this horrid valley where you can't stand up straight under the clouds. I wanted to scour Teller off me with a Brillo pad. I wanted Benjamin to be eighteen again and we'd be down out of the wind where the row of Granny Smiths grows into the hill. Oh, and this time I'd be silky and slow and wouldn't scare him off like I did. I'd say, *It's such a sweet time for this, Benjamin, won't you?* I'd say, *Here now, Benjamin, there's nobody in the world but us.* And then he wouldn't have to run crying and leave his boot, and me there with my shirt ripped up the seam. And then it wouldn't have been his cousin who got to me first, in those cabins out on Highway 2, after the wedding when I was so miserable.

What was I going to do next . . . get warm? Shine my life up? I'd been bunched there so long my joints didn't work right. And there, before I'd decided on a single thing, came Benjamin again. And of course I thought the same thought I was always having, which was, *Why have you come back to me?*

But he wasn't coming back. He'd only wound up in the center of the maze again.

"Get in the car!" he hollered.

"I'm OK here," I said.

He charged across the mud, then pulled up short in front of me. He'd looked half put-together when he'd left. Now he looked half undone, filthy and wild in the eyes.

"You're in this," he said. "And you've got to *get in the car.*"

"In what?" I said. "What am I in?" But I'd find out soon enough.

Benjamin peeled me off the porch post and took me down to the Buick. The road was nothing much, two furrows and a mangy strip of field grass beaten down by rain. He jammed down on the accelerator and it was only the ruts that kept us going straight.

"What's wrong with you?" I said.

We came to the end of the rise. The canyon mouth was out there in the distance like a black eye, and down below where the hill bent away to the right, closer than I could believe, was all that water, fields and fields of it roaring past. Then we crested the last hill. Benjamin slowed and I looked front.

There smack in the middle of the road was Teller's truck, pointed square at us, stopped dead, and there in the mud beside it, face down, was Teller.

 7

CARL PRUDHOMME

Wednesday.

I woke on the cot in my office, still in uniform, a thin light seeping through the blinds. A phone rang in the distance, then stopped. I'd managed to call Carla yesterday, but I hadn't let on about finding the Willys. I'd promised to come home again and I'd broken that one too. I sat up the rest of the way and my back howled. I was wet from yesterday, or from a sweaty sleep—this much water in the air, nothing dried right. I'd go back home and take a shower and think of something to tell Carla.

Then Kooser backed through the office door with two cups of coffee and a sorrier-than-usual look.

"You've got some business," he said.

The man was waiting for us with a duckboat. I knew him from somewhere—maybe I'd gone to school with one of his kids, he was that age. But he only knew me as the one you called when you found a body lodged between two of your birch trees.

"It was my wife that spotted it," he said. "She was looking out the pantry window to see if it was still raining."

His lawn tailed away from the house, then dropped off sharply the way it did at Carla's. Between there and the near end of the hedgerow lay thirty yards of sluggish water, out of which poked some swollen fenceposts and the top half of an ancient swing set. The hedgerow was a mishmash of trees and undergrowth, but where it came close to the yard the trees had been pruned and tended, and there, slumped like a cast-off peel of tractor tire, was Teller.

"I told her she was nuts, you know? I told her she'd been cooped up too long," he said. "You want me to row you out?"

"Thanks, Mr. . . ."

"Darwin," Kooser piped in. "Sorry, this is Larry Darwin, works down at Equity Supply."

"That's all right, Mr. Darwin," I said. "We'll manage."

Kooser poled us across the water and wedged the boat against the manicured trunks of Larry Darwin's birches. Teller had always been a stubborn, barrel-chested weight of a man, but dead he'd grown twice as heavy. We almost tipped over hauling him in. The dead sometimes look resigned, but Teller looked utterly familiar, the dark Stoltz brows fretful as ever, the lower lip furled as if he was saying, *Just my luck.*

Kooser collapsed to the seat and hung his head. "I'm just sorry as hell about this, Carl," he said. "If I'd known who it was . . ."

"Who's going to do it?" I said. "I'm the only coroner we got."

"Looks like the water beat him around some."

"Looks like," I said.

We hefted him from the boat onto a blanket. Larry Darwin leaned over my shoulder for a closer inspection, shook his head, then edged away to the house to report back to his wife, who was still plastered to the pantry window.

"Carl," Kooser said. "You want me to call Epping, or what?"

"Get the old man," I said. "Don't let him send the kid. I can't bear the kid. And listen, don't, you know, say anything yet."

Kooser nodded and slouched off toward the patrol car.

Sperry doesn't generate enough stray bodies to justify a morgue as such, so the undertakers—Epping and Epping,

Muldoon, or in a pinch Bevis and Dowling (though Bradley'd had a grudge against Fred Dowling that went back to the '40s)—they come where we are, and it's a rotten sight to watch their black wagons creep up a mountain road or back with supreme patience down the boat ramp at the big lake. You don't need an autopsy very often, was Bradley's theory, but if you did, you did it back at one of the mortuaries. I'd learned this miserable end of the trade at Bradley's side, listened often enough to him zeroing in on the damage of record. *Cause of death,* I could hear him recite in his chamois-smooth baritone, bending over the clipboard where he'd affixed the paperwork: *Another goddamn drowning. Clean and simple.*

I felt for a moment like the two dead men had me out-numbered.

The clouds were starting to break up, but the wind was no less raw. That moment's perfectly hinged in time: the smell rising from the saturated ground, the moldery light falling against the mountains, the silence in which I began to wonder if I might be glad to see him dead. Kooser was far up at the end of the drive talking on the radio, and Larry Darwin had seen enough for one morning.

I knelt to Teller and loosened his collar button—he'd always looked so backwoods with the top button done and no tie, but you couldn't tell him a thing. Then I straightened his head on the blanket, and saw, in the pale place above the ribbing of his T-shirt, two plum-colored ovals at either side of his windpipe, two fresh medallions the size of thumbs, hung where they didn't belong.

 8

CARLA PRUDHOMME STOLTZ

"Carl, don't you take me up in that thing, I won't go," I said, but he had his way.

The dark was pressing around us and we roared off, hell-bent on surviving. Carl kept trying to soothe me, except it was all too loud and he didn't know what to say but *There's nothing to be afraid of, Carla.*

How could I tell him what was wrong? That Benjamin was trapped down there, that I couldn't bear to leave him, even if it was true I'd locked my door against him and prayed he wouldn't come splintering through the old wood. . . .

It was because I wouldn't put my hands on Teller. Benjamin said, *We've got to drive him to the river,* and I knew what he meant, but no way, I couldn't help him do that. Benjamin said of course I'd help him with the lifting because it was too much of a weight for just him, and I turned around for the house and all I could see was smoke twisting out of the chimney and blowing away.

Benjamin turned me back around by the shoulder and said, *It was him that came at me, Carla,* and I said, *Don't tell me how it was,* and he started in again to tell me, and I said, *Don't, don't,* and he could see by now I wouldn't help him, and I walked away with the mud sucking at my shoes.

Then he was outside my bedroom door, saying he'd brought the Buick back and stuck it in the barn because the road was too much of a risk now, begging me to listen to reason, but I turned up the radio and listened to the Country Giant and sat on Teller's side of the bed and pretty soon it got dark. And where was he when Carl came up the stairs? . . . I don't know . . . hidden away someplace.

If only Carl could've taken us both away, both Benjamin and me, that's what I was thinking in the helicopter.

I let my head fall against Carl's shoulder and that seemed to content him. It felt like we were kids again in the back of Mama's old DeSoto, Carl bolt upright like always, and me stretched out beside him, not asleep, not awake, braiding the fringe of Mama's car blanket in the dark.

So I stayed at Carl's that first night with Carl thinking Teller was out at his mother's. Carl came in with me and made me promise I was all right. He knew better than to believe me, but he wanted to hear it because he couldn't stay up all night holding his weird sister's hand when the rest of the valley was washing away. So he went off and I laid down on the couch and thanked him for leaving me alone. The cars went *shushing* down First Street in the rain. I tried not to think about Benjamin outside my door saying, *Can I count on you, Carla? Can you get your mind straight on this, Carla?*

In the morning I sat at Carl's dinette and told myself I was wicked to sleep like I did, not having any dreams of it or anything, just sleep, heavy as a load of dirt. Wicked for never loving him, which was the start of everything. Except I didn't feel wicked, only crusty-eyed and doomed. You don't guess for a minute you'll be quit of a man like Teller that way, but now that it had come and happened, I knew it was the awful something I'd waited for all my life.

The phone rang.

I knew it was Benjamin after me again and I knew I couldn't possibly talk to him yet, even if I'd have to later. It rang and rang. *Oh, don't,* I said. *Please.* But finally I grabbed it off the hook and smothered it against my stomach and after a little while I tried to hang it up, but there was Carl's voice rattling in the receiver.

"It's you," I said. "I had to catch my wind."

"Where were you?"

"Just . . . I went out."

"You doing better then?"

"Carl," I said.

He promised to come back that night and I said, *If you want,* and he got off the line. I put a muffin in the toaster oven, then tried to eat it but the butter made my stomach swim. It was hours later, when the dark was creeping around again, that I realized Carl hadn't said a thing about Teller. Not one word.

I sat up waiting for him, praying Benjamin wouldn't call, afraid to take the phone off the hook. But nobody came and nobody called.

So it wasn't until Wednesday morning that I saw my brother again. He stood just inside the door like he didn't belong in his own apartment. I could tell he thought he knew something.

"Carla," he said. "We found Teller in the river."

How I wanted to act surprised for his sake! How I wanted to fly into tears and make him put his arms around me and settle me down! But I was never a good enough sister . . . all I could get out was "I knew he wasn't coming back."

Carl looked hurt. He kept banging his hat against his leg. He only had a few hairs in front and they were stuck down with sweat. His eyes were baggy and gray underneath.

He went over and looked in the icebox, then sat at the dinette and folded his hands. I couldn't think of a thing to do except go over and sit across from him.

"Carla," he started in again. Oh, now it was all going to come roaring out and he'd rub my nose in all my weaknesses and tell me I'd ruined it all, absolutely everything he and Mama had worked so hard for . . . and I'd lose Benjamin just like I'd lost Mama and Teller and there'd be no one else for me.

He reached into his top pocket and unfolded a piece of paper and set it before me.

"Put your name down here," he said. He'd made a little X for me to sign next to.

"What is this?" I said.

"We're going to have him cremated," Carl said. "Today. Quick as you can imagine."

 9

CARL PRUDHOMME

If Bradley Vaughn thought breeding and a taste for duty and faith in the Almighty's good-heartedness were all he needed to keep the valley safe . . . or if Mother disguised herself as a war widow and washed her hands of men, and then, in a perverse twist of logic, caused Carla to believe marriage was her only salvation on earth . . . or if people commit their every worldly possession to the fortunes of the flood plain . . . then I say, *Let them all believe no harm can come from it.* Lord knows, it's hard enough to believe in anything.

It's just that I've run the string all the way out on what I can believe about myself.

Bradley would've been in his element tonight. This was the good retirement dinner that should've been his eighteen years ago. The Elks Club was crawling with well-wishers. By the time the roast beef came, the Scotch had melted my horror down enough to hide behind a respectable-looking face.

Half the people in town got up to speak. Bless his heart, Kooser told them about the time I chased Billy DeFrank through Ackerman's pig farm. Everybody laughed. Retirement had turned Kooser jovial as a baked apple. He told them what a great guy I was to work for, and said he hoped we'd have the time to drown some worms together now.

Then the mayor smiled his way to the microphone. If they have a book on mayoring, he'd gone through it and underlined the choice parts.

"I don't hardly need to remind any of you," he began, "how Sheriff Prudhomme started off his long tenure in office. Western Montana was ravaged by floods that spring, of course, and it was only the cool heads and commitment of men like Sheriff Prudhomme that averted a true catastrophe. . . ."

I stared down from the head table and most of the audience disappeared into the lights and smoke. But they were out there still, working on the last of their cream puffs and coffee, pleased with themselves for showing up, but short-winded from the heavy food and ready to stand up and move around.

Finally it was my turn.

I looked back at Carla, who'd been sitting by me. She wore green velvet, with a necklace of silver fetishes I'd bought her down on the reservation. The red in her hair had gone to straw over time and her face had gathered weight. She smiled and let her gaze fall to her folded hands. To the people out front she must have looked serene, proud of her brother in his moment of honor.

I felt the blood rush to my cheeks. I wanted to open up and let fly. I wanted to scald their ears with all I'd never said. *You should know things about me,* I wanted to say. *You should know about deceit. You should know what happens to a house built on sand. . . .*

Instead I thanked them for the plaque and withstood their flurry of applause. It was none of their fault. Let them believe I was deserving.

When we could finally get away, I drove us home. Carla laid her head back on the seat and hummed like she was in another world. Here it was spring again. The last islands of corn snow lingered in the borrow pits, glowing under the full moon. I knew that moon would encourage someone's temper to boil over tonight, as it always did, but already it felt like none of my affair. I left the county road and steered through the half-frozen ruts of our long drive, and pulled up by the lilacs.

Carla got out and snugged her shawl and waltzed slowly off to the house. I stood at the fence a minute, looking out at our expanse of fields, dotted black with Christmas trees reclaimed so long ago from Teller's misery, their heavy smell riding up to me on a chinook wind. And Benjamin Stoltz, what had become of him? Maybe his family knew. He'd left here suddenly for Butte, and Butte for Reno, and Reno for San Jose, and after that the rumors go dead. For a long time I'd made it my business to know.

Far off, something howled, dog or coyote, I couldn't tell. In a few weeks the work would begin again. Crews would press through the rows, shaping the limbs with rapid blows of the machete. Most of the trees would pass for good. The rains would come, then the months of sun and dust. We'd harvest and pull stumps and plant again, and 1982 would throw its lot in with all those others.

The back door opened and Carla called out, "Come on inside now, Carl," her voice no different from Mother's.

What choice did I ever have? I thought for the millionth time, starting up toward the house and its ghosts, toward Carla who has spared me from loneliness.

The Oriental Limited

Lillian Wallace

I

10 SEPTEMBER 1924

A fine prairie grit had sifted into the Pullman and settled on my lips in the night. I cracked the curtain to the aisle. The safety lights were still on, a sickly green. Everyone was asleep, Charles included. I collapsed back to the berth, mad at myself for waking, and too restless to even shut my eyes. I didn't have a prayer of pacifying myself. I wished I could just peel back the bedclothes and let myself into the bottom berth beside Charles, without it waking him. I'd never seen him in bed—only once stretched out on our blanket at the boat races, his hat down over his eyes. But wouldn't sleep treat such a man kindly? Wouldn't his face look heavy and far from worry? I'd crawl in and lie on him light as a comforter, my lips grazing his cheek. Then the miles would disappear.

Of course, I couldn't do anything of the kind. All I could do was wait in my berth and be mesmerized by the tick of the rail-ends. All I could do was what I'd *been* doing for the last ten days: trying not to imagine what might've happened to my two brothers.

Never had I pictured myself on such a train—I'd never ridden anything grander than the Lake Street El. Even down in Galen's room, helping him pack, I never asked myself why it was he and James who struck out for a far-off place they'd seen in an ad. To be honest, it had not been the best of summers. I'd yet to settle on what I'd do that fall—try my hand at college again, or keep the job at Marshall Field's (I was a salesgirl in the luggage room—this I was actually beginning to like) . . . or sharpen my thoughts on marrying Charles. Maybe I did envy them a little, for knowing what they wanted so well. Maybe I did wish they'd leave off planning their expedition long enough to see I could stand having a little direction myself. Well, what could matter less now? In went Galen's rubber boots, his hiking knickers, his good suit, his good pen, Father's Kodak, some copies of *The Saturday Evening Post* for the train. Then at the last minute he shuffled it to make room for a big coil of rope.

He looked up sheepish, smiling. *"Mother,"* he said. We had ourselves a little laugh. Worrier that I was known to be, I couldn't hold a candle to her.

These Pullmans were spanking new, according to Charles. Modern, stable as battleships. I'm speaking now of the Monday before last, the night of the First. Charles and Mother and I sat under the canopy at Union Station, killing the last few minutes before James and Galen were to disembark from the Oriental Limited. Charles wasn't so keen on the modern things *I* thought we should talk about—the up-to-date marriage we'd have, say, or matters of a sexual nature—but he believed in Progress; often I'd hear him say how these were first-rate days to be alive. It had now been exactly a year since Father's death (we had the good grace not to call attention to the anniversary), and in that year Charles, who'd been our long-time friend and James's benefactor at The Carthage Company, had stepped in and become the family adviser. Mother never lacked for a considered opinion of her own, but she took Charles's word on anything that had been Father's province. Money, for example. She made sure he looked after whatever remained of Father's investments. Earlier this summer, he'd persuaded Mother she could succumb to a few of the conveniences, and so she'd allowed herself an electric refrigerator and an RCA. Both on installment. "I'm sure Jonathan's spinning in his grave," she said, attempting a carefree tone, but from the look in her eyes, you'd think she was actually picturing it. But I could tell she loved to sit by the radio with her eyes closed, listening to Gounod or Puccini on KYW. . . .

Well, Charles chatted on, keeping us company. He sat on the bench between us, tapping his hat against his knee, telling Mother how cosmopolitan the railroad had gotten—they had their own greenhouses and put out fresh carnations and asters in crystal vases at every meal. It was fine as eating downtown at the Palmer House. Father hadn't taken her to the Palmer House in years, of course, and James wouldn't have thought it a smart way to spend his money, but she took in Charles's words without a ripple, maybe less rapt than usual, answering from that store of politenesses she'd amassed over the years with Father. Charles had no idea the distress she was in, no idea what she held in check as she waited, out in public like that, for James and Galen to fill the portal from the tracks.

She hadn't told him one thing about their letters having stopped. Nor had I.

A week later (the night before last), Charles and I returned to Union Station and boarded the train ourselves. Mother's sister, my Aunt Viola, had arrived from Racine by then and Mother remained home in her care. There were last admonishments for Charles, then she raised up on tiptoes to kiss my cheek, and I thought, pulling away, I'd never seen such a shaken-looking face on her, not even on Father's account (so drawn-out was his dying), and I thought, *Lillian, you're making a miserable mistake leaving.* But the truth was, I couldn't bear not to, once the chance had presented itself.

Last thing, she surrendered the packet with their letters, smoothed out and paperclipped in order. She stood over me while I cracked my bag and tucked them in a safe place.

"Mr. Meechem's well aware of every word they wrote," she said, more to Charles than to me. "Still I'm sure he'll have need to see these himself." (Mr. Meechem was acting superintendent of the Park. He began his wires, his letters, *My dear Mrs. Wallace . . .)*

It was late and the berths were already made up. Charles and I had little to say to each other now, after a week of bolstering Mother's spirits, of conjuring up new excuses for encouragement. Charles insisted I have the upper—no one would bother me up there, not to mention that it had the superior mattress. Charles knew these things. He squeezed my hand and snapped me in. I didn't argue. I only wished it'd had a window, but under the circumstances, this seemed too petty to mention.

The first night a window wouldn't have mattered, for I dropped into a black sleep before we'd logged three-quarters of an hour toward St. Paul. This night past, however, I lay imagining the country outside growing drier and emptier. From the Glacier Park Hotel, the night of their arrival (the 17th), Galen wrote, *Prairie dogs stand up to watch us thunder by, but nothing else pays us any mind. Everything looks starved for rain. The cattle seem very thin. Once in a while you see a cowboy off against the sky. The mountains appeared at midday, but for hours they seemed no closer. . . .* Where James had only said, of the train: *The food was good and the prices were reasonable. Got in here on time altho at one point we were 45 min. late due to new bridge construction.*

Two letters, side by side in the same mail, addressed *Mrs. Flora Wallace, Miss Lillian Wallace.* I thought: Of course they'd write two letters. And how they showed off who they were! James the born engineer, ever the one, like Father, to say: Yes, he believed life was working out the way he'd intended it should. His script was squarish, the Palmer Method loops as boxy as if he'd inscribed them with a template. Galen's writing wandered above the line, extra words cribbed in on the slant, correcting, coloring what he'd started off to say. He wouldn't rest until convinced no one would misunderstand him. He was only twenty-two (eighteen months older than me), not so cheerful as James but happier (jubilant!) when there was cause. He'd gone off to college and enrolled in the general course, Western Civilization and all that, but the spring of his second year he switched direction and followed James into mechanical engineering—a surprise to all except Mother, who claimed to know everything there was to know about us. This past year, James had put aside part of his salary and sent him on to M.I.T.

Every day for a week, letters or cards.

When we got in from work at night, Mother set tea water to boil, then composed herself at the table in the kitchen while I read them aloud. She stared at the sugar bowl, on the listen for words of caution. From James's letter: *Just leaving Many Glacier for Granite Park. We are both O.K.* From Galen's: *Spent the afternoon tramping about, climbing up a mountain back of the chalet—Goat Mountain. We only went up about a quarter of the way. Had to hustle to beat the band to clean up and get into dinner before 7:30 when the dining room closes.*

From another of Galen's: *We are enjoying ourselves very much and taking no chances of injuring ourselves.*

"Well and good," Mother would say, snapping to.

If I *had* foreseen any travel for myself, surely it was a wedding trip with Charles—north to Mackinac Island for a week at the Grand Hotel. I had a slew of pictures of it from *Collier's,* also the rotogravure. The longest white porch in the world. I imagined there'd be orchards in ferocious bloom, boats to watch crossing the straits. But that seemed to lie a ways off in the gauzy future. In any event, I'd hardly ever left Chicago, and certainly never saw myself on such an errand as this. Not heartsick, not having to guard myself so among such cheerful, nosy people.

Charles said we were going to Montana on a family matter. His tone was so forceful no one inquired further.

We weren't even engaged, not strictly speaking, though at home it was taken for granted. Mother believed twenty-one was a good age for a woman to marry. (She'd been past twenty-five herself when Father had undertaken his furious courtship . . .)

I'd turned twenty this spring. Charles was thirty-eight.

That he was roughly twice my age disturbed others more than it did me or anyone in the family. Adelaide, my one dearest friend, teased me relentlessly. "God, Lillian," she'd say, "you might as well marry Reverend *Utzinger!*" (the mossy old pastor we'd had before Reverend Koenig). So then

I'd have to say disparaging things about Eddie Stovall, the boy she was threatening to run off with. Really though, Charles's age wasn't a thing I dwelled on. He'd always been there—to me he seemed simply a full-grown man. But, all right, why not someone my own age? Why not one of those pretty, floppy-haired boys Galen ran with? Was Charles a curious destiny Mother'd planted in me long ago? Yes, I had these thoughts; they just didn't stir me up.

More often, I'd wonder what Charles saw in me. I was anything but the fancy stuff he could find downtown: storkier than was called for (I made a point of taking off my shoes when we danced), not terribly quick with the bright comeback or generally (despite Mother's years of intermittent hammering) adept at the social graces. I watched for a sign he was tired of waiting for me to grow into something marvelous, but Charles was a model of patience. And whenever it was just us alone I felt no qualms at all about our partnership. He had a smooth and gracious face. (Once in a while, I could see it transferred to my own sons.) Though not imposing in height, he struck people as prosperous and well-informed. Even here on the train, strangers naturally gravitated to him with their questions. *What river was that?* a woman asked. Charles left off calming me long enough to say, "The James," and tell how it ran south and joined the Missouri at Yankton. If anyone was the least concerned about our morals, they had only to look at Charles. They'd see how decorous he was, the image of a chaperone.

If it weren't for Charles I wouldn't have been on the train at all, I'd still be back in the eye of Mother's desperation with nothing useful to do, eclipsed by my Aunt Vi, who'd gotten in after dinner on Friday. This was Mother's elder sister—exactly the kind of busy, top-heavy woman I'd cringe to find approaching my counter at Marshall Field's. There was no hiding from Viola. Her voice caromed off the hardwood and sought you out. Once, I'd heard Father call her *The Steam Turbine*—this to James, not to me, certainly not to Mother, who was another person around Viola. She was a harder-forged Christian than the rest of us, that was for certain.

Lillian, she told me (years and years ago), *the devil has eyes sharper than any hawk, he's watching you for the least opportunity.* . . . (I believed this, and even after I stopped believing in devils, I still felt scrutinized. I'd find myself composing detailed rationales for every step I took—though I guess that's not Viola's fault.)

I favored Mother's younger sister, my Aunt Mae. She was only a bit older than Charles, an unmarried lady who worked for a book publisher. She'd packed off to New York in 1904, the same year I was born. To my knowledge, she'd never come home. Still, I had pictures of her, and letters galore—she'd singled me out, taken me on somehow. Mother spoke of her gingerly. "Your aunt's so . . . *footloose,*" she'd say, which was hardly the right word, even I knew that. But this was as close as she'd come to passing judgment on Mae—in front of James or Galen or me.

Mae's letters to me were wonderful gossipy things. *Don't you dare tell your Mother, Lily . . .* she'd write, then describe some rendezvous, some passing wickedness. Now that I was older and aimed at a crossroads myself, she'd started talking about my coming to New York. "We'll sign you up at City College and you can stay with me . . ." *And study what,* I wrote. My first two terms had been an aimless business, a swarm of things that seemed not to concern me. "Or just come and don't go to school, then. We'll find you a job. Dear girl, what's to lose?" Often Mae sent us books she'd worked on—travel books primarily, or someone's memoirs. Though they sat handsomely on the shelf alongside the Richard Harding Davis and the Mary Roberts Rinehart, I was the only one who ever read them. Mother disliked hearing any talk of Mae's career. I suspected there was more to the story of her leaving home. *Precipitous,* Mother called it, but beyond that she was closemouthed. Mae wrote, "You may ask your Aunt Viola about it sometime." I realized that I'd never heard Viola so much as speak Mae's name, and I didn't have the nerve to ask. But then, I didn't really have to.

Anyway, it was Viola who'd come when Father began his final decline, and she came now. She'd no sooner breezed past me in the vestibule and flown across the front room to embrace Mother (Uncle Malcolm trailing behind, counterweighted by his wife's luggage—*missionary bags,* I called them, clunky things) than I could tell how I'd been displaced at Mother's side, and felt immediately dull for not remembering how much water lay between the generations.

But relief poured in with such a rush I didn't care. I slipped out the front door and down the stoop and dodged across the avenue into Garfield Park. I hadn't been out of the house, it seemed, out into the moving air, for days.

Strike me down for thinking so, but it was a pretty evening in Chicago. The wind had vanished and there was no inkling of fall yet, except for a stillness lying on the railings and the branches of the maples like an invisible weight. Headlamps were coming on. Across the grass floated the sound of a cornet, not a song, just runs of quavery notes, someone warming up to play. Years ago she'd send me out front, *Lillian, see if the boys are coming yet. Lillian. . . .* I'd squint off toward the park, relieved of the problem of amusing myself. The faces bobbed and mingled and disappeared. I counted to a hundred, hugging my arms. No one, no one, then finally James with his felt cap and dark round glasses, his back thin and straight. And Galen skipping and fidgeting along beside, listening, a ball glove bouncing from his belt. Then James drawing up and stopping across the avenue, spotting me and waving, his other hand palm out at Galen's chest while the automobiles passed.

Once, after James had left for the Army, Galen was ambushed by some boys from Fulton. It was nothing terrible—they'd turned out his pockets and taken a fifty-cent piece and a tiny gold, one-bladed pocketknife Father'd given him, then held him down and cut the buttons off his shirt with it. He was fifteen, stringy, obedient, no fighter. He came through the gangway and in the back to his room, clutching the buttons grimly. He let me follow him in. I took a needle and poked the dirt from the holes and started sewing them back. Galen hunched on the bed, asking me what he'd done. That was the worst of it for him. *It wasn't you, Galen, it could've been anybody,*

I said. *You just happened to be walking there.* But I didn't know that for a fact. Maybe it was him. Why did I get migraine? Why was it *our* father who was withering away? Galen hung his head, mystified. "There," I said finally, handing over the shirt. "Nobody will know." Of course, some of the buttons didn't hold and Mother got the story eventually. "You come straight home from now on," she told him. "I was," Galen kept saying, "I wasn't doing anything."

I walked clear through to the conservatory and down around the lake. I didn't see a soul I recognized, but gradually my thoughts milled and settled. By the time I'd looped back to the house, Uncle Malcolm's Peerless was gone and the face of the house was covered with shadow. I pictured them back in the lighted kitchen, Mother turning out her heart to her sister. I stopped and sank to the steps. It was only then, as sudden as that cornet slicing the air, I began to hear my own dark thoughts about James and Galen, separate from Mother's.

The next morning was Saturday, which happened to be the morning the *Tribune* printed the notice about Galen and James. I'd not found it in time to spare Mother. Aunt Vi had spread the paper open across the oak table. There were the two pictures: James's from when he was in the Army, Galen's from this June. They almost looked like twins. Under the headline it said in lesser type, *Fear Brothers Have Met Death in Crevice.*

"It's a sin," Aunt Vi said.

No one at the Park had said they were dead, no one had mentioned crevices. What could we think but that they'd still appear! That all the confusion distance brought on would dissolve just as abruptly . . . *while traversing the brittle shale formations, which readily become dislodged . . .*

"They don't know a single thing," Aunt Vi said, more to herself than to me. "Those morons."

I broke away and began waiting for Charles.

He stopped by every morning now, helping to write our wires, only going to his office for a few hours midday. The

Carthage Company had been more than kind about this, Mother insisted. Today I met him at the street. Charles hardly ever got his back up over things I said—he'd only smile and let them flutter past the way he did when I was twelve or fourteen. But even *his* patience was brittler now, and I'd been up since way before it was light working out a passionate little speech. . . .

Charles latched the door of the Buick, and stood rubbing his ring.

"Lillian . . ."

It wasn't in me to be coy or flapperish. I told him I couldn't stand it. I told him this was a thing I'd decided on.

He took a new bead on me and his breath seeped out. Moments later we walked up the stoop and Charles launched into a speech of his own: "Flora, believe me, I know what a help Lillian's been to you here," and so on, laying out the proposition—of course not letting on it'd started with me.

Quick as that, an idea I'd been afraid would sound disrespectful in my own voice—all right, *foolhardy*— was received and accepted without complaint.

If she'd shown me the least resistance . . . this was the same mother who'd tried her level best for weeks to cajole the boys out of their plans, everything short of forbidding them, which she simply couldn't accomplish any longer. James was almost thirty, after all, her main support (Galen's and mine as well). But if she'd said, *Lillian, dear girl, I can't bear to have you gone,* or, Lord, anything of the kind, I'd have stayed.

I couldn't stand it in the berth another minute. The dressing room was at the end of the car, but I didn't want to bother with it. I wriggled into yesterday's clothes and swung my legs out of the berth.

I let Charles be.

I made my way back through the observation car, opened the door and stepped onto the deck. The wind snapped around the sides of the car, cool and dry-smelling. Straight east there was light enough to tell the sky from the wheatland, to watch the two pearly streaks stretch back into the flat country we'd left overnight. I stood at the railing awhile, waiting, trying not to think ahead, my arms in goosebumps and the hair flying across my face. The door gave a click behind me and I shot around, expecting it was Charles come to say *There you are . . . better get inside now.* But the glass was empty, the latch only jittering with the rails.

 2

Mother waited until morning before wiring the hotel, though, logically, there were no more trains they could've been on. Four days plus a Sunday had elapsed since Galen's last message: *These postal cards are on top of the menus. We are just leaving Many Gl. for Gr. Park. We are both O.K.* But neither of us vented any worry. We went to work, we had our ordinary suppers, we took our walks in the evening. The streets smelled of cabbage and sausage, of tires and the stale warm air rising off the sidewalks. Mother clipped along as usual, surveying the life of the neighborhood, but minus her customary murmurs of interest. Each night something would strike her wrong. A raised voice carrying from an upstairs window, a couple necking in the back of a passing taxicab. In the year past I'd known her to complain about the West Side going to pieces—"Since the war," she'd claim. Now she didn't say anything. She stopped mid-block, her chin turned to stone, then wheeled around for home.

How easily we resumed the practice of not thinking our worries aloud. I could say we'd learned this during Father's sickness, for it certainly was the rule of the house then. But it was older—it came from who we were. *James is my strength,* Mother'd say. *Galen is my delight.* When I was still in the crib (according to James, our historian) she'd say, *Lillian is my little dream.* I can't imagine such playfulness in her voice, I can't imagine her bending over me, buttoning my gown, laughing. I was the easiest of her babies, the least troubled by croup or fits of unexplained fussiness, that's all she'd grant me. Maybe she thought, *Here is one I can let be. Here is one who will know things on her own.*

When I got older she began to think, *Lillian's the image*

of myself. My headaches (we never called them migraine) came on the same wicked spring week I turned fourteen. She took this as confirmation—and began to suspect it wasn't her best attributes that Providence had passed to me. Her steadfastness, say, her unornamented cast of mind, her musical talents. But instead the very shortcomings she'd persevered against since her own girlhood: being seduced by worry, or not believing what she believed deeply enough, which was a worry itself.

She'd had the headaches, too—gruesome, day-long bouts of pain and vomiting. But they'd vanished after she'd given birth to James, and even now she included this blessing in the catalog of things James had done for her. Privately, though, she felt an act of will had been involved, that once there were children she mustn't give ground to such indulgences. It's true she didn't judge me outright. She took me to Dr. Canfield for medicine, and when it didn't do enough, she brought me again and made sure he tried me on something stronger, codeine and ergot finally. Even so, I could feel her holding back some of her sympathy, I could feel her bristle when he called this a nervous disorder.

When the headache came, I'd lie in seclusion upstairs, my head in wet packs, wishing I was buried in the earth. In summer there was the bright clatter from the streets to blot out, in winter the clamoring radiators. I'd try to breathe without the slightest movement, and even then I felt on the verge of pitching off the bed and flipping end over end. I'd pray I'd keep the pills down long enough for them to work and carry me off. When I woke, time would've passed, a great stretch of it, making a before and an after. Mother had mentioned a dream the headaches had given her—she'd be clinging to the seat of an old-fashioned trap (the sort her grandfather drove) as it hurtled through a corner on two wheels, while their cargo of Ball jars cascaded endlessly from the back, shattering on the cobblestones. But if I had any dreams I remembered nothing of them and didn't care to. I felt light in the aftermath, reprieved and cleaned out. Instead of rushing to join the affairs of the house, I'd tarry in bed—nearly floating, my senses strangely honed. I'd feel, for a while, that I was on the edge of knowing things.

Often I'd wake to piano music coming from down in the front room. No one played except Mother—if James and Galen had showed no inclination that way, so be it, but in my case I knew it seemed more irksome testimony against me. Mother sight-read easily. Sheets of classical pieces lay in the bench, but she seldom brought them out anymore. Instead, I'd hear her roaming through the Congressional Hymnal, testing the first lines with her voice. *The light of God is falling / Upon life's common way.* The piano was kept in tune and her touch was pure and firm. Everyone said how well she played, imagining what a great refuge music was for her. But fresh from sleep one afternoon, I was suddenly privy to a secret of hers. There was nothing of passion in her playing. It was all technique, as much a habit as setting the kettle on to boil. And then, lying in that subdued light, near but apart from her, I understood the rest of it: that it was no different for her church-going, her faith, that (as James would say) she was only covering her bases.

After that, whenever she said *God this, God that,* I heard how she meant not the one who kept His eye on every sparrow, who listened to every lisp of a girl's prayers, but something else—Providence, The Way of Things. No one would guess, though. When Father became so sick he could no longer walk down to the church with her, she went between James and Galen, and sat in the same row down on the right as she had since they'd come to the neighborhood in the '90s. She could be counted on to serve coffee, to make collections for the Auxiliary—she was a great organizer, everyone said. She accomplished these things as if they were enough, as if they quelled her wondering and her worry. But I knew what I knew, and it seemed I was the only one to catch the flash of annoyance that interrupted her sadness when Reverend Koenig talked of Father's ascension to his reward. Of course, I kept it to myself.

That Sunday before the boys were due, we asked Charles for dinner. He sat at the head of the table where James normally presided (before him, Father), carving the pork roast that had bathed the house all afternoon with a sweet, cloistered smell. James had planned on cutting the vacation close—he was due at work Tuesday morning. Charles and I joked about how he'd be at his drafting table bright and early while poor Galen was still buried under a mound of sleep.

It was just then Mother spoke up. She asked Charles to drive us to the station the following night. Ordinarily, they'd just take the El.

"That's fine, Flora," Charles said.

"How could I manage without you?" Mother said.

As Charles looked away, pleased, patting his lips, her hand went still around her water glass, her chin stiffened as it had in the street. No matter what we did or didn't say to each other, *she knew.*

And imagined she might forestall it by appearing at Union Station in person.

As I said, she waited all night, thinking . . . I don't know what. But Tuesday, with the first wire, and the first reply, all she'd stored up burst out. *Spurred on by the frantic appeals of Mrs. Wallace, rangers set out to find the brothers.* By the time Charles and I left Chicago, they'd been out of touch for eighteen days. First it was Mr. Griswold who wired, the one in charge of the east side of the Park, then the Superintendent himself, Mr. Meechem; then the Park Service in Washington; then Secretary Work of the Interior Department. So calm and serious. *Our rangers are experienced men,* Mr. Meechem wrote, *imbued with the spirit of going out to accomplish the task assigned to them. We are nearly always successful in this work.*

Now the house was awash with people. Women from the Auxiliary, Mrs. Deegan (shrunken, asthmatic widow of Father's partner), the new pastor, and a procession of well-intentioned others. Mother reported what facts she and Charles had culled from the crossfire of messages and laid out in a semblance of order. Though I'd have thought just the opposite, with each recital her voice sounded less frayed—as if familiarity made it tolerable, as if knowing exactly where they'd been and just what they'd done there made up for not knowing where they were at this moment.

As James wrote, the train had arrived on time. He and Galen had stepped off at Glacier Park Station and crossed to the hotel. This was a mammoth log edifice, dozens of rooms around a three-story lobby, buttressed by 800-year-old Douglas firs. A good bit fancier (more expensive!) than they'd expected. And the guests, the ones they could see socializing downstairs, were city-dressed, weary-looking businessmen and their wives.

Though it'd rained earlier, now the sky was streaked and broken. Their room had a view of Mount Henry. Galen: *James says he has never been this happy.*

In the morning they rode one of the red, open-topped buses thirty miles north to St. Mary, switched to a motor launch and made the last ten miles to Going-to-the-Sun chalets. Galen carried a brown government map (the same one tacked to the corkboard by his bed all summer—now Mother and I had only the sketchier map on a pamphlet the railroad put out). This was the afternoon they hiked the lower slopes of Goat Mountain. The waitresses that night were dressed like Swiss milkmaids.

The following morning they joined a guide and a train of horses and rode twenty or so miles over Piegan Pass to the hotel at Many Glacier. Though even James wasn't used to riding anymore, it seemed this was the way to see the Park. For long stretches it was quiet, except for the breathing of the horses, the shifting of the tack. The wind blowing down off the lower reach of Grinnell Glacier was cool and scented. Both boys were stiff that night but slept easily.

Wednesday they hiked seven miles in to Cracker Lake, fished, and returned to Many Glacier. It'd rained every day so far, then cleared. Where the trails were low-lying and ran through forest, they were full of mud. Today it didn't clear. They wore slickers and fished in the rain awhile, then circled the lake to where the horse parties stopped, and had lunch. *Tea, bread, bacon, Julienne vegetables.* On the way back, Galen tried again; in five minutes he'd caught a trout of about ten inches, but after that there were no more strikes.

Thursday and Friday the weather moderated. Iceberg

Lake one day, Josephine and Grinnell Lakes the next. The fishing picked up. They took Kodaks of each other, James on one knee blowing on wet kindling, Galen perched on a chunk of dark rock, round-shouldered, staring off with what James called his Percy Bysshe Shelley look.

Saturday they left Many Glacier for Granite Park chalet. It was longer than they'd hiked so far. But now they weren't sore anymore. Their packs were light and they didn't have any blisters. The suitcases had already been checked at the hotel and would be waiting for them at Glacier Park Station a week later.

(Those bags—brand-new matching Republics with their initials. My contribution, six dollars a week out of my check until December . . .)

Well, James and Galen came off Swiftcurrent Pass mid-afternoon—in terrific spirits, whooping and breaking into a run. (I didn't know this for a fact, of course . . . but wasn't the trail all downhill from the pass to the huge stone chalet, wouldn't the sight of it all be enough to take even James out of himself?) They got in before six, had trout and potatoes in the dining room, then sat outside until it was nearly dark. Galen fell to talking with a couple from Brooklyn, New York, an importer named Taussig, and the woman's sister, Celeste. Galen took to her right away, a slender, jaunty girl my age, who rolled her own cigarettes in dark papers that smelled of licorice. Galen talked a streak. He ticked off their entire itinerary, told her about school, about watching Dazzy Vance pitch against the Braves in Boston that May, told her he had a sister named Lillian who was a model—poor Galen, the closest I'd come was demonstrating Hoovers in an appliance show. When he'd stop, she'd lean in and touch his wrist and he'd go on, breathless. (I can see him, in over his head.) James had to come downstairs twice to remind him they had their longest hike the next day. Finally, Galen said good night and followed his brother upstairs. (We didn't know this either, the part about Celeste. All Charles and Mother and I knew of that night was that they'd signed the chalet register, that they'd booked a room for the following night at Lewis's Hotel, down at the base of the mountain, on Lake McDonald. And that they'd never checked in.)

At twilight our train left the Indian reservation and pulled into Glacier Park Station. It was a long boisterous stop, with much movement of luggage and people milling in the aisle. We would continue on to Belton on the west side, where the headquarters was. But this was where James and Galen had gotten off and taken their room at the hotel, where they'd written us. All afternoon I'd studied the mountains, first a smudge along the horizon, then a fine band of gray-blue that seemed not to grow for hours. I thought of Galen sitting here where I was sitting, his eagerness spilling over, James at his shoulder, steady, soaking it up.

Lights were coming on. Charles leaned close and asked wouldn't I like to get out and get some air?

No. All day staring ahead and now I hated to leave the train. The mountains felt immense and ominous. Their shadows buried all the buildings and reached past us into the plains. I couldn't bear to see myself standing down on the apron gawking like the others.

"You go," I told Charles, but he took my hand and stayed.

It was sometime after nine, thoroughly dark and clouded over, with a blustery wind, by the time we reached Belton. The chalet stood on a rise across the way, festooned with antlers. Charles saw to the bags, then draped his jacket over my shoulders as we walked.

"Are you going to be all right, Lillian?" he asked me in a gentling voice.

Don't worry about me, I wanted to say, but I only hugged against him and kept walking.

The boy at the front desk was Galen's age, though heftier, with tiny, insolent eyes and a voice not even Charles could hurry.

"It was Mr. Meechem himself that made these arrangements," Charles said. "As I understand it."

The clerk blinked at us. "Oh right," he said. "It's about those boys."

Charles wouldn't let him say another word. We registered and moments later Charles had dropped me off at my room and gone to his, after which, he said, he intended to see about the telephone.

The room was freezing. I could still feel the clerk's eyes running up and down me . . . *sister of those lost boys.* I felt so stranded I could hardly get a hold of myself. Down below, the station lights went out, leaving only a single hooded lamp at either end. Beyond the station, night loomed, burying a wilderness of ledges and careening water. Lord, how could I chase the morbid thoughts from my mind?

I crossed the hall to Number Twelve and knocked lightly. I needed him to say he wouldn't have dragged us here if he didn't think there was *every reason for hope,* which is how he'd put it back in Chicago. I needed him to say *Go to sleep now, Lillian,* I needed to feel his heart thudding against my cheek. But it seemed he'd already gone to make his call.

 3

Mr. Meechem glanced up from the map, distracted for a moment from describing the searches. He was a tall man in a brown uniform, forty or thereabouts, with tipped, cowled eyes. *Gaunt,* Mother'd say if she saw him, her word for how Father became, so sallow and sick-looking. She couldn't trust men who weren't full of face and prosperous through the midsection, men like Charles. Yet you couldn't distrust Mr. Meechem's face. It looked only sleepless and troubled—didn't I look the same myself?

"Miss Wallace, Mr. Wicks," he said, "I want you to know . . ."

Charles jumped in, "The family realizes you're doing everything possible." But the way his voice slid off you'd think he meant otherwise.

Mr. Meechem frowned. A deep groove materialized between his eyebrows.

He'd spent a half-hour patiently running down the parties and who led them, locating each with the tip of his pencil: Sun Camp to Sperry Glacier, Lewis Hotel to Sperry Glacier,

176 / David Long

Avalanche Basin and up its headwalls, Snyder Creek Basin, Mineral and Camas Creeks, up the old trail to Logan Pass, the whole area at the north end of McDonald Lake and up McDonald Creek toward Granite Park. The other chalets and hotels and camps had long since been contacted, the guests interviewed. By now that notion we'd held to at first, about them simply altering their plans, had fallen to pieces and blown away.

"It pains me terribly," Mr. Meechem said, "but the truth is we haven't turned up so much as a collar button."

Charles straightened and started telling him what The Carthage Company was willing to offer in terms of financial backing. Mr. Meechem took this in, nodding, then explained how since this was a federal preserve, they weren't in a position to accept private money.

"But it's not only that," he went on, "we're just not speaking of expense at this point, Mr. Wicks. I could send a hundred more men out, beyond what's already there, and it would still be, well, largely a matter of luck. I'm not sure you fully appreciate the kind of terrain . . ."

He broke off with Charles and looked at me, working up a fraction of a smile.

"No, about all we can do, at this point, is to figure out what they were *thinking.*"

Charles nodded and sat back down.

Now Mr. Meechem opened the file on his desk and picked out a telegram and held it at the tips of his fingers but didn't look at it.

"They stayed overnight Saturday at Granite and left there, but didn't ever check in at Lewis's, we knew that much. Since then, we found a man who works for Mr. Lewis—he was deadheading a string of horses up that trail, and says he remembers passing a couple of boys about their ages. One of them—he doesn't remember which—said he wished the man was going the other way with the horses . . . that was about eleven, eleven-thirty.

"And now just this morning I've had another wire from Mrs. Wallace. Apparently two men from Chicago called after seeing the piece in your paper out there. They didn't know the boys, but they were also guests at Granite Park the night of the twenty-third, and remembered talking with the Wallaces. What they recalled them saying was that they were headed down for Lewis's right away. This was about eight o'clock, which jibes with what the man from Lewis's said, and of course that's what it says on their itinerary."

Now he slipped Charles the telegram, then went on, "Which I guess brings us to what you were telling me on the phone last evening, Mr. Wicks."

"Charles?" I said.

And so here it came out that Charles had called James and Galen "romancers." He'd told Mr. Meechem all sorts of things: how they'd pored over the railroad's flyers for the Park *(See the Switzerland of America!),* how they'd carried along a rope they planned on using to lower themselves down precipices. *(Precipices? James and Galen?)* He said that back in Chicago they'd bragged about climbing in to a lake that wasn't named, somewhere in the vicinity of Granite Park, and naming it after themselves.

Of course, I stared at Charles, stunned.

"Lillian . . ." Charles started in on me.

None of that's true, I said with my eyes.

"First of all, the rope, Lillian," Charles said.

"That was her doing, Mother's," I said. "They took it to humor her because neither of them can swim. She made Galen promise they'd only fish one at a time and only with the rope tied around their middle."

"Lillian, for pity's sake," Charles said. "I'm not making this up."

"You make them sound like, I don't know . . . wild men," I said.

Charles snugged his lips, so disappointed in me.

"Miss Wallace," the superintendent said, "I know how terribly difficult . . . let me try saying this another way—the way it looks now, what's become of your brothers pretty much depends on who they are."

Charles was adamant about seeing the trail. Mr. Meechem said he'd made arrangements. He drove us in his own Ford, from Belton along Lake McDonald to Lewis's Hotel where we'd have lunch and switch to horses.

The road was full of ruts and washouts and soft places where the wheel wanted to jerk in his hands. It fell back from the lake at times, cutting into stands of cedar. The clouds broke overhead, splattering sun into this dense, quiet stretch of forest. I would've liked to tap Mr. Meechem on the shoulder and ask him to stop—I could almost picture myself walking a little ways off into that mossy, mysterious light. Under happier circumstances. Now and then Mr. Meechem turned sideways and said something to Charles, and Charles shook his head thoughtfully, but didn't turn to repeat it for me.

Then we were at Lewis's.

Well, I thought it would feel momentous and sad—twenty years of chasing James and Galen, and here I'd reached a place before them. I should've been overcome, leaning on Charles for support. But it seemed a perfectly ordinary day at Lewis's. I watched a workman sawing fence posts at the edge of the drive. Horses sidled at their tie-ups, rope slapped loosely against the flagpole. Inside, there were more introductions, lunch to eat, a thick stew with cornbread and huckleberry preserve. There was talk to make across the table. (*Thank you, yes, the Pullman was quite comfortable . . .*) I watched Charles lift the cornbread to his mouth without it crumbling. He caught my eye and fashioned a courteous smile, which I returned. But inside I was wondering if my head still felt all right, if there was any of the squeezing and trembling that came to tease me before the headache. Too much time had sifted by already, too many days of respite. But I glanced around the table at Charles, at the other men, everybody chewing and nodding and staying off the heart of the subject, and I thought, *Lillian, don't, not at a time like this.* Suddenly I knew that as soon as we finished eating, Charles would take me aside and try to talk me out of riding up the trail with the others. He'd say, "Lillian, you've been through so much, I'm sure Mr. Meechem will understand . . ." when that wasn't what he meant at all. So I excused myself right then and went to change into my pants.

There were five in our party as we left the hotel: a burly ranger named Waddley (Waddell?) in front, then Mr. Meechem, Charles, me, and a man from Lewis's in the rear with a rifle tucked into his saddlebag. The first miles we were on the road still, scarcely climbing at all. The creek lay to our left, low and riffled in its banks, with the mountains poking straight up on both sides, great bare walls of rock. Granite Park was too far to make today, some twenty miles, but Charles had insisted on getting the feel of the place. He rode upright, scanning solemnly. Now and then he craned around to see how I was managing, then looked away. My horse clicked along like a sleepwalker, oblivious of my hands on her reins. I felt as much in a dream myself. (I couldn't see any of what I was seeing without hearing myself pass it on to Mother. *The bottom part is certainly well-enough traveled, and even after the road leaves off the trail is wide enough for a horse to gallop . . . though of course we rode quite slowly.*)

Finally, at a spot where the trail cut high above the creek, which had narrowed to a gorge, Mr. Meechem halted us and announced this was where we'd turn around. He seemed almost shy now, apologetic.

"Well, now you can see it," he said. "You can see how it makes all the difference whether they stayed on the trail."

Charles nodded, but his eyes seemed crimped and jittery. We all just looked out, thinking our thoughts.

Finally Mr. Meechem started in again, "From all I can gather, these boys appear to be quite . . . well, methodical, Mr. Wicks—they stuck right to their itinerary. You know, a lot of the people—most of them—they come up here and don't even *have* an itinerary. They just . . . we get a number of people who do have some misguided notions, Mr. Wicks. But frankly, these Wallace boys seem so cautious, so mindful . . . and then, too, twenty miles is a stiff hike for city boys, even downhill. You wouldn't think so, Mr. Wicks, but a lot of people find downhill takes more out of them . . . so I don't see that they would've gone to the extra exertion of making any side trips, *on purpose* is what I'm saying. Maybe other days, but not that particular day, you see? Not to dispute what you were telling me, Mr. Wicks."

I'd never seen Charles so at a loss, so out of his element. He worked the flat of his hand on the pommel, staring off.

Mr. Meechem watched him a while before speaking again. "I can see where a person would want something named after him, Mr. Wicks. I understand that completely. But I can't think of any lakes that aren't named. There are a couple of small bodies, not even lakes really, over by Snyder Creek, but that's over on the other side of Mt. Brown, and a search party's been through there already, in fact, several times."

Now he reined his horse around and faced me.

"I want you to know how sincerely mystified I am. I just don't have a thing to go on."

The other ranger and the man from Lewis's had drifted up the trail a bit, and now Charles broke off from us and trotted their direction.

"If it was *one* of them, of course," Mr. Meechem said, quieter, just to me. "It wouldn't be nearly so hard to see if it was one of them. I try to understand how they'd both fall into the same ravine, or off the same cliff . . . I can only see that they'd be one behind the other, not side by side. Now they could've climbed down by the creek, that's entirely possible—it's awfully slick by the falls, and I can see where one of them might've lost his footing . . ."

"Galen," I said, though I hadn't meant to say it out loud.

Mr. Meechem studied me. "I believe I heard you to say that neither of them could swim, but you see in creek water like this, Miss Wallace, it doesn't matter a great deal how well a person can swim. It's terribly cold and fast."

Either would have jumped for the other, though . . .

"But then," he said, "we've had good men and dogs up and down both sides, all the way to the lake. I'm not at all convinced that's the answer."

My horse twitched away and Mr. Meechem reached a hand out and caught her mane and she dropped her head immediately.

"There's also . . . you'll understand how reluctant I am to express all this to your mother, Miss Wallace, but there is the question of bears. It's not uncommon to come across a grizzly in this part of the Park, and they're a fearsome creature, you can rest assured of that. Unimaginable power, Miss Wallace, five or six hundred pounds most of them, and they tear through terrain like this at a gallop. But then, I've had no reports of anyone sighting grizzlies anywhere near this trail that particular day, or that week even . . . I'm not saying it didn't happen, but here again, you see, I have trouble imagining both of your brothers being attacked and leaving no trace."

Up the trail, Charles's hand darted against the gray tumbling slope across the valley, pointing, scooping circles in the air. The ranger and the man from Lewis's sat back in their saddles, half-looking.

"I hate to ask, Miss Wallace," Mr. Meechem said, "but is there anything else you can tell me?"

If Mother were here she'd fill his ears! But really, I couldn't imagine her here, so far torn from home, entertaining so grim a picture as James and Galen clawed and dragged off as carrion. I didn't know how I should endure it, either— *me!* Yet I found I was able to keep away that sick and drowning feeling long enough to think. In fact, it seemed that ever since we'd come to this promontory, I'd felt only patient, cut off from time and harm. It was as acute a feeling as any I'd ever waked to and savored after a headache . . . and it seemed to quicken with Charles at a little distance. I heard the water breaking through the gorge, the air bristling through the firs, the long snuffling breaths of the horses. Back in Chicago when she'd want to know so much from me, I'd beg myself to say if I felt any presence of them (whatever it was worth to believe in such an intuition) but I'd have to say *No.* I felt nothing of them on that trail, not even their absence. The only presence I felt was my own—and not the one I always was, but another that seemed as if it might expand into the great broken distance looming around me. . . .

"Miss Wallace . . ."

"I'm sorry," I said. "I don't know what they did. I don't even know why they came here."

It was just a holiday, I was going to say that, too—what did it mean, though, a holiday, a vacation? Such weightless words. I couldn't look at all I was looking at now and not think some craving brought them here, even if I'd never know what it was . . . even if they never knew.

"I'm sure your mother's a devout woman," Mr. Meechem said suddenly. "As devout as mine is."

He seemed poised to go on, to divulge something from his own life, but he went no further. He shook his head. "I'd give anything to know what happened here," he said.

 4

A week after Charles and I set out for home, Mr. Meechem called back the search parties. He left four men out after that, then two, professional hunters. Indian summer came. He promised they'd stay out as long as the weather held, scouring the slopes below the chalet. Telegrams and letters flew back and forth, Mother's begging for some detail to be rechecked, Mr. Meechem's more delicate and fatherly than ever. But there was nothing to report. Mother and I returned to work. For a few hours each day we were spared each other's company.

In the meantime, Charles and the company lawyers had contacted the Great Northern offices in St. Paul, and Mr. Louis Hill himself had offered a thousand dollars reward for news of James and Galen. (In addition, he had sent Mother and me each a pass good for unlimited travel on his railroad. A token of good faith, in his words. Mother studied hers sadly. I dropped mine in my purse and didn't give it another thought.) The membership of the First Congregational Church pitched in six hundred, and Mother's employer, Mr. Atwood Sr., added a final hundred. Seventeen hundred dollars in all.

Now Mother set about having a poster printed.

I can't name the moment, but sometime during that dark,

tense month of October, she stopped believing they'd fallen or drowned or been mauled. Thereafter, the only solution she'd abide rested on what she called *foul play*. On the last day of the month, she received a small packet from Mr. Meechem containing the only items any of the searchers had found: a silver pencil, a tortoiseshell pocket comb, and a strip of silky material that appeared to be the lining from a hat. The next day she wrote back: *I am in receipt of the articles you sent me, none of which belongs to my sons, and I am returning them under separate cover. They may belong to the murderers or the kidnappers.*

At first when I got home, she pressed me constantly, saying I'd been her eyes, her ears—as if it had been *her* idea to send me. But right away she grew impatient, only keen for items out of line with what the government had told her. She might as well have come out and said, *Lillian, what are they hiding from me!* She stopped wanting to know how brutal the landscape seemed and focused instead on the roughness of the people. Not the guests so much—she was persuaded they were other Easterners and Midwesterners on vacation, people of a like character and class as James and Galen. No, the ones who worked thereabouts—she'd learned that crews of men were blasting a road through the middle of the Park. She'd heard that some of these men were foreign, Russians in particular. Then one evening Charles told her how bootleggers and smugglers of opium and who-knows-what-else trafficked through Belton.

Oh yes, she said, she'd suspected as much.

"Why did you *tell* her such a thing?" I complained to him once Mother had excused herself for the night.

"Because," Charles said, "it's true."

We were still at the kitchen table—bright and close as it was, it seemed the only place we could bear to sit and talk. Charles had come straight from work, as take-charge as ever, but now it was half-past ten. His shoulders were angled like a coat hanger and the charm had seeped from his voice.

"No one else tells her these things," he said. "You don't think the Park's going to advertise how unsavory it is. That close to the Canadian border? Not for a minute."

"I wish . . ." What *did* I wish? That I wouldn't be the last to see what people like Charles saw right away. Really, I was weary of it.

"Lily?"

"Is that what you think happened?"

He leaned and took my hand across the table, wrapped it in both of his.

"Lillian, all I'm saying is, that's a very rough area. A place like that *breeds* . . ."

"No, but Charles, what do you think actually . . ."

He gave a tired smile, then looked at our hands for a while and didn't answer.

Finally I slid over and kissed him, a little dried flower of a kiss.

"Thank God, nothing's happened to you," he said in a minute, touching the skin on the back of my neck, stroking it as if it were a china cup.

"Nothing has," I said.

His eyes closed. "You don't know," he said. "I had such plans for your brother." I touched his mouth and he didn't go on. In a moment we heard Mother creaking down the hall above us, turning into her room. Then the house was still.

The next day, Mother began to talk about James and Galen being abducted to work in the mines. Uncle Malcolm had long since come and driven Viola back to Racine. Mother'd never succumb to calling her—long-distance was extravagant and desperate in her view, even now—but Viola called every second night or so, while supper was on the stove.

The ringing jolted her.

She drew off her glasses, let them drop to the front of her sweater. She stared toward the archway—as if it would be that strange hour, not day and not night, when, somehow, *they* would call.

I'd have to fly in to the telephone table and put a stop to it. "Lillian," Viola'd say. "You put your mother on," and finally Mother would gather herself and come.

It was Aunt Vi she first broached the business of the mines with. Copper, silver, bauxite, weren't there wildcat operations all through those states? Wouldn't skilled engineers such as James and Galen . . . ? Of course, Viola encouraged her—there was no limit to the treachery in men's hearts, after all. Mother got off the phone bristling with Viola's insights, and stayed that way through supper, but later when we were simply alone in the house together, nothing to do but get our clothes ready for the A.M., she kept looking to me to bolster this mood, but I couldn't work myself up like Viola. I tried picturing how such a kidnapping would happen—part by part, the way Mr. Meechem saw the two of them coming upon a crevice. It was possible to imagine Galen carrying on about their talents, back at one of the hotels where he might be overheard by the wrong party, but after that it broke down. Even Mother had trouble finding a purchase on this notion, and after a few days she let it go, settling for a less exacting theory: that they'd reached the road above Lewis's and been taken outside the Park in an automobile. For what purpose, she couldn't say.

On the tenth of November the posters arrived from the printers. This was Mother's thirty-first wedding anniversary, as it happened, though it was days later I remembered. I wouldn't have remembered at all except that at work an older man had stopped in to buy a traveling case for his wife and had wanted it monogrammed. I happened to say, "Oh, FMW, same as my mother's," and got to thinking, once he'd left, about the initials James had woodburned into the top of Mother's thread box . . . then about how good James was about presents and dates. Still, not remembering spared me wondering if I should mention it or not.

Anyway, the posters: I think, if there'd been money enough, she'd have sent one to every sheriff and every post office in the country. As it was, she confined herself to the Northwest states, also Alberta, British Columbia, and California as far south as Sacramento. Fifteen hundred posters in all, two heavy bundles wrapped in brown paper and string.

That night, Friday, sixteen of us convened in one end of the church basement, Mother's friends from the Auxiliary for

the most part. I was youngest by thirty years, except that Mrs.
Tiebloom had brought her daughter, a retarded girl named
Leah, who was Galen's age. There was an urn of coffee, as
always, and Mrs. Androes had baked a plate of tiny me-
ringues, but no one would walk over and take the first one.
Mother sat under the best light, addressing envelopes long-
hand, flanked by two other widows. It was such a clamorsome
place ordinarily, scene of endless receptions and potlucks, but
the talk was close tonight, ranging not much farther afield
than the business of folding and stuffing. They'd all called on
us that first week, one or two at a time, bracing Mother with
brave encouragements, and she'd let them. Hadn't she been
to their houses on like errands? But after two months, with
nothing new to report, you could hear how no one knew what
tack to take.

I'd ended up alone at a table with Leah. With a huge
attentiveness, she separated the stamps from their sheets and
stacked them in piles of ten, humming a hymn I couldn't think
of the name of. Neither of us spoke. Every couple of minutes
I looked past her toward the stairwell—Adelaide had given
her word she'd come and help (or at least keep me company!),
but she hadn't appeared at our house earlier and Mother
refused to wait. After a while I gave up. I listened to the
ripping of the stamps, the straining of the folding chairs. I kept
working my stack of posters down, watching James and Galen
disappear again and again between the creases. The job took
longer than we'd imagined, but no one left until it was done.
Fifteen hundred envelopes in a canvas sack. Charles would
come by with the car in the morning and haul them to the post
office. I found myself almost believing it was work that
needed doing.

Mrs. Tiebloom gathered up her daughter and said good
night to us on the steps, and the two of them headed off under
the streetlights, Leah hugging her arms and swaying, humming still.

"Your friend never came," Mother said as we walked.

"No," I said, almost adding, *She must've gotten a better offer.*

We went on quietly, Mother no doubt reflecting on the
constancy of *her* friends.

Adelaide would call in the morning, I felt sure. But she didn't. Nor Sunday night when we usually commiserated about work. Then, Monday afternoon at Field's, I saw her next-youngest sister, Annabelle, make her way into the luggage room. She was an intense, frizzy-haired girl, given to long furtive silences. Now she came as if on a mission. She thrust a note into my hand and darted off. Inside were a few lines of Adelaide's slapdash scrawl:

> *Have done the terrible deed! Don't say a word. Wish us all the luck. A.*

Four weeks, five weeks. Mother would get that look and ask if I believed we ought to have more posters printed. *Please don't ask me these things,* I'd wish, *I don't know any better than you.* But finally I'd say, "I think we've sent enough."

"I know you do, Lillian," she'd say, the flutter of her head, the sigh expelled into her curled fingers telling me how different in kind it was for a mother.

"If I thought for a single minute . . ." she'd go on—but how could she admit she was afraid for our resources, that a line had to be drawn somewhere?

The second week of December the postmistress in Sisters, Oregon, wrote Mother to say she'd displayed the poster in a prominent spot beside her window and that everyone who came in paused and looked at the boys' pictures with great interest. Her heart went out to Mother, she said, and she prayed for a merciful outcome.

"Well, Lillian . . ." Mother said, as if to say: *You see, you see? Our messages are striking home!* And right away she retired to Father's immense roll-top desk and wrote a reply to the woman, which ran to several pages.

In the next day's mail came another such note, from Jordan, Montana, and a third from Cougar, Washington, signed Miss Amanda Robbins. Mother read them, solemn and excited, both. Investing faith in the posters was only what a wise woman would do, this first trickle of mail said. Nothing desperate at all. She could shut her eyes to all other notions of what'd happened to the boys (Mr. Meechem's most of all).

What a surprise and a comfort to glimpse this web of attentive, Christian women in far-flung outposts.

I said I'd write the thank-you to Miss Robbins and you could see Mother balk at farming it out—wasn't it her duty, and there were just the three to do. . . . But I went ahead and wrote it before she could speak up, and when it was done I took the atlas down (already it fell open limp to the double-page map of Montana) and looked up Cougar in the privacy of my bedroom. It was as far from that trail over Lewis's as Niagara Falls was from here! A tiny place, on a black squiggle of a river. *What hope in the world was there that any spark of news would land in Cougar, let alone James and Galen themselves?* But instead of following this thought, which God knows I should've done, there I was imagining myself opening a little post office in the morning, firing up the stove, handling my allotment of mail, fitting the letters into their slots. Maybe I'd have an apartment in the back, maybe a pair of spotted horses to watch from the window, and beyond them the river choked with logs. . . .

What can be said of the dreary holidays that followed? The gritty, wind-driven snow tearing at us on our way down the street to church, the furious radiators in the early-morning dark. Mother resisted Aunt Vi's offer to have us up to Racine —it was bad enough we should leave the house unattended while we were at work each day. An argument ensued between the sisters (as much of one as you'd ever hear). Mother stood squinting into the shadows of the front room. Aunt Vi railed in the earpiece. "I don't imagine . . ." Mother said. "Sister, I . . ." Why couldn't it have been Viola who went East and never came back, not Mae? *She'd* have lent us some reckless cheer, at least. But that's the way, isn't it? Mother finally agreed that Viola and Uncle Malcolm should drive down the Saturday after Christmas. Friday evening Mother rallied to make a fruitcake (awful, sweet thing!), and while that baked, we changed the bedclothes (though Viola'd been the last to sleep in them), ran the Hoover, and otherwise tried to make the house presentable.

One by one I snapped dead leaves off the aspidistra, but

couldn't decide where to stop, and pretty soon had a bare spindle of a stalk with a few leaves dangling at the top. Nothing looked very good in the front room anymore. I'd done pretty well at not remembering Christmases past—you can keep things from speaking to you, you can put your mind elsewhere, that's one thing I'd begun to know. But the room had a taxidermied look. The antimacassars seemed shriveled and brittle, the draperies—if I so much as brushed by they'd rain down motes of dead air.

"*Lillian . . .*" she was calling. Why hadn't I smelled the burning cherries?

"Oh, maybe it's not so bad," she said, prying at the tin. "Maybe, don't you think we can dust it with sugar . . . ?"

But it didn't matter. A fresh storm swept through in the night and Uncle Malcolm refused to make the drive.

Thank heavens, I thought. The snow eased off by early afternoon, but the day stayed heavy and cold. Mother couldn't get settled into anything to do. She'd never admit to being relieved about her sister, but Aunt Vi would've only gotten Mother farther off into God's perspective on our trouble, and the last thing she needed was another theory to stand against her own.

What I said earlier was true: she begrudged every minute away from the house. But I had to get outdoors!

"Going to Sullivan's," I shouted, already dressed, not waiting for an answer. But once I was on the street I walked straight past the grocery with no more than a glance at its steamed windows. I walked uptown along the park, and soon I was standing on the drifted sidewalk opposite Adelaide's old apartment. Since that one scribbled message I'd not heard a word from her. The other three sisters still lived at home. Lights were scattered around the building, even Christmas candles burning in a few windows, but theirs were dark. Annabelle would have a room to herself now, it occurred to me. I wouldn't have gone up anyway, I guessed. Maybe I wouldn't ever again.

I crossed at the next corner and moved closer to the storefronts where the wind had swirled a hollow. I thought

of Adelaide sequestered in a room with Eddie Stovall. I had
no idea where—wherever it was, it was the only place she'd
ever craved to be. I remembered how angry she'd gotten at
being denied. It had begun to ruin her. Nothing mattered but
dropping off the deep end with Eddie. I caught myself trying
to imagine them in that room, Adelaide's boyish little body
all taken up with his. I tried to hear the promises they'd give
each other when no one was around to say they were foolish.
But I felt squirmy picturing such things. It was life with
Charles I ought to have been imagining . . . it wouldn't take
place in a room with a bare bulb hanging over a hodgepodge
of sheets, that much I could see. There would be music,
children . . .

It was colder now. No one was on the streets. I walked
a while longer, fighting the wind off the lake. Then I stopped,
in the middle of the block. The stores were closed. Ahead, the
buildings of the Loop made a ragged blot against the bottom
of the sky. I wiped at my eyes. Suddenly this seemed a terribly
pointless expedition.

"Charles called," Mother said, soon as I'd peeled the scarf
from my face.
"Is he coming over?"
"I'm afraid he wants to take us out."
"Tonight? I hope you said yes . . ."
"You go," she said.
It was no trouble picturing the solitary evening she'd
already mapped for herself. I'd be ten minutes out the door
and some innocent errand would take her back to Galen's
room (there was a perennial disturbance in the spread where
she gave in and sat and stared at his radiator). "No, please,"
I said. "I'm sure he wants both of us, I'm sure that's how he
wanted it."
"I couldn't possibly . . ." she started in, but couldn't find
a reason she'd care to offer aloud. She frowned at me stub-
bornly. Wasn't it just evident? Why on earth should she have
to explain these things to her only daughter?
But then—heaven knows it was nothing *I* said—she

straightened and touched a hand to her hair and said, "Well, if that's what Charles wants." So that night we dressed up and allowed Charles to squire us downtown.

The Aberdeen was legendary for its roast beef, carved at the table from a linened cart, but Mother ordered white fish in a cream sauce, forking apart each bite to check for bones. Charles would favor the Aberdeen for an occasion such as this —it was old and spacious, with a soft glitter of lamplight and cut glass. The waiters wafted among the tables like spirits. A ten-piece band entertained from a riser surrounded by poinsettias, the only sign of the holidays.

Charles seemed to shine here. Now and then a horn player stood and took a few bars of solo. Charles lifted his chin, looking off with a rapt smile. He'd as much as declared the evening a breather, a few hours of timeless time. How I wanted to share his mood. Driving here, three in the front, we'd followed the same route I'd walked that afternoon: what a sudden lift I'd felt as we rolled past the block where I'd stopped and turned for home. I'd taken it as a favorable omen. I knew I didn't have much talent for evenings on the town, but Charles was so absolutely at ease, especially tonight, I managed to believe I'd do all right.

If Mother drifted for long, he drew her back. At home I couldn't come up with any safe subjects, nothing not already drenched in our lives—let alone say it so cheerfully . . . I'd still hear James chiding Galen and me for our moods. . . . *Cheerfulness is one of our unshakable functions,* he'd quote some English writer.

When dinner was over Charles asked Mother if she wouldn't like to dance. It seemed the last thing she'd agree to, but there she was thanking him, rising from her chair with only the slightest constriction of her lips. Charles came and squeezed my shoulder and apologized for abandoning me.

"Don't go anywhere," he said.

"No," I whispered. "Of course not."

But soon as I'd lost them in the swirl of dancers, I did feel marooned. I urged myself not to be a ninny. I sipped at trying to imagine I belonged here, trying to put on the look James would've worn. Carts of fruit and torts hummed by. The band played "You're So Grand." Everyone was happy.

Suddenly I stood and plunged off toward the ladies' room, two skinny, glaring enclosures full of smoke. The mirrors were lined with smart-looking women, rippled waves, cloche helmets, round cool faces. I felt as though I'd stood frozen on that exact spot before, equally out of my depth, then I remembered that dressing room on the Oriental Limited, which had been packed like this, day and night. These were the women who'd boarded in the cities, the ones who adorned the club car, their backs to the windows, as if the prairie outside were as void as the space between stops on an elevator. How much happier they'd seemed in the dressing room, where the windows were frosted, where the jiggling of the floor was cause for great amusement.

Suddenly I was back in that blowing space between the Belton station and the chalet, with Charles's coat lying heavily across my back and his arm circling my waist, hearing the firs grate on each other in the dark beyond the floodlights. And there was Charles whispering gravely, *I know you're tired, Lillian, you can rest in a little while,* when it was only confinement I needed to be quit of—that and not knowing anything. Upstairs in bed, hours later, I was still cold. The wind strained at the eaves. I heard the window sash bucking in its frame, but no other sound anywhere in the building—most of all that impossibility I'd worked myself up to hear: the rasping latches of two doors, his across the hall, then mine (of course mine was locked). Instead there was the desk clerk's lifeless voice *. . . here about those lost boys, sister of those lost boys.* As if that were all one would need to know about me.

There was a commotion in back now, the slap of a stall door, the sound of a choked-off cry.

Everyone went still at once. For a moment all we heard was the band's drummer, a dull syncopation beating through the walls. Then came a burst of retching. *Dear Gawd,* so one said. Then a little sputter of laughter. A raspy behind me snapped, *What a waste of good booze.*

laughter, then the conversation was back at full strength. Water was running, people clattered through their bags. The girl was still being sick in the background. Now a moment of fierce dizziness spun through me, as if it were me with my knees down on the tiles, far from home. I couldn't get my breath . . . I grabbed at the shoulder next to me, a shelf of cool satin. The woman started and jerked back as if I'd reached for her throat. Before she could find her voice I snatched my hand away and pushed out through the double set of doors and flew back toward the ballroom.

Charles had just seated Mother and was still on his feet, eyeing the tables to see what had become of me.

I was sure Mother was about to say how Charles had done his duty to an old lady, but I didn't wait to hear it, and tugged him straightaway to the dance floor. I kicked off my pumps and pressed against him until I felt my heart settle. His cheeks still smelled of witch hazel. His lips were beside my ear, but for a long time he only hummed, or whispered how much he enjoyed dancing with me.

Finally he pulled back to look me in the eyes, and I thought he'd say it was already time to go back and keep Mother company.

Instead he smiled, almost forgetting to move his feet.

"I think it's time we were married," he said.

The first instant I thought, *Oh God, yes, right away, just as soon . . .* but this had scarcely blossomed when I imagined abandoning Mother to that house —*impossible.* Where did he have in mind for us to live? For years he'd stayed in an apartment at his club, which naturally I'd never so much as laid eyes on. So I had yet to say anything when he went on, "I thought maybe in the spring. How would the end of May seem?"

The Grand Hotel, I thought. *Whitecaps on Lake Huron, the endless white porch . . .*

"Oh, Charles," I said. "I don't see how. With Mother . . ."

But he knew what I'd say. "She needs something happier to think about," he answered patiently. "Otherwise, I'm afraid . . ."

He spun me gently.

"Don't you agree?"

I buried my head against his shoulder. *I'd like to,* I thought. But she wouldn't think of anything but them.

The clarinet made a long tumbling run and the song finished. Charles let go and clapped a few times, that shining contentment still lighting his face . . . such a far cry from the last forlorn note hanging in my ears. The bandstand cleared. He turned back to me and whispered, "Your shoes, Lillian," then we were threading our way toward the table where we'd let Mother languish, and in those few moments I thought, *How can I possibly tell her this?* But as soon as I saw her again, saw how she sat watching me approach, I knew I didn't have to say a thing, for they had talked it out between them, dancing, or long before.

The first mail of 1925 brought a letter postmarked Butte, from a man named L. Roy Watson, who'd at one time worked for Pinkerton's and later for the Anaconda Copper Mining Company, as a detective. He was without a job at present and felt sure he could be of use to us. He'd need an advance of four hundred dollars against salary and expenses.

Mother wrote back the same (but politely condensed) version of the story as she'd given the postmistresses and all the others (the coming of the year's end had triggered a rush of curiosity, as many as fourteen cards some days). To Mr. Watson she added, much as she regretted to tell him, the official reward money was all she was in a position to offer. This seemed to put an end to Mr. Watson's interest.

But shortly afterwards we heard from Wm. Turkel of Missoula, Montana.

I have recived from Mr. Meechem of the Glaciar Park the areal map wich I have show it to a man by the name of George More wich he claims to be a trailar and a trapper for abaut 25 yr, he claim that he is able to find some trace of the said brs. dead or a life, if the reward was still in force, he would start out on the job in searching the minute he would get the notice, he wrote, and a great lot more, involving around-the-world help from the Veterans of the Spanish War, of which he was a member of the highest standing.

Mother looked stricken. It was as if she'd turned her back for an instant and found her front room occupied by a pair of men off the street.

"Throw it away," I said. *"Please!"*

And she did, then and there, crumpled it and dropped it in the trash. But later when I bent to dump the potato leavings from supper and thought to pick it out and have another look, it was gone. *What have you done with Mr. Turkel's letter?* I wanted to ask her—but then I didn't want to know.

Next came a letter, not from those towns out West where the posters had gone, but from Michigan. A man named Dickinson claimed the boys were working for the Salvation Army in Grand Rapids.

He'd first seen James the night before Christmas, on a street corner near the mission, leading a group in song, and again this past week inside the mission. On both occasions there'd been a younger man with glasses beside him, clearly under his care. He said James had on the uniform of an officer. And there was (Mr. Dickinson said) a woman, Mrs. Hubbel, a higher-up with another organization, the Volunteers of America, who'd also seen James several times and would swear to the truthfulness of all he said. "The boys looked well and proud of their part, I don't know what the game is but it looks a matter of choice on the face of it."

"What the game is?" Mother said.

Well, this business unraveled in no time. One phone call and the Justice Department sent an agent to Grand Rapids and found Mr. Dickinson mentally unbalanced, in their words, a notorious testifier to conspiracy. So that was that. Still, there were those two days—it was February now, the streets glaring with thaw—when she had to trouble over this story, sifting and weighing the particulars: the singing voice, the uniform (which, want to or not, she couldn't help connecting with his second-lieutenant's uniform from the war), the image of Galen hovering at his side. And which was harder to bear? Imagining them holed up in Grand Rapids—oblivious of her suffering (and mine), for whatever reason she couldn't begin to name—or shutting her eyes on this picture of them, which, false as it was, gave a certain enticing light?

But outside of the letdown, she bore this Mr. Dickinson no ill will. She seemed to have decided that enduring wild tales was an ordained part of getting the boys back. Having the letters just stop (the way *theirs* had), that was the awful thing.

What did she believe then, alone there at the kitchen window, watching bright sheets of water slide off the roofs, hearing icicles work loose and shatter on the cement?

In that time following Father's death, I'd wanted to talk about him with Mother, but she recoiled from the most innocent reference. James had to take me aside finally. *"Lily,"* he said, more stern than I was accustomed to seeing him. "I can't imagine what you're thinking. You're going to have to show her more consideration."

"He's my *father,"* I said, "I can't just pretend . . ."

But yes, I would have to, that was how it was handled in this house. Whatever I had to say, I had to say it to Galen on the q.t. (Oh and Galen was a good listener, better than James, who always assumed I'd come for advice. But it was hard for Galen to see past Father's illness, back to a time when he worked, when his face was full and confident. Sickness terrified Galen. "Rub my feet, won't you?" Father'd ask, for he kept losing the sensation in them. We would oblige, one or the other of us. But you could see Galen shrink from touching him, and of course later he'd nettle himself for this failing. So when I'd have my talks about Father with him, about riding in the Armistice Day parade, or what he'd said about spotting Mother for the first time at the band concert in Sturtevant, Galen listened happily. But sooner or later he'd bring us back to what had become of Father. "Can you inherit that, do you think?" he'd ask. "Is that what's going to happen to me?")

I'd thought it would ease with time, but I was wrong once more. It hadn't yet reached the point where I could even say, "Wouldn't Father have just loved this Katzenjammer?" with any hope she'd let down and say, "Oh yes, wouldn't that have tickled him . . ." or some such. And when I thought of the bigger things, marrying Charles, say, with Father not there to watch and approve, it did seem as though a good bit of the point of doing it had been lost. But by now I'd learned the lesson of letting Father's name lie. So when it came to the boys, I knew not to bother her with the everyday thoughts I had about them. In the forum of the kitchen or the front room, the only times we actually said *James* or *Galen,* we meant the objects of the search, the faces on the flyer. . . .

But truly, what was she thinking that day, posted at the window? *Is it melting where you are, too? Is everything breaking up and running with water?* As if, beyond all else, it was winter that had kidnapped them and insured their silence?

 5

Before long it was cold again. Charles was off to New York on business. He didn't think he'd be back until the end of the month.

Meanwhile, there were other sightings. Reno, Nevada. Susanville, California. Ogden, Utah.

I followed them out of a Kresge's store, the man in Utah wrote . . .

I bluntly addressed them as "Hello Jim and Galen Wallace". The tallest one denied as that was their names—stated his was Henry—it was hard to secure information from the shorter of the two, while not exactly sullen he was quite reticent. I insisted that they allow me to take a Kodak view of them. My rooming house was nearly opposite on the same street. . . . I insisted that they cross the street while I ran in and secured my camera. . . . I subsequently made two views of them outside a theatre. I know you will find the likeness to be striking. Please write me at . . .

The snapshots were stapled to a second sheet stamped with the man's name, and stamped underneath, slightly askew, it read:

Ocean to Ocean Walking Tour
For Health, Not Wealth
To Attain and Impart
Friendship and Good Cheer
To Acquire Knowledge

They were taken from the street, so far back half the marquee showed. A shadow of the man's head lay in the foreground like a pothole. But they were good enough to tell it was just two boys bumming together. Two silly boys, caps and knickers. No relation, anybody could see that.

And so I thought: *All right now, this is the end of it, this is when she comes to realize . . .* but she took them back from me and away they went into the accordion file where no harm could come to them.

When they should have been shredded and tossed out to the wind.

"Mother, I can't bear . . ." I started to say.

"I know, Lillian," she said, hushing me.

She took my hand and smoothed it against the tablecloth. I don't think we'd touched in weeks.

"Brothers are a wonderful thing in nature," she said. "A thing to behold."

How tranquil her voice sounded—it was unnerving. Her glasses hung on their chain. She stared out with dry, stationary eyes, but the skin underneath them had a livid cast.

"People desire to see two brothers, do you understand? Two boys who come from a good home. Who are quite obviously devoted to each other."

"Mother, couldn't we . . . ?"

"It's up to us to forgive people for what they think they see, Lillian." Her fingers rubbed and rubbed, my skin was numb under them. "We have to keep the best possible attitude," she said. "The Lord has His . . ."

She broke this off and gazed into the dark part of the house. "His mysteries," she said.

I felt my entire rib cage tense against what was next—it could be anything in her present frame of mind.

But she only picked up my hand and fanned out the fingers. "You know, you ought to do something about these hands of yours, Lillian," she said. "They look so raw . . . you need cream on them."

Abruptly, she stood and left the kitchen and came back in a minute with the jar of palm oil from her dresser. It was greenish and felt like fat going on.

"You'll be wanting to get down to business on this wedding," she said then.

"Yes, well, Charles was saying . . ."

"Summer is the time you'd want it," she said. "I'd certainly have chosen that myself . . ."

It was well-known that she and Father had been obliged to marry in November—and that the matriarch of Father's family, whose failing health had brought this about, had lived on another two years, long enough to hold the infant James on her lap, however briefly.

"But I should think you'd want to avoid June, wouldn't you?"

"June would be OK," I said.

"It's up to you," she said. "But I should think you'd care to . . . I don't know, wait a bit. You'd want a day you could be certain of, weatherwise. Sometime on toward August. Wouldn't you think?"

Oh, August, I thought. *So close and sticky.*

In a moment I said, "I'd kind of thought we might hold it outside . . ."

"What, the wedding?"

She got to her feet and looked about the kitchen, but there was nothing to put away, so then she just stood, fingering the tatting at her neckline.

"No, I'm sure Charles would want it in the church," she said finally.

"I was hoping maybe Aunt Mae could come," I said.

"Oh, I don't think so," Mother said.

"I could write and ask . . ."

"No," Mother said, "I don't think we should trouble her to come all that way."

I'd already allowed myself the improbable thought of having Mae stand up with me—I'd imagined how much better I'd feel with Charles's weight on one side, Mae's grace and fire on the other.

"Well, maybe if we . . ." I began to offer. But I could see now how it wasn't the money or the distance.

"She won't come," Mother said.

It was quiet in the kitchen after that.

In a while, Mother went on, not looking at me, "And if she were to—I mean, if she were to let us know ahead of time that she intended on coming, then Viola wouldn't be able to come. She'd have to stay up there in Racine and of course she'd feel we'd done this to spite her, don't you see."

I didn't.

"After every kindness she's done for us," Mother said. "Well, I don't know what we'd do."

She sat, heavily. "But, after all, it won't be a problem. . . . Mae won't come here."

Now she fixed me in her sights. "This isn't the kind of world where you can pick and choose among your responsibilities. I know how you've idolized her, but believe me, Lillian, you can't leave people in the lurch and then just . . . expect to run home whenever you want. . . ."

Her voice had gotten as spiteful as Viola's, but the effort exhausted her. She sagged against her arms. "You have no idea the shape your grandmother was in," she said. "It was shameful . . . Mae might just as well have stuck a knife in her."

And so I had that glimmer of what my aunt had chosen and been accountable for all this time, but I couldn't bear to hear a word more, not tonight. I guessed it would catch up with me soon enough.

Then came the letter from Mr. Jules Harvey.

I do not, by any means, wish to create any false impressions, he wrote. *But I am greatly interested in this case. You may be certain, Mrs. Wallace, that I am a God-fearing Christian man.*

It was typed on sheets of thin letter paper and contained no overstrikes:

I have been doing some scientific research with an instrument that will indicate among other things, the location and states of health of people through the law of vibration. It is on the order of the Abrams Law. To go into detail would take too long and probably not interest you at this time. Suffice it to say that I took the vibration of these two men, your sons, from their published photographs.

James is dead and is buried in, or near, Hinsdale, Montana. He seems to have met with an accident about September 1, 1924, but was not killed instantly. His vitality gradually lowered, until he died about January 1, of this year. There seem to have been wanderings. Sometimes your sons were together, then at other times they were at some distance from one another.

Galen had a short period of lowered vitality about October 1, but does not seem to have met with an accident and, save for that brief period, was, and still is, in good health. The indications are quite strong that Galen left James during the months of October and November, but rejoined him again in December, and remained at his side until the hour of his death. After that, Galen seems to have wandered.

January 15 places him in Plains, Montana, the 20th across the border into Idaho. On approximately the sixth day of February he appeared in the vicinity of Pasco, Washington, where he still is. I have no detailed map of that area and thus am unable to give his location with certitude.

You may be assured, Mrs. Wallace, that I will keep in touch with Galen every day between the time of this mailing and your receipt of it, as he may yet make many moves. And you may be assured as well that I understand your position. It is no light matter for any person to believe in something unknown.

Mother read it over and over, then put it down and was quiet for a long time. Finally she said, "You'll have to write him, Lillian."

I told her I couldn't possibly.

"I believe you are mistaken, start with that," she said. *"I am sure you are a man of the highest . . ."*

I could feel her hands kneading the back of my chair. "I can't," I said.

"I am not able to believe that such an instrument is capable . . ."

Imagine a woman talking through a closed door, not sure if anyone's there, that's how she sounded. Meanwhile, my eyes crept across the onionskin. I was not immune to thoughts of Galen wandering the world. A newborn Galen, it would have to be, a Galen stripped of the memory of us, a Galen too tender . . .

Where is my wandering boy, Father would sing.

I sat at the table and didn't move.

The next day Mother didn't go to work.

"There's no such thing as the Abrams Law," she said that night. "There's not a mention of it anywhere."

"You didn't believe . . ."

"I've taken care of writing him," she said.

But before he'd had time to receive hers, a second letter came from Jules Harvey. It was alone on the floor of the front hallway, lying in a slash of light, the way you'd see it in a dream.

I take the liberty of writing to let you know that your son has left Pasco. This does not surprise me greatly, Mrs. Wallace, as the nature of the vibrations appeared volatile, suggesting a state of excitement or restlessness.

However, I was taken aback by his rate of movement. Ordinarily, I make my readings once each day, in the evening (you'll forgive me if I tell you that I pursue this research on my own time, though I should also say that late evening is the most reliable part of the day, since there is less interference from the sun's radiation). In this instance, (the night of the 23rd), I was obliged to make new readings every two hours.

I was at a loss as to how to explain this activity, but now believe that his path of movement corresponds with the Great Northern rail line between Pasco and Spokane, Washington. The final reading (taken at 4:45 this morning, the 24th) shows that he has either disembarked or that the train itself has gone onto a siding.

You may be assured that I will keep you up-to-date.

Of course, the following day was Sunday.

Whatever comfort it was to occupy her regular pew at the 10:30 service, or to linger downstairs for a time with Mrs. Tiebloom and the others, it didn't much compensate for there being no mail delivery that day. Back at home, she tried busying herself with the newspaper, and later some kitchen work, but nothing would take hold. Viola called at her usual hour, around dark. I listened long enough to hear she wasn't going to mention Mr. Harvey, then slid out of earshot. Shortly after that, I heard her on the stairs. I ended up eating a corned beef sandwich, alone in the kitchen.

No letter came the next day, either.

Tuesday's mail consisted of a card for me—from Charles, a tinted view of the Brooklyn Bridge:

Will have to stay on two extra days, sorry to report. Due in Friday night, rather late. Miss your shining face. Love to Flora. C.

Mother looked it over and handed it back. "He's a fine man, Lillian," she said. From the look on her lips, she wanted to say more. She seemed on the verge of issuing me a warning, about the treatment of Charles, I felt sure. It would have to wait, though. She was tired, her thoughts taken up with Mr. Harvey's pronouncements, and his silence.

Tuesday was her night for church Auxiliary—I'd let myself hope for that little respite, but she gave no sign of getting ready to go.

"Isn't it time you . . . ?" I said.

She cast around the front room for the reason to stay home. "Why don't you go instead," she said finally.

We looked at each other.

I couldn't bear the thought. She dropped it there and was quiet, but a few minutes later she was back on the subject of Charles. Out of nowhere, she was telling me what a foolish plan it was to wait for summer.

"A man loses his patience," she said. "Believe me, even a godsend like Charles."

"Mother," I said, "I don't think Charles . . ."

"I should think you'd want it taken care of."

"I do," I said. "Of course I do."

What should I think? I'd already begun to wait the way she'd asked me to. And there was that worse obstacle, which was picturing her rattling around this house alone from that day forward. I didn't know why she'd urge it.

Unless she thought that if I was with Charles she'd always know where I was.

"I've looked it up and your birthday falls on a Saturday this year," she said. "I don't see why that wouldn't be the time."

"That's not even a month from now . . ."

"Oh, a month. A month's an eternity," she said.

"I don't have a dress or anything," I said.

"Don't buck me on this, Lillian," she said.

"Well, I don't mean to," I said. "Really, I'm just confused . . ."

"There's nothing to be confused about," Mother said. But she was looking away from me, and didn't say any more. And a minute later I could tell the mood had already blown past.

I thought to myself: if we can make it one more day without hearing from that man . . . then on Wednesday:

I regret I have nothing new to give you, Mrs. Wallace. The state of restlessness I referred to in my last message is still present, yet there has been no further movement. I am rather unsure how to interpret this, but I see no immediate cause for concern.

You stated in your letter: "A widow is an easy prey . . ." I want you to know that I am not motivated by hope of financial gain, as regards the published reward for the return of your sons. I should refuse it if it were offered. You may think of me as one who believes (I may say fervently) that there is more to know than we yet know. Science is our window into God's machinery, Mrs. Wallace, and I am referring to all the branches of Science, not just the so-called "official" kinds.

I do sincerely hope you'll not resent my intrusion. I have taken the liberty of speaking directly with Spokane's Chief of Police (a man named Hugo). He knew of your sons' disappearance through a Justice Department communication, he said, and agreed to canvass the local hotels. Of course, it is possible, perhaps likely, that Galen is using another name, or that he is unaware of his identity. Such things are known to happen.

I cleared the plates and washed them, then scoured the sink, and after that went straight to the bathroom and scoured the tub and basin, and it occurred to me then that I might get out Father's brushes and buff our work shoes, which I did, four pairs altogether, but still it was only quarter to eight with an expanse of evening before us. Now she was stationed at Father's desk with her box of note cards. The pen was still upright in its holder. I could feel how she'd turn in another instant, searching me out. I knew how her voice would be, what she'd make me attest to.

"I'm going up now," I said.

I bent over and kissed her cheek.

"You must be awfully tired," she said, not looking at me.

"Yes," I said.

But I wasn't. It was hours before I fell asleep (imagining myself tucked against Charles), and not long after that I was awake once more. The blood sang through my head. I could not possibly stay where I was.

I walked past Mother's door, keeping to the side of the runner where it wouldn't squeak.

There seemed to be nothing to eat but hard-cooked eggs, heaped in a blue bowl, shells off. I put the water on the stove and sat down. I thought of James across from me, tappi spoon around the top of his two-minute egg, and spilling salt on the oilcloth and drawing circles in it with his finger. I thought if you could freeze such a moment and study it, you'd find all you needed to know about them. And what would I have been doing, across the table, that said as much? Staring at them, I guess. I still was. I prayed Mother was good and asleep. I wanted to be left alone and have my thoughts stray where they would.

It was two-thirty, then three.

I set my cup in the sink, switched off the kitchen light and angled through the dark toward the stairs, but stopped in the center of the front room, and knew that what I most wanted to do was go back through the kitchen to Galen's room. I wanted to walk into the middle of it and look at his things and see how much I could bear.

I worked the latch quietly and let myself in, not reaching immediately for the light. The radiator was on. The air had a thick smell, wool and old glue and steam leaking at the valve. This had been a spare room for years, while the boys shared the room at the top of the stairs. We used to call it the maid's room—a distant joke of Father's. It was where they'd moved me when I had scarlet fever and thought I would die, the same year Viola had lent me the fear of hellfire. Still, this had been Galen's refuge a long time now. A trunk of his things was gone already, most of his books and papers, his pictures of us—it was in storage at the rooming house in Cambridge. But what else of his might I find stashed here, if I pulled out a bottom drawer, or rummaged under the bed? The streetlight at the end of the alley grazed off the painted brickwork next door, cut across Galen's desk and threw a white wing of light up the corkboard where the map had once been pinned.

I lowered myself to the edge of his bed and began to run my hand over the ribbing of the chenille, but the covers suddenly stirred and there came the rasp of interrupted breathing.

"*Jonathan?*" she said. The voice was cracked and hopeless, a little girl's voice.

My hand froze on the spread.

"Who's there . . . ?" she said, up on one elbow, but not

awake. She sucked at her lips, rolled and settled under Galen's bedclothes, and was still again.

I flew back out to the kitchen, then to the telephone. *Oh God, Charles, she's sleeping in his bed . . . Tell me what I . . .* The name of the hotel was right in front of me. The Brunswick on Sixth Avenue.

I waited and waited, my heart still thudding, then when I got through, the night clerk refused to ring his room.

"Oh believe me," I said. "He won't mind when he finds out who . . ."

The man could scarcely hear me. I tried to point my voice without raising it.

He relented finally. I heard the tiny bursts of shrilling in the earpiece and pictured Charles throwing back the blankets and planting both feet on the carpet before he answered, and then his voice coming on, stern at first.

But the ringing just kept up.

"Are you sure that's still his room?" I said.

"It's still his room," the man said. "He's just not in it."

"Well, would you . . ." I started to ask, but I couldn't say any more, and let the phone drop back on its hook.

The front room lay in a cold fog. The joints of the chair cracked under me like ice. *I'll just sit here another minute,* I thought, hugging my arms, *and then when I feel all right I'll go upstairs and lie on the bed, and in a while it will be morning . . .* but I couldn't even begin this stretch of waiting. A moment later I had the long-distance operator again.

A half-dozen rings, then my aunt's voice, sleep still on it like burrs.

"This had better be good," Mae said, not the least angry, I could hear, only curious who'd want to drag her from a good sleep at quarter past four.

"My dear Lillian," she said. "Are you here in New York?"

"Well, no, I . . ."

"Of course not," she said. "Let me put some water on."

I smothered the mouthpiece and listened frantically in the direction of Galen's.

"There," Mae said. "Now . . ."

We talked for an hour, maybe longer. I forgot the house.
I felt my shoulders drop. Her laughter seemed a miracle, nine
hundred miles away.

"Well, it's another day, Lily," she said finally. "I can see
the gulls already."

"It's still night here," I said, pulling back the curtain.
"Starting to rain."

"There's pink all up and down the bridge cables," Mae
said. "The tugboats are heading out."

I didn't answer, picturing it.

"Don't despair," she said.

The boy looked sick. He stood shivering on the top of
the stoop, rain spilling from the bill of his cap. Mother
pushed through the foyer past me and took the telegram.
The boy bunched his shoulders and scuffed down out of
the light. I watched him retrieve his bicycle and wobble up
the block.

"This came across *hours* ago," Mother said behind me.
It was hard to see how she'd have gotten it any sooner—we
were only just home, her hat wasn't even off.

She held it in two hands, like a sheet of lyrics. The
envelope had fallen to the carpet.

*Galen headed east stop strong life signs stop Sandpoint Idaho
stop*

J Harvey

I read it over her shoulder, then straightened and backed
off.

"It's Friday tomorrow," I said. "Charles will be home."

No response from Mother.

"Maybe we should meet his train. Well, I know it's late,
twenty past eleven, but . . ."

She turned and disappeared into the kitchen.

First thing in the morning, the same boy from Western
Union, thin as a prayer.

Your son eastbound stop Libby Montana stop more to follow stop
J Harvey

"Lillian?" she said. I knew what she'd ask next. I couldn't stay home with her.

"What about Mr. Atwood?" I said.

"Oh," she said, as if I understood nothing. "He'll just have to fend for himself."

"Mother, I can't not go to work."

She cast me a glazed, scowling look. I froze, feeling a desperate need to turn to James and ask what I should do, or to Galen for a moment's sympathy—though, of course, if they'd been there I wouldn't have had to ask. A moment later I took off running for the El.

It was still ages until summer, but the rain had shaken people loose, it seemed, sending them down to Field's to look at luggage. They gabbed at me from all sides. What did I think of their steamer bookings? Weren't customs agents a rude lot? Did I know there were sleeper compartments on airplanes now? A woman suddenly interrupted herself and stared at me and finally asked if I was OK. Tears were running out of my left eye.

I'd not had a headache for weeks, only two since Christmas, the milder sort I'd try to carry on in spite of. Now I knew I was in trouble. I knew I wouldn't get home in time, I'd be holding the side of my head and running.

She wasn't the least surprised to see me. As if I'd been outside pouting all this time.

"Look at this!" she said, waving another sheet of telegraph paper. *"Lillian. He's coming."*

"No, don't," I said. "I can't think, I can't possibly . . ." I pushed up the stairs and banged into my room.

I could hear her calling from the landing. I crammed the pillow over my face and prayed she'd stay outside and let my medicine begin its work.

I woke once before it was fully dark, and sat straight up in a panic that I'd overslept for work. Slivers of light throbbed off the bottles on my dresser and smeared trails across my eyes when I squeezed them shut. I grabbed for the quilt and let it swallow me. I woke again, later in the evening. The pain had moved some distance off, but it was there still, flashing like heat lightning along the horizon. I didn't sit up this time. A slit of light burned along the bottom of my door. I believed I heard a man's voice now—such as you'd hear declaiming through the radio speaker, though far more pure and not muted by the flooring but here in the room with me. *All the world,* it said, *all the living world is divided in two. . . .* I stared out at the light slashing my own room into two black halves, and though the words felt momentous I couldn't hold them together long enough to understand them; then I was off again. When I woke next time all was quiet. There was only the usual scratch of light under my door, cast by the tiny, paper-shaded bulb at the head of the stairs.

I remembered then what night it was. I tipped the clock and read it. Half past ten.

No time for pinning my hair or frowning before the mirror. I eased myself off the bed. Downstairs, other lights were burning—randomly, lights we never used. Mother was nowhere in evidence. I called for a taxi and slipped my coat from the front closet and stood waiting, staring at the fringe of the rug. I should've still been upstairs in the dark—I felt shaky and exposed. She'd appear in a minute, I knew she would. I'd look up and she'd be coming toward me through the glare. I slid into the foyer, then outside. The rain had nearly quit, and it was not so cold as it had been. Steam rose and drifted from the railings. The park lay in soft black shadow, with no remnant of snow. Suddenly, it seemed, April had come.

I raced down into the main lobby and saw that it was 11:40 now. Charles would have carried his own bag. He would've moved briskly through the stream of people, not losing any time casting his eyes about for me. He'd have found a cab— already he was likely pulling up at the curb outside the club. But I charged down toward the portals to the tracks anyway, sick to think I'd slept that much too long.

There wasn't even a last trickle of passengers.

A pair of old redcaps stood conversing by the chained gate.

"You can save your hurry," one said.

I didn't follow.

"No one coming through here for a long while," the other said.

I tore back to the ticket windows and heard the story confirmed. The rain had washed out a trestle near Defiance, Ohio. Westbound traffic was being rerouted through Ft. Wayne. There would be long delays.

I resolved to wait. If it took until daylight, so be it. I'd revive and go down to the apron by the tracks. I'd watch him make his way through the aisle, I'd run and slide my hands under his coat and tell him about Mother. He'd listen then, touching my hair. People would stream around us.

And I wouldn't say anything about calling him, not then and not ever.

Now that I was certain he was coming and knew how I'd act when he arrived, now that it was simply a matter of killing time, the panic finally started to trickle away. How overwrought I must've looked tearing across the station, my coat flapping, my hair flailing out behind like a gypsy's. *You're something,* I thought. I took the nearest seat, ready to get on with the night. But I was up again in a minute. All I could think to do was walk, up the stairs and down, one end to the other. People were still about, a few families, a gathering of men by the side doors, in out of the rain.

I came to rest again opposite another string of gates, and realized this was the bench where the three of us, Mother and Charles and I, had waited that first night of September. Charles had talked about the amenities on the train, the linen and silver, the fresh-cut asters. I'd barely said a word, thinking of that golden week Galen would be home before going on to Cambridge. Mother had sat in this exact place, her eyes on the archway, blinking back a mist of premonitions.

Now, as if deposited there by Providence, two boys did come swinging through the portals. They were tall and slen-

der, each with a bag. One had round-rimmed glasses. If they'd
dozed through the last hours of drizzle and darkness, they'd
roused at the outskirts of the city and shaved and slicked their
hair. They talked steadily, looking straight ahead into the
vaulted space of the station, coming with quick, synchronized
strides. They passed so close I might have touched them. The
glasses were wrong, of course, the lenses much too bulging
for James . . . the bags were wrong as well, checkered paste-
board, terribly frayed at the corners. But what a sadness anyway! I shifted on the bench to watch as they swept amidst the
other travelers. I found myself weeping frantically. They
weren't my brothers—even so, Lord, weren't they dead?
What could it matter if they shrank away in a clean bed, month
by month, or dropped in a crevice with only God's eyes on
them? I felt seized with this vision, surrounded by strangers
passing into death. The couple opposite me with the baby
sleeping across their knees. The man boarding up the news-
stand. Those others with bowed heads and rain on their shoulders. Sixty or eighty years, what did it matter, not a soul in
Union Station wouldn't have gone through what James and
Galen had. This bleakness gusted straight through me. I felt
if I didn't jump to my feet and run headlong I'd begin scream-
ing terribly. But I didn't move, and scarcely a moment later
everything I could see looked commonplace once more, utterly lacking in the power to shock me. No one had seen.
Now I stood, gently, and caught a last look at those two boys
as they climbed the stairs and disappeared. The light sent
sparks flying from their hair.

It was at this point in the night's progress that the final
boarding call came for the Oriental Limited, departing west.
I'd not heard the others. Before me there was a final rush of
embracing and pulling apart. I dug through my bag and in a
moment I'd located the square of heavy paper representing
Mr. Louis Hill's goodwill toward Mother and me. I can't say
I hesitated . . . how long does it take a bent stick to break?
I took a seat in the coach, and before I was stung by the first
serious misgiving I felt the shudder of movement bang
through the couplings. Eyes open, I settled my head against

the velvet pile, shivering with a monumental, terrifying joy. Presently, the lights of Chicago fell away. I wasn't proud of myself, nor, for once, was I ashamed. Moving west, it came to me that in all the time ahead I would miss those who were mine to miss, but I came to know, too (as Mae had known), that I wouldn't be stunted by it. And as for Mother and Charles, who belonged to each other and whom I loved, when I got where I was going I would write them the first of many letters.